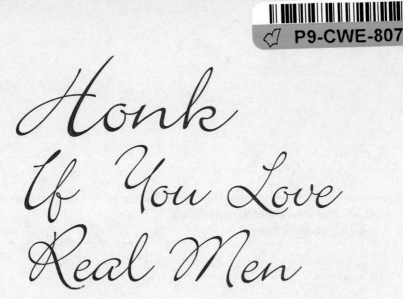

Honk
If You Love
Real Men

**Don't Miss This Other Sexy Anthology
from St. Martin's Press**

Burning Up

Honk If You Love Real Men

FOUR TALES OF EROTIC ROMANCE

Carrie Alexander

Pamela Britton

Susan Donovan

Lora Leigh

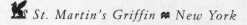 St. Martin's Griffin ⚜ New York

www.stmartins.com

Library of Congress Cataloging-in-Publication Data

Honk if you love real men / Carrie Alexander . . . [et al.].—1st ed.
    p. cm.
    Contents: Naughty girl / by Carrie Alexander—Wanted: one hot blooded man / by Pamela Britton—Have mercy / by Susan Donovan—Reno's chance / by Lora Leigh.
    ISBN 0-312-33916-X
    EAN 978-0-312-33916-6
    1. Erotic stories, American. I. Alexander, Carrie.

PS648.E7H66 2005
813'.6080803538—dc22

        2005042786

10 9 8

CONTENTS

Naughty Girl

Carrie Alexander

Chapter One

The man had abs that could stop traffic. No need for safety cones or warning flags.

The blazing sun had bronzed him like an Aztec god. Against the fluorescent orange of an unzipped safety vest, his brown skin gleamed with sweat. Dirt rimmed the corrugated muscles. They flexed in rippling perfection as his arms swung high, freezing against a diamond flash of sunshine before he brought the pickax down to slam it into the crumbling edge of the pavement. A cloud of red dust rose, caking his jeans. They hung heavily off his lean hips, the downward drag producing a gap at the waistband between his hipbones and flatiron stomach.

The carved shoulders and the hard jaw were admirable, but it was the gap in his jeans that had tormented Estrella Ianesque's imagination since the road construction had begun. She'd fantasized a hundred times about the pulse and fullness and hot satin skin promised to her if only she could slide her fingers into that tempting gap.

She rubbed at the bus window with her sleeve, moving around

the smudges to get a better view. At twenty-six, she was too old for panting against the glass, but young enough to squirm with a tingling blood rush of desire for a road construction worker.

And daring enough—perhaps—to make plans to act on that desire.

The question was *how?* To him, she was only another staring face in a vehicle window.

Brenda Ventano nudged Estrella's arm. She was a big-haired redhead who rode the city bus to her job as a waitress at a little coffee shop on Alvarado Boulevard. "I haven't seen a better chest since Brad Pitt stripped to his skivvies in *Thelma and Louise.*"

"Yes, but he was a callow boy." Estrella's tongue curled around a puff of warm breath. Maybe she wasn't too old to pant. She pressed a fingertip to the window, wishing she could melt glass and reach across Highway 201 to stroke the worker's body, making one long leisurely trip from lip to navel before her fingers spread to take hold of his surging penis. "*That*—that's a man."

"A mighty fine man."

Estrella's head tilted against the window. "I wonder who he is. What's his story? I think he's so . . ." She couldn't finish. There was no one word to describe him.

"Sexy? You and every woman on this bus with a pulse."

"Uh-huh."

After a minute, Brenda nudged again. "Want me to find out?"

"You can find out?"

"I have connections."

"What?" The word popped out in soprano. Estrella's heart drummed.

In the distance, the truck-mounted stoplight switched to green, and one of the crew flagged on the halted traffic. The bus lumbered forward, edging past the barrier of orange-and-white-striped barrels. Estrella's eyes followed the sun god, appreciating the fine-tuned mesh of strength and thoroughbred grace as he swung the ax up and down, up and down, a mesmerizing rhythm that got her thinking of what it would be like to have that driving force between her thighs.

"My neighbor's husband worked with a city crew until he hurt his back," Brenda said. "He might know, or at least know who to ask. If you want, I'll try."

The bus picked up speed. Estrella looked forward with a fevered face. "What good would a name do?"

"It'd be a start."

"A man like that probably has women flinging their bras at him from passing convertibles."

"You backing out?"

"He's only a fantasy." One she'd love to make true.

Brenda pushed the hairpins deeper into her pouf. "Right. He's not a match for the likes of you anyway. You're going better places, *muchacha*."

Estrella shrugged, temporarily dismissing her rock-solid goals. "I don't want to actually *go* anywhere with him." Her gaze slipped sideways, dreaming out the window to avoid the reality of the smelly bus and her drudge job, a necessary means to an end.

"Except to bed?" Brenda's knowing laugh sputtered like a tailpipe.

Estrella smiled to herself. "He doesn't look like a man who needs a bed to make my fantasies come true."

"Is he there?"

"I can't see." Frustration scraped at Estrella's nerves. The bus was moving too fast, grinding gears with a nauseating whiff of diesel. "Why are there so many men standing around?"

"Have you never looked at a construction site before? It's a law that five men must stand by and watch the one who works." Brenda settled back and honked into a tissue. "Damn allergies," she added gummily.

Estrella decided to skip lunch at the coffee shop. The day's schedule was already too busy. Eve was going on a business trip, and Estrella had a list of chores that would have to be finished before the airport departure at two.

She gazed outside as the bus rolled past the barrels and flags marking the end of the construction zone. Missing her usual morning's eye candy would make the day that much longer.

Suddenly he was there. Striding over the dirt berm that had been created for the widening of the road. His boots dug deep among the chunks of earth and stone. Uneven footing, but his chin was high, his eyes on the swaying fronds of the palms that bordered the boulevard.

Dark eyes, Estrella believed, to match his black hair.

In her imagination, they were seeing eyes. Really seeing. Eyes with so much fire and knowledge they would melt her insecurities as easily as her bones.

"Drum," Brenda said in her ear.

Estrella's head gave a quick nod, but she didn't look away. Every detail must be memorized. The height, somewhere over six-four unless her perceptions were distorted by his sheer presence. There was the fit of his jeans over his firm ass and thighs, the swing of his arm, the vitality in his strong profile.

Today he wore a shirt—a wifebeater. Horrid name. A chill

chased across her warm skin. She shivered, distracted from her perusal until his head turned and she caught an unexpected glint. An earring? Why hadn't she noticed that before? She didn't know if she liked the thought of an earring, although that wasn't as bad as tattoos. So far, she'd spotted none of them, thank you, Jesus.

Huh. Not that *her* preferences mattered. He exuded the confidence of knowing himself, of being sure of his place in the world. She was envious of that. It had taken her years to feel halfway sure of her choices.

He looked toward the bus as it drove away. At her window? Estrella's hand went to the collar of her polyester blouse, as if she could catch the hope and longing that leaped into her throat.

The bus moved beyond range. She scoffed, getting her senses back. He hadn't been looking at her. She was a nobody.

"Drum," Brenda repeated. "That's his name."

Now that he was out of sight, Estrella could concentrate on the conversation. "Drum? What kind of name is that?"

"Dunno. Maybe he's a musician."

"What else did you find out?"

"Not a lot. Supposedly he keeps to himself. But you were right. He has lots of women."

Estrella's stomach twitched. "Of course."

"Even a Hollywood agent stopped once, to give him a card."

"He's a wannabe actor?" *Too bad.*

"Kris's old man didn't think so. That was only a story he'd heard once about Drum, along with the gossip about the women who holler their phone numbers out of passing cars. Heh. Or other invitations." Brenda nudged elbows. "The guys like to be on Drum's crew, 'cause they get plenty of boob flashers."

Estrella groaned.

"That doesn't mean Drum likes that type of woman," Brenda said. "Only that he attracts them. Easy to see why."

"He does look like the Calvin Klein version of a road crew worker. Most of them are short and stocky, kind of grizzled."

"Kris's hubby sure is. The guy looks like he stuffed a six-pack under his grimy T-shirt. Where Drum—"

"Wears his sex-pack well."

Brenda chuckled. "*Sex*-pack?"

Estrella pressed two fingers to her grin. "Oops. Did I say that?"

"Yep. That man's got you unhinged. Never thought I'd see the day, but I guess it took a Grade A prime beefcake to catch *your* interest, huh?" When Estrella didn't respond, Brenda peered closer, a tissue wadded under her reddened nose. "What's the plan?"

"How do you know I have a plan?"

"You always have a plan."

Estrella blinked. She and Brenda had met on the bus, discovered they lived within a few blocks of each other, and become friends. At first, fresh from her divorce and the accompanying trauma, Estrella had kept their acquaintance casual. She wasn't ready to trust.

Brenda's warm acceptance and caustic attitude had won her over. They'd never sat down and had an actual heart-to-heart, but during the course of the year Estrella's past had leaked out: the early marriage that had blossomed into a huge mistake, the troubles she'd had in breaking it off, the eventual decision to start her life over, even if she had to leave everything that she knew and begin at the bottom, alone, hundreds of miles from home.

"Eve is going out of town for a week."

Brenda's penciled brows arched. "And?"

"She's leaving me the Miata."

"That trippin' red convertible? You're kidding me!"

Estrella nodded. "She trusts me."

"You get to take it home and everything?"

"No. She doesn't trust me that much. She thinks the car would be stripped bare in ten seconds flat in our neighborhood."

Brenda laughed. "Ack. She might be right."

"I'm only to do the chores in it. Knowing Eve, I'll have a list of exactly where to go and what routes to take. She may have even calculated the mileage. But that doesn't mean I can't . . ." Estrella flipped a thumb over her shoulder.

Brenda closed her open mouth. "Mm-hmm, girl! You're gonna drive by the construction zone and catch Drum's eye."

"Maybe."

"You'll have to dress different."

Estrella looked down at her pink polyester. "Ya think?"

Brenda was calculating the situation with her reddened eyes pulled into slits. She squinted at Estrella. "You gonna throw your bra at him?"

Only under more optimal circumstances, Estrella thought with an extra fillip of anticipation, though she said in an utterly calm way, "Course not. But I'll come up with something."

The bus had slowed with a wheeze of the brakes. Estrella swung up out of her seat. "Here's my stop. I'll see you tonight, Bren. Pop an Advil so you can make it through the day."

"I'm already dosed up." Brenda sneezed into the damp tissue. "Bud nod flyin' as high as you."

Estrella laughed as she skipped down the bus steps, as light as the churros her mother used to make every Saturday morning—

crisp golden dough, sizzling with hot sugar. She'd been practical and hardworking for too long. Why not find a way to entice this Drum person to share the fantasy?

Jesse Drummond wasn't sure how many times the tempting bit of fluff had passed before he noticed, but once he had, he was looking for her continually. When the red Miata reappeared and his jackhammer sputtered out of control for the third or fourth time, Tea's head came up. Jesse's coworker switched off his machine, took out a grimy red bandanna and wiped the sweat from his brow. "Hey, Drum," he yelled. "You're spittin' gravel. Got somethin' botherin' you, boy?"

"Nothing." Jesse leaned into the machine, the vibrations going straight through him, rattling his bones. They were drilling out an old sewer cap, which would have to be moved back twenty feet.

He shot a glance at the stalled traffic and said it again, to himself beneath the racket of the hammer. "Nothing."

The convertible gleamed in red and silver, freshly waxed and polished. Behind the wheel, the driver's ponytail swished to the heavy bass beat of a popular rap song.

Tea didn't follow the distraction. He shrugged and mouthed, "All right."

Jesse continued hammering while he watched the other man walk away, fighting for balance on the torn-up earth. Frank "Sweet Tea" Williams was a middle-aged former football player from Alabama, a strapping man gone doughy at the middle, whose easy manner gave the impression that he wasn't the sharpest tool in the box. What mattered to Jesse was that Tea had a big heart and a stalwart disposition. He stood up for what was right. They'd covered each other's back since the first days on the job, when their foreman had tried to bully Tea into taking the blame for a cracked water main.

The hierarchy on the road crew was not much different from what he'd faced in prison. Jesse had learned early on to keep his mouth shut until he ran smack into trouble and push came to shove. Then he shoved back with all his might. That had always been enough to maintain his survival.

But he'd been out for nearly eight months now and mere survival was losing its appeal. He wanted more.

Not a woman in a red convertible, he said to himself, stealing another look toward the road. A chunk of concrete gave way and he automatically pulled back, flicking off the jackhammer's switch. That way lay danger. His parole officer had drilled it into his cranium: Keep your cool, do your job, stay out of trouble.

Pussy was always trouble, one way or another.

Especially when it came packaged as a woman who radiated a certain spirited sexiness from fifty paces. Kindness was there too, somehow evident in the shape of her face or the sincerity of her smile, regardless of the flashy car and pounding music.

Jesse shook his head. Hard, sharp women knew the score. Crazy chicks he brushed off like lint. It was the nice ones he had to watch out for. They had a way of getting under a man's skin. Turning his head. Making him lose balance.

Leave this one alone, like all the rest. He heaved the hammer to one side, leaning it against a pile of rubble, then shook the stinging sweat from his eyes. The vehicles in the eastbound lane were being waved on at last.

On the other side of the barrier, the convertible was stalled. The woman's head bent low over the wheel as she cranked the ignition.

Other drivers hit their horns. The ponytail bobbed. As the honking escalated, her slender brown arm rose in the air, flashing a sassy hand gesture.

Jesse laughed, but he didn't move. The car trouble ploy wasn't even original.

Tea lumbered past with two water bottles in his hands, sloshing the contents as he climbed the slope to the stalled car. Jesse heard the deep graveled voice. "Gotcha some engine trouble? Can I help you, ma'am?"

He missed her response, but within two seconds Tea was waving to Jesse, then hunching behind the bumper to push the car out of the way.

"Shit," Jesse said as he took off up the steep slope. Leave it to Sweet Tea to volunteer both of them to play Sir Galahad.

"Put her in neutral, ma'am." Tea grunted at Jesse's arrival. "We got to roll her over a few feet."

Jesse barely glanced at the driver, although he felt her eyes on him as he moved to the rear of the car. The vehicle resisted for an instant, then rolled smoothly over the small stretch of pavement that remained between the traffic lane and the barrels that marked the construction zone.

"Please don't scrape the car," she said, becoming anxious as the nose of the convertible tipped a cone.

"Turn the wheel a little to the left," Jesse directed. "We have to get your rear end clear of traffic." Hell, yeah.

A wary "Eeeep" whistled between her teeth, but she complied. The car coasted to a stop, the right side within inches of the barricade. Jesse and Tea stayed close as the delayed vehicles streamed by.

"Let's pop the hood," Tea said when the flow of traffic had switched to the other lane.

Jesse looked into the pit. The foreman had stepped up to a vantage point to watch them, one meaty hand wrapped around the frame of the earth mover. Jesse lifted a fist in acknowledgment, flashing his fingers. Five minutes. "Uh, Tea. We need to get back to work."

"We can spare five minutes." Tea smiled at the woman behind the wheel.

She did the grateful eyelash flutter of the helpless female. "I don't know what's wrong. The car is kept in tip-top condition."

"Lemme take a look."

"Thank you." She reached for the lever and Tea disappeared behind the hood.

Jesse couldn't keep his eyes off her any longer. "I'm Drum and that's Tea."

Her face tipped up. Her mouth pursed expectantly as if she had to savor her words before she spoke them. From his vantage point, she was all eyes and lips and honey-colored skin. Bare shoulders and arms, more than a hint of rounded cleavage in a plunging neckline, and firm naked thighs revealed by an excessively—and successfully—short skirt. Even her kneecaps were provocative.

Her mouth opened. Lips so pink and ripe, they seemed almost obscene, if only because of the thoughts they put in Jesse's head of what he could do with them.

Tea's head poked around the side of the hood. "That's no way to introduce yourself to a lady." He nodded at her. "I'm Frank Williams, ma'am, and he's Jesse Drummond."

The blow-job lips curved into a smile. "Estrella," she said. "Pleased to meet you, Frank." Her eyes widened at Jesse. They were dark blue, liquid as the pond at his grandpa's farm, where he'd once skinny-dipped at midnight, never again so easy and free. "You too . . . Jesse."

He nodded. Keeping it cool.

"Shew." She fanned her face. "It's hot out here in the sun."

No hotter than you. But that was what she wanted him to say.

An awkward silence swelled, as heavy as the heat rising off the pavement.

Tea's head appeared again. He shot an encouraging look at Jesse. "Sure is, ma'am. Damn hot. Pardon my French."

"Please call me Estrella. I don't know how you stand it, sweating in those orange vests." Her eyes drew a line down Jesse's arm to where he'd loosely clasped his hands over a thickening erection. He hadn't been this unable to control himself since his teenage days as a walking hard-on, when he'd been driven half-crazy by something as simple as the flex of muscle in Jenny Crocker's smooth calf while she crossed her legs in third-hour English.

No wonder he'd never learned his subjunctives.

Tea nodded again at Jesse. "I brought water. Offer some to the lady, Drum."

Jesse found the bottles where they'd rolled to a stop against the convertible's folded roof. There was a bag of groceries, a bucket of cleaning products and a ziplocked bag from the dry cleaners in the back of the car. He moved forward again and held out one of the dripping containers to Estrella.

"Thanks." She took the bottle and rolled it against her neck, then pressed the cold weight between her breasts. Her shoulders shifted and she let out a soft little moan that was so obviously erotic, his balls tightened. "That feels great."

He stared, fixated as the first time he'd opened a *Playboy* and seen a naked woman. Her nipples were bullets, shooting down his best intentions. *Damn.* That thought alone proved that he'd lost it.

Almost angrily, he twisted off the bottle cap and downed half the bottle in one long drink before he went and handed the remainder to Tea, who muttered behind the hood, "What are you waitin' for—get her number. I can't stay under here forever."

Great. The man was a fifty-three-year-old matchmaker in Timberlands and fluorescent orange.

Jesse returned to the driver's side, bending closer with his hands propped on his knees. Their eyes were on a level now, and he was able to appreciate every nuance as Estrella's lips ovaled around the mouth of the bottle. She drank, gulping and swallowing with relish until she caught his eye and became flustered.

She sputtered. "Bad news?" she asked, wiping a dribble of water off her chin with the back of a hand. When he didn't respond—impossible with a a strangled throat—she prompted, "About the car?"

Time to cut and run.

"What did you do?" he asked in a conversational tone. "Loosen a plug wire just enough for the car to stall?"

"Wha—?" Her jaw snapped shut. He heard her teeth click.

"You wouldn't be the first," he said.

Her chin shot up, making the sable ponytail flip. "Does the trick ever work?" she purred, watching his face through slitted eyes as she held the bottle between her breasts again, making them appear even more plump and full.

Surprise. He'd been sure she'd deny the ploy, but maybe she wasn't as frivolous as the rest of them. There was an attractive weight to her, a solid sensibility beneath the centerfold figure and flirty eyes.

He shook his head. "Nope."

Her moistened lips pursed. "That's no fun."

"Welcome to my life."

She leaned her shoulder against the car door, looking at him closely now, the false note abandoned. "Hmm, I'd almost think that's an invitation—if you weren't so humorless."

Humorless? Maybe so. Most of the unessentials had been worn down by the grinding desolation of prison life. But he didn't need humor to give her what she wanted.

Estrella recoiled. Something in his eyes, he realized.

"I'm sorry. I've made a mistake." Woodenly, she handed him the water bottle. "Forget this happened."

He straightened. *Just let her go,* his head said. The rest of him wasn't speaking, only reacting on instinct to her round sexy body. Fortunately, his reason prevailed; he had experience hanging on by his fingernails. "Tell me what you did to the car and I'll fix it."

"I didn't—" She swallowed, not looking at him. He felt the loss in his gut. "Okay, you caught me. Check the distributor wires. That should do it."

"Done."

"I gotta apologize for Drum—Jesse, that is," Tea said to Estrella while his partner fixed the car and slammed the hood with more force than necessary. "The guy's been in—" Tea caught himself, aided by a glare from Jesse. "The guy's lost his touch. He forgets his manners around nice ladies like yourself."

"I'm not so nice," she mumbled, watching Jesse through her lashes. "And I certainly do apologize for the trouble I've caused."

"It's no bother helpin' a pretty girl." Tea's chest expanded. "Been a long hot day and this was the best part of it."

Jesse hadn't known that Tea was such a sweet-talker. The rambling stories about his football glory days and the head cheerleader girlfriend might even be true.

"Let's cut this short." Their boss was barking at them from the shallow pit.

"G'day, ma'am," Tea said, tipping his helmet as he departed.

Estrella took her hand off the key to do a finger wave.

Jesse hesitated nearby. "Go on and see if the car starts."

She looked as if she wanted to speak, but she simply nodded and turned the key in the ignition. The engine came to life and she goosed it for emphasis. *Vroom, vroom.*

"Thank you," she said, blinking her big shining eyes at him. Her expression had sweetened. Either she'd already forgotten her moment of alarm, or he'd miscalculated the reaction, the way he tended to, seeing slights even where there were none.

"Look," he said. "I shouldn't have been so—"

"No, you were right," she blurted. "The car—that was just a silly ruse. Please don't tell your partner." Her face puckered. "I don't want him to think badly of me. It was just that I saw you working here, and you really caught my . . . what I mean is, there's no denying you're sexy as hell, but still, I don't know what got into me—"

Her voice cut off and they looked at each other with an awareness that zinged like the current in an electrical line, each of them certain they were thinking the exact same thing.

Him, getting into her. Burying himself deep in the tight wet welcoming heat of her pussy.

Her eyes were glassy. The apples of her cheeks reddened. The tip of her tongue had flicked out to lick her top lip and was apparently stuck there.

She was waiting. For him. To make a move.

He didn't. He *couldn't.*

"I'm there." She pointed to a high-rise apartment building just off the main boulevard, a tower of glass and steel. "The tenants have an outdoor pool, if you want to, um, cool off after work."

He resisted the steady pull of attraction. Futile. "You don't want—"

"But I do."

He tried again. "You don't know—"

"All the better."

Aha. Despite the hints of her being a nice girl, she was looking for a straight-up fuck. Check your emotional needs at the door.

In that case, he *could,* even though he shouldn't.

"Tonight, maybe?" she suggested, gunning the engine again. The vehicles in the right lane were moving, and she switched on her blinker, intending to join them. Her face still seemed youthfully innocent, but her mouth was inviting. *Inciting.* "If the sign isn't wrong about your, you know, equipment."

"What? What sign?"

"That one," she said, giving one more sassy ponytail toss as she drove away.

He looked in the direction she'd indicated, toward the warning and safety signs that dotted the construction zone at frequent intervals. The bottom of his stomach dropped out, but dammit if his cock didn't swell, ready to meet the challenge.

The sign read:

MEN AND EQUIPMENT WORKING.

Chapter Two

The encroaching smog from the inland valley had smudged out the sun an hour ago, leaving the sky the dusky purpled blue of a bruise. Estrella winced when she rubbed her arms. Her skin was tender to the touch. She felt pummeled, as if the unanswered stretch of restless anticipation had manifested as a physical pounding.

She stood on the spacious balcony of the sixteenth-floor apartment. Her view to the pool, a blue rectangle set in an illuminated white concrete frame, was obstructed only by the dusty brown fronds of a row of palms. The binoculars had long since been abandoned.

Her shoulders slumped. Jesse Drummond had left work hours ago. He wasn't coming.

She should've known. Her attempt at seduction had been a laughable failure. He'd seen right through her with his diamond-cutting gaze.

Her fingers curled around the pitted edge of the stone railing cap. His forbidding demeanor should have been off-putting. Honestly, it *had* knocked her off balance for a minute or two. But she'd been drawn straight back to him, inexorably. Beneath the hard surface was an intensity that fascinated her.

Maybe too much. She didn't want another "passionate" man in her life. Her volatile ex-husband had left her with an appreciation for calm routine and quiet.

But Jesse . . .

He would be an experience of short duration. Flame to her moth, and afterward she would be burned free of the craving that had taken hold at the first sight of him.

She leaned over the railing, searching the pool area one more time before she gave up the last sliver of hope.

A figure moved out from beneath the palms. Her heart leaped. Was that him?

There'd been little activity at the pool after five. She'd waited there for more than an hour, her skin prickling at every sound. But no one had arrived except a couple of caftan-clad women carrying cocktails. They'd sat under the cabana awning and played cards, sending her arch glances until she'd scurried away, certain they suspected her of loitering under false pretenses.

False pretenses? She was full of them.

Didn't matter, not this time.

Estrella pushed aside the misgivings as she watched the solo newcomer wander around the pool's perimeter. *Had* to be Jesse. She straightened, pressing her knuckles against the ache in her chest, barely holding back a shout of greeting. Excitement wasn't sophisticated. She wanted him to think she did this all the time. Or at least now and then, she amended, catching sight of her less—

than-refined self in the gleaming glass of the sliding door as she went inside.

"Never mind." She closed and locked the slider, careful not to leave fingerprint smudges.

The descent of the elevator took forever. She hurried through the atrium in the lobby to a side corridor that led to the pool. But once she was out the door, she hesitated. Could she actually go through with this? Have sex with a virtual stranger merely for the physical satisfaction?

She wasn't old-fashioned, only inexperienced. Well, perhaps old-fashioned too. She'd been raised by strict but loving parents, who'd given her little reason to rebel. When she'd arrived at the age where sexual feelings were as inevitable as a rising tide, Tony had come into her life, overwhelming her with his devotion. There had been little question that they would get married as soon as her parents allowed.

But now Tony was gone. Her parents were far away. At last, she was free to make her own decisions.

"I want this," she whispered, creeping through striated shadows toward the pool. The air was clotted with the astringent scent of chlorine and the overly sweet honeysuckle that climbed the thick block wall surrounding the pool.

The sound of splashing water reached her. She stopped, no longer hidden, but safe in the darkness beneath the palms.

She sucked in her nostrils. *It was Jesse.*

As she watched, he bent and swished a hand through the water, making it lap at the border of Mexican tiles. His hair swung forward against his jaw, smooth and silken, shining clean. Of course. He'd gone home to shower and change. His shirt was a crisp white cotton, worn loose and untucked with only a few of the buttons done up and the sleeves pushed up to his elbows. His dress shirt, she thought, touched that he'd worn it for her.

He stood tall, searching the facade of the building. She half raised her hand, an involuntary *I'm here!* Her voice was frozen in her throat.

With only a cursory glance around him, Jesse stripped out of the shirt, kicked off his shoes. In one motion, he lowered his pants, either taking his briefs with them or proving that he'd gone without, because when he stepped out of the discarded garment he was entirely nude. And head-to-toe glorious.

Estrella shrank to a crouch. Not to conceal herself. Simply because no strength remained in her legs. She was drained of all but the ability to stare.

No, he was too grand for that. She must *behold* him.

Behold his beauty. The animal grace. She'd thought he'd looked good sweating on the job with tight jeans the perfect foil to his blatant masculinity. Now he was unrestrained.

And awesome.

Maybe she was unworldly and too easily amazed. But there was no denying her reaction. Desire was a thunder inside her.

Jesse stood poised at the edge of the pool for only a second or two, but to Estrella the moment was huge. He was starkly beautiful, a masterpiece of carved muscle and taut sinew. Golden-brown skin was set off by the black furring at his chest and between his legs, where a thick penis hung, its size and potent virility drawing her gaze like a magnet. In that one instant, its proportions swelled and she realized with a mouth gone dry that he was already . . . already . . . *ready.* And that she could have him if she dared. Have his fully aroused cock thrusting inside her, filling her to the hilt, touching deep, driving her wild.

Estrella swallowed. Beads of perspiration sprang up all over her body. The congestion of moist heat turned her armpits and panties into jungle zones. Her thighs slid against each other as she leaned forward, hands clasped, neck extended, eyes wide.

Jesse Drummond wasn't a fantasy. He was real. He no longer looked like an unattainable model posing for effect. She could see now that he wasn't sculpted, oiled and plucked to perfection. His body was hard, veiny, scarred. As unequivocal and severe as the bleakness in his eyes earlier in the day, when she'd become scared and pulled away from their flirtation.

He'd acted then like she hadn't affected him. But hard evidence: he was here.

And even if the risk was great, she had to find, somewhere inside herself, the confidence to be his match. The reward of that would be unforgettable.

Jesse dived into the pool. What luxury.

But as he swam its length, the warm water parted to his stroke like a woman's thighs. He soon realized that he preferred the ocean. Wild and untamed, an element to conquer. Swimming pools were too civilized, although they had their uses.

He reached the wall and flipped, gliding underwater before he surfaced and returned to an overhand stroke. His muscles warmed, stretched, blood pumping through them instead of sinking straight to his erection.

When he turned his head, he saw her through the rippling water, walking at a diagonal to the pool, on a course to meet him at the opposite end. So—she had decided to join him, even after the scare tactic of his strip-down. He put his head down and swam hard, welcoming the pull of it in his shoulders. If he didn't burn off some of his energy, he'd drill a hole right through her.

He surfaced a short distance from the wall. She was poised to flee, though she stayed put, wearing the same clothes as before—a sort of knitted halter top that cupped her breasts like basketball nets and the creased denim miniskirt. The hem of the ruffled flounce rose higher across her rounded ass, making him want to reach around and flip it up. Her legs were slender and brown. Her feet were bare.

She wet her lips. "Hello."

He lifted his chin out of the water. "You didn't run."

Lashes lowered, she traced her big toe over the colorful coping tiles. "So you knew I was there?"

Small voice. Frightened?

He should let her go, untouched. But he wanted to be selfish. "Yes."

"How did you get in?" After hours, the outside gate was locked, making the pool accessible only to the tenants, through the apartment building.

"Climbed the wall. I hope you don't mind that I took a swim."

"No one's around." She frowned. "That is, you're welcome. I invited you, after all. Most guests—" Big breath. "—wear suits."

"I didn't have one."

"That's okay. I'm not complaining." Her smile quivered a little, then became smugly serpentine. The knowledge of his naked body reflected from her eyes. He almost laughed, but then she scrubbed her hands on the sides of her skirt and he knew she was still nervous.

He speared his arms through the water, moving closer. "Join me? Water's warm."

"I don't have a suit either."

He laid his palm on the pool surround. "Does that matter?"

She lowered herself, holding her skirt tight around her thighs with one hand. After a moment's hesitation, she sat and dropped her legs into the water. "I'm weighing my options."

"Underwear?"

"Yes," she said, her face suffusing with humor. "Unlike you."

Taking advantage of her distraction, he reached over and lifted her skirt, just a quick peek, but she let out a yelp and shoved it down, kicking him away. "Bikinis," he said. "More than they wear on the beach in Rio."

She forgot her modesty. "You've been to Rio?"

"I was all over the world for nine years. Merchant marine. Got the job when I was nineteen and looking to get away from trouble."

"How old are you now?" Her eyes were huge.

"Old enough. Are you?"

"I'm not as young as I look. That's just my round face." She tucked a hank of her loose hair behind her ear, curling the ends around her finger before she realized the gesture was girlish. She tossed her hair over her shoulder, tilting forward with her breasts swaying inside the slings of the halter. Her nipples were erect, two shadowed bumps teasingly visible in the open slivers between the woven threads.

He ran his gaze over her body. She was short, curvy, bursting with wholesome goodness like a commercial touting the healthy benefits of fruit. "You're round all over."

"Obviously you don't know women. A comment like that won't get me to strip."

"I like round."

"Such as?"

"What do you want me to say? Balloons and merry-go-rounds?

Forget it." He glided closer to her dangling legs, slipping a hand along the back of her calves. "I like round female bodies. Round tits, round butts, round thighs."

"Round tummies?" His bluntness had made her blush, and her voice was hoarse, but she wasn't giving up. "I have a little pooch."

"A little pooch? Like what, a poodle?"

She smiled, shaking her head very fast so her hair loosened and fell around her face, curving into two dark parentheses against her rosy cheeks.

His fingers crept along her leg. "Let me see."

She tightened her thighs. "Not yet."

"You're uncomfortable?"

"I don't *know* you."

He thought that was the point. "You know my name and my job. More than I know about you."

"My job . . ." She looked up at the building and sighed.

"Must be important," he guessed. "To afford that convertible and this place."

Her brow scrunched. "Is one job more important than another?"

"EMT. Firefighter. Social worker. Schoolteacher."

"Well, yes. But lawyer over construction worker?" She shook her head. "Not to me."

"Are you a lawyer?"

"Mercy, no. My job isn't important. Especially tonight."

He stroked her leg. Firm, supple flesh. She worked out. In an expensive gym, he supposed, puffing on a treadmill in a coordinated outfit. Except the image didn't quite fit.

"What's important tonight?" he asked. His voice rough.

"Do I have to say it?"

"Only if you want to."

She looked at him, a direct stare. The lights around the pool made stars in her eyes.

"Sex," she said. And then bit her lip.

Jesse surged up out of the water like an erotic Neptune, his thighs and prodding erection the trident that cleaved her body. She was startled, but she opened to him. Her head flew back; her back arched. Her widespread thighs clasped at his hips. He pressed into her, hard and dripping wet, holding himself up out of the pool on arms that encased her like steel bars.

His mouth covered hers before she was able to draw breath. The slam of pure sensation was another shock. She responded instinctively, melting against the heat of his massive chest. He couldn't use his hands, so every molecule of his dominating force went into the kiss. And she ignited. She burned.

"You mean fucking," he said with a ferocity that curled her edges. His face was right there, strangely exciting, made of jutting bones and scraping skin. Eyes black as sin. Hot breath. Even his lips were hard as his tongue speared in and out of her mouth. "That's all you want from me?"

He didn't let her answer, only pressed deeper with his driving tongue. There was some fear, but for the most she was deeply, darkly aroused. Every inch of her body was alive with a gasping pleasure, but the hottest pinpoints of sensation were at her nipples and especially her clit, where the sensitive nerve endings had knotted into a hard little pearl that worked like a hair trigger, sending her senses reeling each time the ridge of his cock ground against it.

"Just a boy toy," he said. "I should be insulted."

"You want it as much as me."

He put his head beneath her chin to push her head back, saying, "What gave you that idea?" as he opened his mouth on her throat.

She gripped his hair. Her jaw sawed, but the only sound that came out was an "uh, uh, uh," as he bit small hard kisses over her neck and shoulder and along the slope of her chest. Her nipples were on fire, aching for the relief of his wet mouth. But he didn't continue. His shoulders hunched and with a splash he dropped into the water.

The abandonment was sudden. She didn't move for an instant. Then came the hot stab of awareness. Her hands plunged to her skirt, shoving the denim—patched with damp—between her open thighs because his hands were on her knees and, oh God, his face—

"Don't be shy." He inhaled. "I know you're aroused. Your scent gives you away."

She focused where she could without breaking into self-conscious giggles. "I am shy. Sometimes."

"I might believe you—" One long arm snaked out, wrapping around her butt and pulling it to the very edge of the tiles. She heard the zip at the back. "—if you hadn't gotten wet so fast."

Gulp. "Shy girls want sex too."

Don't be passive. Take charge. She lifted her hips and dragged the waistband past them. He helped remove the skirt and she plopped her ass down, raising her legs and pushing the garment away, chill bumps popping up on her exposed thighs as the air met her slick skin. His hands worked easy strokes into her muscles, glidingly warm. The caress was about more than seduction.

"Besides, I learned to go after what I want," she added. She met his eyes, saw the amused respect in the lift of his brows. Emboldened, she leaned down to rest her hands on his shoulders and launched herself into the pool with a gleeful shout.

In a swirl of waves, he caught her around the waist. She squirmed about, laughing, keeping her knees together so he had to put the other arm under her thighs to hold her high against his chest. She felt like the queen of the circus, riding aloft on the elephant's trunk.

They bobbed together as Jesse propelled them deeper, keeping his face lifted to hers, his gaze searching. "Tell me what else you've gone after."

"Freedom," she said without thinking.

"From?"

She looked away, answering him only in her head. *Fear.* Her greatest relief after the divorce and her move West had been to know again what it was to live without fear.

Then why was she finding Jesse's fierceness such a turn-on? She would not let herself be lured into an obsession. On either of their sides, she realized. Her craving was as powerful as his.

"Oh, you know. Freedom from—" She rolled her bottom lip, trying to keep her head while at the same time she was starkly aware of the vise of his arms around her, holding her wedged against his body. And the capacity in him—in all men—to turn their physical mastery to violence. "*For.* Freedom for an education."

"Doesn't every American have that?" His chin hitched. "Even if some of us waste it."

"I had extenuating circumstances."

"Huh. Big words. Showing off the education?"

There was a teasing gleam in his eye, leading her to suspect that he might be the rare blue-collar man who wasn't intimidated by her intelligence or ambition. Or white collar, she amended, thinking of the night school advisor who'd tried to direct her to acquire an "easy" degree.

She was beginning to feel more than lust for Jesse. She slid against him like warm butter, dipping lower in the water. "I want to know about you. How long have you been on the road crew?"

"Since I— Not long. Eight months." His nose pressed against her collarbone. He licked her skin. Hard, pressing fingertips moved across her bottom, stirring her hunger. "Are you asking me when I intend to move on?"

"Is it true that a Hollywood agent scouted you?"

He snorted. "That was nothing but a load of bullshit. But how did you hear about it?"

"Oh . . . I made inquiries of knowledgeable sources."

"Uh-huh. You plotted to get me here."

"Does that bother you?"

"Not as long as I had a choice too."

"Had?"

"I've made it." He set her against a corner of the pool, having slowly paddled them out of the deep end. The water came up to his chest and she could have stood too, except that he held her in place with his body, pinning her like a butterfly with her arms and legs outspread. The inset steps were nearby, but she didn't even try to reach for them. Instead she slithered against him, catlike.

He let out a groan, half pleasure, half resistance. "Time for you to make *your* choice."

She worked her arms down and with a flourish pulled the crocheted halter top off over her head. Her breath caught short as her breasts tumbled out, shining wet, glowing pale as a blue moon in the dancing reflections of the water. *Please think I'm sexy. Think I'm wild and outrageous.*

Jesse looked at her breasts, then at her face. His expression was raw. Hungry—so hungry, the tangible need of it rolled off him like heat from the sun—but, somehow, reluctant.

She forced out her voice. "I say—"

"Wait." He lifted one breast in his palm, his thumb brushing leisurely across the nipple, making her shudder as small detonations went off inside her at every stroke. Her body flowed with sensation. She could come, she thought, if only he'd take her into his mouth and suck until the rapture ran through her hard and fast as a river.

"Before you decide, I should warn you." His eyes bored into hers. "So you can change your mind."

"I won't."

"Listen." The flat of his hand covered her breast like a shield. "I've been in prison. I'm an ex-con."

Chapter Three

The night took on a strange resonance as Jesse's words echoed in Estrella's head. She was hyperalert to the swish of traffic beyond the walls, the shimmy of the trees, the warm silk of the water. And especially to herself. Skin so alive, it twitched and crawled, the chorus of blood singing in her ears, the push-pull of her desire.

Then there was Jesse. He didn't back off.

"Is that supposed to scare me away?" she asked, barely keeping the wobble out of her voice.

His gaze lowered to her breast, where he turned his hand over, gently scraping his knuckles over her tender flesh. He scooped water onto her, and she was amazed that it didn't evaporate into steam.

"It should," he said, sliding his fingers over her slick skin before pulling away. "Scare you."

"Why? Did you do something really bad?"

"They don't send a man to prison for being good."

"But you were innocent." She tried to smile. "Don't they all say that?"

"On TV, yeah." He looked at her, his head still down. The angle seemed predatory and she wondered what he would do if she tried to stop, to leave. Although his confession had given her the option, he didn't seem like a man who would let go easily. She might be making a mistake.

"I was guilty," he said.

"Of what?"

"Assault."

She shrank, giving herself a half-inch of space to slither down the pool wall until her toes touched bottom and she was shoulder deep. "What kind of assault?"

"I beat up a guy."

"Why?"

"I won't make excuses to justify it, if that's what you want."

"There had to be a reason."

"A woman," he said with reluctance.

"Ohhh." Not what Estrella wanted to hear. She crossed her arms over her breasts.

Jesse took note with a flick of his lashes. "It was a stupid bar fight that meant nothing. I never saw her again."

How could he say it was nothing? That was what her ex, Tony, used to say: *I didn't mean to. It's nothing, just a little bruise.*

She pointed her chin at Jesse. "Must have been serious if you went to prison for it."

Slowly, he pulled an explanation out of himself. "I'd been involved in petty crime when I was young. Stealing cars, that kind of crap. Two convictions. I did some jail time for the second one, and when I got out, it was strongly suggested to me that I join the army to straighten up. I was too bullheaded for that kind of regime, so I picked the merchant marine instead. Got a different kind of discipline there."

"So this time, when you, uh, ran into trouble—" She nodded, getting it. The state had a version of the three-strikes law, where there was no lenience for a third violation—maximum sentence, no matter what the extenuating circumstances. "—that was the third strike?"

"You're faster than I was. Sure you're not a lawyer?"

Her mind was spinning in another direction. Although he'd given her a small amount of space, she was still hemmed in by his broad chest and the cage of his arms, which were braced against the lip of the pool. She should have been frightened. But when she looked at the contours of hard muscle, what might have been intimidating remained arousing. Her fantasy wasn't going away that easily.

She inhaled. "How long have you been out?"

"Getting scared yet?"

Exhale. "I was wondering if this is your first—?"

"Nope. It's been nearly eight months."

"Of course, and there are all those women catching sight of you in your handsome orange vest and throwing underwear out of cars with their numbers on them."

One corner of his mouth twitched. "I'd be fired if I was caught making time on the job. I'm walking a narrow line with my crew chief as it is."

"Then why are you here?"

He took his time answering. "Turns out you're irresistible. And maybe I like trouble a little too much." He studied her face. "But I don't think you do."

"Hmm. I guess you're right. But for once I couldn't help myself, and besides—" She ran her finger along his chest the way she'd imagined doing only days ago, except instead of continuing below the water line, she made a curve upward to trace around his bulging pectoral. His brown nipple had beaded and unconsciously she fluted her tongue as she looked at it, then gave her upper lip a slow lick. "—every hardworking girl deserves a night off."

She put both hands on him and rubbed his chest. His skin flinched. "Make that a night to remember," she said.

He took a step back, looking at her, amazed. The pirate's earring glinted at his ear. "Are you sure?"

She nodded, keeping her mind on one track only as she slipped into position against his chest.

"I'm clean," he whispered, his mouth against her hair as he cradled her.

"That's good. Because I'm feeling kind of dirty." Her tongue flicked against his nipple. She inhaled his scent—hot male and black tar. "That's *my* confession: I want to be dirty." She thought of him on the work crew, every muscle in use, glistening with sweat and grime. Of the words she'd already used and the ones banked inside like embers, still to be said.

Go ahead and say it. You want to fuck.

Good girls didn't speak that way.

No, but she was fed up with being good.

Fuck me, Jesse. Please fuck me. Make me dirty.

She didn't quite dare. "Is that enough of an answer?" she said instead. "Can you help me out?"

"Help you out? I'll manage." He lifted her into his arms again and she went without a moment's hesitation, meeting his mouth in an unbridled kiss. His hands roamed over her body—breasts, belly, butt—as he shifted her in his arms each time he found another area to pet and squeeze. Even before they broke the kiss, he had reached for the elastic waistband of her bikini panties and snapped it. The undergarment floated away and she realized with an absurd shock that she was nude in a pool overlooked by a hundred or more windows and she didn't care if the occupants of the entire building watched her get it on.

Tomorrow, she would care. Tonight, she wanted Jesse.

And Jesse's hot mouth, and Jesse's blazing tongue, consuming her like fire. His fingers, not reluctant, oh not at all, two of them spearing through her swollen labia, pushing into her tight clenching opening until they were lodged inside her three knuckles deep. Her buttocks tightened and she rose several inches out of the water, almost clambering him like a tree trunk, driven by an instinctive need to get away from the sudden invasion even though it felt good. So damn good, she was almost crying for it.

She hadn't escaped anything. The fit was too tight. He worked his fingers in and out, and she rode them, urging a faster rhythm with small jerking motions of her hips, feeling absolutely licentious in her abandon. His knuckle ground against her clit and she whimpered at the stinging pleasure, biting into his shoulder with her nails, bearing down on a galloping climax.

The water lapped at her bottom, wantonly spread. Sweet Santa Maria, she was almost completely exposed!

Sensing her alarm, Jesse moved them into deeper water, pressing her against the wall for more privacy. She leaned back to brace herself, arms outstretched and shoulder blades sawing as she rode his plunging fingers like a valkyrie into war, the water churning and frothing all around.

He nuzzled between her breasts. "You are a dirty girl, aren't you?" He tilted back, goading her. "Do it. I want to feel you tremble as you come on my fingers."

The hot flush of embarrassment produced by his command was no match for her need for relief. But she couldn't quite let go. She wanted to beg him to please not do this to her, so fast and blatantly, but if he stopped now, she might die.

Jesse kissed her, his breath hot as he whispered, "Don't hold back." He moved in tight against her, one hand secure at the small of her back, the other busy between her thighs, and, when his mouth found her breast and sucked her nipple deep into his throat, finally then she felt the irresistible pull and relentless pressure as her senses wound so tight, there was nowhere, no further, to go. The pleasure snapped and she flooded with a copious release.

She howled. Her body jerked; her arms flew up.

Jesse's face nudged hers. "Hold on to me."

She obeyed, hugging him. He kissed her ear, her neck, whispering soft words she wasn't able to comprehend right then. His fingers slipped out of her, and for an instant there was a hollow ache before she was bathed by the soothing warmth of the water. Washing her, but not clean. She wasn't ready to be clean. Maybe never again if this mindless bliss was the reward for being dirty.

Slowly, she came back into herself and realized that they weren't through. The thought was a wonderful surprise, like finding a forgotten gift under the Christmas tree after the others had been opened. She might even be able to have him all night. Her intention had been to entertain him upstairs, but now that the moment had come—come like a steam train—she wondered if she really dared.

She had gone this far, so of course she dared. Why not? Her mother had always said, In for a peso. . . .

Though she doubted that her mother had intended *this*.

Gradually Estrella's vision cleared, as did her head. She blinked and looked around at the empty pool deck and the border of landscaping, beginning to focus on the public aspect of the location. Titillating, but dangerous in all sorts of ways. "We should go up."

"Your apartment?" Jesse grimaced. "I'm in no state." As if in agreement, below the water his erection bobbed against her, sending a shock through her system. They definitely weren't finished.

"I'll be your shield," she offered. "I just want to get out of the pool before we end up arrested for public indecency."

He came close to smiling. "Yeah, that's all I need on my record."

She blinked. *Okay, here I am asking an ex-con into an expensive apartment that's not even mine, with an open invitation to perform unspeakably lewd and lascivious acts upon my naked body. Can I get any more risky?*

"How do we do this?" Jesse asked.

"We find our clothes, for starters." She pushed out of his arms and paddled toward the steps, remembering she'd tossed her top somewhere in the vicinity.

Jesse stood and stopped her when she'd climbed halfway out of the pool to reach for the abandoned garment. "Estrella." His arm crooked around her neck and head, pulling her toward himself. He kissed her. Sweetly, with a gentle tongue.

She passed a hand over her face, ostensibly swiping up the droplets. "What was that for?"

"You're safe," he said. "I'm not dangerous."

"I know that." And she did. Not with one-hundred percent certainty, because that could only come over time—which they didn't have, she realized with a pang—but there was something inside her saying that Jesse wasn't like Tony. His gallantry might be grudging, and he showed little emotion, but he would never hurt her. She felt safe with him. A minor miracle, that was, after the length of time she'd gone when she'd wanted no contact with men at all.

Safe, but quaking with an anticipation that verged on trepidation. Make sense of that.

She grabbed her top, then swam to the deep end to find her skirt, taking the opportunity to cool her fevered body. Jesse climbed out of the pool as he was—sporting an erection that had scarcely subsided. Attempting to appear oblivious, she watched him out of the corners of her eyes while struggling into her wet clothing.

Oh my goodness. The sight of his engorged penis was riveting. Enough to bring a woman to her knees.

Estrella lurched suddenly off hers as he approached. She staggered and he caught her elbow, keeping her steady as she led the way inside beneath the lush trees and towering palms, finding the set of keys she'd zipped into her skirt pocket. Once inside, she peeked into the atrium lobby, found it echoing and vacant, then took his hand and rushed him through to the elevator, a compartment paneled in stainless steel with diamond-patterned quilting.

The walls were reflective. She peered closer, pushing wet hair out of her eyes. Not bad, though she was sodden and bedraggled while Jesse remained arrestingly sexy. Since he hadn't dried off, his wet skin had already soaked through his shirt and trousers, making them clingy and transparent in various appealing spots. Especially those areas that highlighted his virility.

She started to thank the gods that they were alone, but luck wasn't with her. A hand reached through the elevator doors just as they were closing.

Jesse stepped back, pulling her in front of him. An older man nattily dressed in a fitted suit entered the compartment, took a look at them and spun on one heel to face the doors, his narrow face hollowing in disapproval. He punched in his floor. Fourteen.

Complete silence. The elevator rose. Estrella couldn't help but stare at the back of the third passenger's head, where his closely cropped silver hair revealed a pink bald spot. She willed him not to turn around. She was in no state to withstand questions.

Jesse pressed a fingertip to the small of her back. The touch felt like the burned head of a matchstick applied to a bruise. She had to smother a yelp.

The other man glanced over his shoulder. "Been swimming, I sec."

Estrella recognized him, but not by name. "Yes, we had an impulsive dip." She plucked at the sagging yarn of her top. It dripped like a used dishrag. Even though Jesse wasn't as wet as she, a puddle was forming around their feet. "I'll be sure to, um, wipe up the elevator."

"Hmph." The man looked at Jesse and raised a supercilious eyebrow.

Jesse must have responded with his own look, because the tenant quickly faced forward again. Estrella's eyes went to Jesse's reflection in the steel doors and met the hard black glare that she found strangely exciting. She was reminding herself to breathe when his hand dropped to her rear end. She tried to reach behind herself to grab hold but he avoided her. Seconds later, he lifted the back of her skirt. A wash of cool air touched bare skin. Her panties were missing.

She elbowed him. Jesse's left hand closed on her shoulder. His right grazed her exposed bottom. She cleared her throat. The tenant moved his head slightly, trying to see without actually turning to look.

Estrella pasted on a pleasant smile, praying for the elevator to move faster.

"I've seen you before," the man blurted as Jesse traced a finger along the seam between her cheeks.

Oh God. She was in trouble now.

"Aren't you the—?"

"Here we are," she interrupted. "Fourteen." *Bing.* The elevator doors slid open. "Have a good evening."

She kept an ungiving smile on her face as the man departed, exhibiting a quizzical look as if he wanted to say more. She'd only been in and out of the building every weekday for more than a year, but she supposed he'd never seen her as a real person. Fortunate for her, at the moment.

Jesse squeezed her ass as the doors closed, and this time she turned and socked him in the rock-hard gut. "There are mirrors all over this elevator. He might have seen!"

"He was a prig. You should have flashed him."

"*You* should have flashed him."

"Didn't want the guy to get too excited."

"He'll be complaining to the condo board as it is."

"What's to complain about? A beautiful tenant, spicing up his ride in the elevator with a little gratuitous nudity?" Jesse caught her around the hips, rucking her skirt up beneath his fingers.

She smiled, pushing it down in front. "You *are* beautiful, in a ruthless way."

"No, you are." He nodded with his chin. "Look."

She swiveled her head to take in the steel-and-mirror enclosure, and saw multiple angles of her naked butt, pale and marbled against the contrast of his brown hands. With a helpless moan, she buried her head against his chest.

"Pretty little dirty girl." He palmed her cheeks, pressing her closer against the fullness at his crotch. Lazily she rocked her hips. His erection had subsided somewhat, but she soon felt the swelling and lengthening that signaled how well his equipment worked. Her own warming arousal answered as her mind filled with erotic images of what she could do once she had him in private.

Or had him right there, right now.

She tried to shake away the temptation. The hell he wasn't dangerous. He made her forget herself.

And his damned talented fingers were tickling between her thighs again.

Estrella's head snapped back. A terrible thought had cut through. "Security cameras!"

Jesse immediately pulled down her skirt. At the same moment, the elevator stopped and the doors opened on the lobby—empty, luckily. She stared out, dumbfounded for a moment before it occurred to her that after the other man had exited, they'd forgotten to press the button for sixteen. The car had automatically returned to the ground floor.

She slapped at the panel, closing the doors, then hit the sixteen before looking up. Sure enough, there was a camera high in one corner, filming their every action. She cringed. *Please don't let there be one at the pool.*

She pointed the camera out to Jesse. "You're a bad influence on me. Look at all the trouble I'm in."

He laughed, the bastard.

"Maybe I should show you what it's like," she said. "See how you enjoy being at *my* mercy."

He held his arms open. "You can try."

"You think I won't?" With a mighty shove that moved him only because he allowed it, she backed him into a corner and attacked the front of his shirt, giving it a good wrench that popped a couple of buttons. They pinged off the stainless steel paneling. *Clean-up on Elevator One.*

"I'll sew them back on," she said while staring at his naked chest.

His laugh made a number of muscles ripple. She wasn't sure what she'd said to get him to laugh—she wasn't thinking too clearly again—but she hoped he'd do it often. Her hands reached out, spreading over his chest like a Braille reader. Watching him ripple was nice, but feeling him ripple was better.

She stroked the corrugated slab of his stomach. The heaviness and heat below his waistband drew her, but she resisted by traveling upward. Jesse gripped the steel rail that circled the enclosure and rested his head against the wall while she experimented on him, prodding and petting, tasting and teasing, peppering small kisses over the expanse of warm rounded muscle until she reached his shoulder, where she scraped back the damp cotton and opened her mouth wide, making an unabashed glutton of herself as she slurped with her tongue like a child with a melting ice cream cone. A moan rumbled in Jesse's chest.

The elevator stopped; the doors opened. Reluctantly Estrella raised her head. She hadn't even managed to get his shirt all the way off. Only his biceps were—

Her eyes widened. Ice crackled in her veins. An inch below the glistening skin where her mouth had been was a tattoo. Somehow, she'd missed it up to now.

Maybe she'd blocked it out on purpose, she realized, as the bottom of her stomach dropped out. It wasn't a large tattoo—only a simple line drawing that had faded to the point where she had to stare to make it out. A curling wave, vaguely Japanese in style, with a moon above.

Not a threatening tattoo, so why had she backed all the way across the elevator? Why was she reaching for the doors, to be sure they didn't close and trap her inside?

"What's wrong?" Jesse said, coming toward her with his shirt hanging off his forearms.

She stiffened. He stopped.

"You have a tattoo." It was nothing. *Nothing.* No reason to get all psycho.

"Yeah. And a couple on the other arm too." He lifted his right shoulder to show her. "Just small ones, from years ago."

She didn't want to look. Or explain. But he deserved something, because suddenly her entire body was a Popsicle. Her teeth would be chattering if she hadn't clenched them so tight. "I'm s-sorry. I have a thing about tattoos."

"I don't get it."

"An aversion."

Jesse frowned. "They're only tattoos."

The doors started to close and again she put her hand out to block them. "I can't help it. I know it's irrational, but they turn me off. Tattoos remind me of some—they bring back bad memories."

Jesse was breathing heavily. He clenched his hands. "I've had them all along. Why would they matter now?"

There was no good answer for that. She looked away, her previous trepidation rising too high to deny. One foot edged over the elevator threshold into the hallway. It was all she could do not to bolt. "I didn't notice before. You're very tanned and I . . . I . . ."

She was miserable. And even though the hot animal attraction was gone, she could still remember every bit even if she couldn't feel it. She hated having to leave him, aroused and frustrated.

But that was what she must do.

"I'm sorry," she said, looking into his eyes and pleading for an understanding that she knew he couldn't offer. Given her open provocation, she'd be lucky if he didn't follow and break the apartment door down.

Jesse shook his head in disbelief. "Estrella . . ."

"I made a mistake," she said. "Good-bye."

And she turned and ran.

Chapter Four

I freaked," Estrella said two days later as she stood over her minute electric range top waiting for the kettle to heat. "And I'm not talking about having second thoughts and backing out. It was a full-fledged panic." She poked her finger near the spout and winced at the burning metal. No whistle and only a wisp of steam, but her stinging fingertip didn't lie. She picked up a potholder and tipped the kettle over the teapot.

Brenda snuffled, not thrilled about the prospect of tea, especially green tea, even though Estrella had explained that the quality of its flavor was all in the precise steeping. Brenda, who read cozy mysteries and believed she knew about such things, had replied that only a jolly round Englishwoman in a cardigan and Wellies should be that concerned with serving tea.

The redhead dropped another Kleenex into the wastebasket. "So what were the tattoos of anyway?"

Estrella shook her head as she measured scoops of loose tea into the pot. "That's not the point. Any kind of tattoo scares me." She felt foolish, admitting that. But after a person has been attacked by a vicious dog, even friendly ones seem risky to approach.

"Get off the pity pot, *chica*. We've become a tattoo nation. Even my Lou has them. And you never said a word. You've seemed comfortable at our house."

"I know. I am, but . . ."

Brenda went off on her own tangent. "I've told our boys they can't get any until they're eighteen, but I doubt either of them will listen to me." Her teenagers were hellions. After Sunday dinner, she usually escaped to Estrella's bachelor-girl apartment, where the three small rooms were austere but peaceful.

"Please don't misunderstand. Lou's tattoos are fine." True, they'd given Estrella a jolt the first time he'd shoved a hairy arm at her out on the Ventanos' front lawn. Her aversion was involuntary, but not exactly a phobia. She had some control. She'd looked into Lou's kind eyes and been able to take his hand.

But Jesse had expected more than a handshake.

"It's in, you know, intimate situations that I'm most—" She waved the tea strainer. "When my defenses are down."

Brenda huffed. "That explains Benny Marx."

Estrella brought the tea tray to her kitchen table and sat down. She'd dated Benny every Saturday night for three months, her only real relationship since the divorce, setting aside a couple of short-term flings. Benny had liked schedules, and she'd liked his predictability. But he'd also liked precisely six minutes of foreplay, the Sci-Fi channel and Taco Bell, sometimes in that order. He had asked Estrella to marry him, out of momentum more than passion, she'd believed. This had been confirmed when the gentle nudge of Estrella letting him down easy had rolled him in the direction of the shoe rental girl at Steverino's Super Bowl.

Estrella distributed paper napkins and mismatched porcelain cups and saucers, mentally ticking off the final seconds of steeping time. Benny Marx had been safe—and about as likely to get a tattoo as he was to go out in the sun without proper SPF protection.

"You know that Benny was a toe in the water." Thirty seconds early, she poured the aromatic tea through the strainer she'd placed on the rim of Brenda's cup. "Drink up. This will be good for your sinuses."

"Like Benny. Hold my nose and swallow?"

"There was no need for swallowing with Benny."

"I don't suppose." Brenda turned her teacup, still looking doubtful. "If he was a toe, what's Jesse Drummond? Or do I have to ask?"

Estrella passed the squeeze bottle of honey. She thought of the wave tattoo. "He was a tidal wave."

Brenda squeezed, stirred, sipped, wrinkled her rabbit-pink nose and squeezed again. "You're regretting letting him go, I can tell."

"Yeah." Estrella sighed. Her fantasies of the roadside he-man had been replaced with endlessly replayed moments from their time in the pool. She hadn't dared delve into what the remainder of the night might have been. "But I think I'm better off this way. For one, lying to him was wrong. For two, his resemblance to my ex is more than a little weird. The physical part is explainable, if I accept that that's the type of man I'm attracted to. But the other—the dangerous, violent thing . . ."

The green tea must have done wonders for Brenda's sinuses because suddenly she got very quiet.

Estrella put her chin on her hand. "Do you think I'm a head case? Like subconsciously I want a man who'll treat me badly?"

Brenda slammed her spoon down on the table. "What did the

guy do to you? If he hurt you, I'll get after him with my hedge clippers and turn his trunk into a twig."

Estrella waved. "No, no! It wasn't like that. Honestly. He was a perfect gent—well, maybe not a perfect gentleman, because that wasn't what I asked for." Ha! She'd asked for a righteous screw, but had backed out before she got it. "He treated me well. This is more about my attraction to his *type*."

"You're sure?"

"Mmm." Estrella felt guilty for withholding Jesse's confession about his stint in prison, but she wasn't comfortable revealing it either, especially when she didn't know the full story. She didn't need to look any more inconsistent, either. That she'd run from his tattoos but not his prison record made no sense.

"Before you noticed the tattoos," Brenda said, picking up one of the flat hard sugar cookies Estrella had put on a plate. She had bought a package of them for ninety-nine cents at the corner market. Her mother would be appalled, but between work and school, she had no time for niceties like baking.

Brenda finished crunching and returned to the question she'd started. "Before the tats, how did you feel about Drum? I mean Jesse."

"I wasn't thinking. I was only feeling."

"Knowing you, that's probably a good thing."

"Wait, now. Mindless sex with a guy I barely knew—how can that be good?"

"Sometimes it just is. 'Cause that's what a woman needs. And sometimes—" Brenda looked at Estrella with her eyes crinkling into mascara-caked slits. "—it leads to the real thing. Hot chemistry is there for a reason, you know?"

"We're not 'meant to be,' if that's what you think. He turned me on from the window of a passing bus. That's hardly a grand romantic beginning."

"Twenty-one years ago, I met Lou in the men's washroom of the Sunshine Superette. The ladies' was clogged as usual. I came out of a stall with a piece of tissue on my shoe and he was at the urinal."

"And it was love at first sight?"

"It was chemistry. But I was halfway gone when he had the decency to wash his hands before coming after me."

Estrella chuckled. "Thanks for cheering me up."

"Maybe you want to spend some time thinking about why you overlooked the tattoos in the first place, and if that's really why you stopped."

"That's *all* I've done for the past two days. Maybe I actually need to stop thinking."

"And start, oh, I dunno, *living?*"

Estrella wanted to protest, but she couldn't. Until Jesse, she'd been existing, which had been about all that she'd thought she could handle. He'd made her want so much more.

Sunday night at Rosa's Mexicali was Jesse's favorite way to finish off the weekend. The partying crowd was absent, leaving the die-hard regulars and the occasional newcomer who looked amazed to have found chili-colored walls and tango dancers pulsing away inside a building with such a drab exterior.

On Sunday night, the band was generally coping with the remnants of their hangovers. They played only slow songs with a lot of desultory sax and more thumps and brush-sweeps than hard drumming. The multicolored lights were toned down to a warm glow and Jesse could hide out in a roomy corner booth with a plate of empanadas and salsa and not be bothered.

Except, tonight, by Sweet Tea. "What about that one?" he said, aiming his beer bottle at a hoochie whose breasts threatened to spill out of her top every time she leaned over to filch from a friend's plate. Her hair was brushed forward around her face, as if being past forty were a crime she was trying not to be fingered for. "She's pretty."

Jesse thought of Estrella's breasts, soft and real. He could still feel them in his hands, taste them against his tongue, like sweet plums. "You can have her."

"She don't want an old man like me."

"You never know."

"You're the one she's checking out."

"Tell her I'm taken."

Tea burped against the back of his hand. "What's that? You're taken?"

Yeah, taken with Estrella, who didn't want him. "I didn't mean anything," Jesse said. He'd had two beers, the chipotle salsa was a green puddle and he was getting maudlin. Time to go.

He didn't move. Weighed down by the block of lead that had been lodged in his stomach ever since Estrella had stared at him with fear in her eyes. There had been a watchfulness about her all along, but he'd sensed she was toying with the aura of risk, letting it excite her. What had happened in the elevator was different.

Jesse grazed his knuckles over the tattoo on his right forearm. Different, and senseless.

"I like the looks of that redhead at the table under the window," Tea said, grinning. "She's built for my speed. But that's gotta be her husband with her."

Jesse glanced over at the couple, catching the wife staring at him. When their eyes met, she turned to say something to her man, then got up and marched across the room toward Jesse. She looked like a mother hell-bent on telling him off. It had happened before. But for once Jesse had to be innocent. Until the irresistible allure of Estrella, he'd slipped out of every grasping entanglement like a trophy-winning running back.

Until Estrella?

Jesse froze his slumped position, but his mind was flipping through his options for escape. Goddamn, he'd *known* going after a woman like Estrella would lead to no good. "Don't look now, Tea. The redhead's coming for you."

Tea got flustered. He tugged on his collar. "Me? What'd I do? She think I was flirtin' with her? I don't want be fightin' with her old man."

The blowsy redhead stopped in front of their booth and put her hands on her hips. She was full-bodied and bejeweled, dressed in black with fringe and spangles, her face as highly colored as her hair. The mouth was loose and generous, but a flinty expression said she was nobody's fool.

"You're Jesse Drummond," she announced in a smoky voice.

"That's him," Tea said with relief.

Jesse leaned over the table to say, "Go get the other one," and Tea was so rattled that he did.

The redhead slid into his spot. "I'm Brenda Ventano. You don't know me, but I'm Estrella's friend."

Jesse nodded.

She looked him square in the eye. "What kind of guy are you?"

" 'Scuse me?" Normally that question was said in a threatening manner, but the woman had been almost conversational, except for the frown lines cutting a deep groove between her hand-drawn brows.

"I want to know if you'll be sweet to her."

Jesse was bemused. "Do I look sweet?"

"Like that matters. My Lou, over there—" Brenda hooked a thumb at the fireplug with a flat-top and tattoos who was currently scowling at Jesse. "He's sweet to me."

"I get the point. But you'd better talk to Estrella about this. I don't know what she told you, but I did nothing to—"

"Yeah, yeah, you were a perfect gentleman. She said. The girl gives credit where it's due. But I'm not asking about the other night. This is for next time. What kind of guy are you? The kind who cares too much, or not at all?" Her eyes flicked up and down him. "I'm guessing not at all. You're not looking for a sweetheart like Estrella."

Jesse shifted, trying to figure out this woman's relationship to Estrella. She was, like him, downmarket. But there was Estrella in that fancy building with the car he couldn't buy without spending a full year's pay. Nothing about her added up, except the way she made him feel.

Which was, beyond the lust, hopeful. Hopeful? Hell. He was past maudlin and into seriously demented sentiment.

He cleared his throat. "You're right. I wasn't looking for Estrella. She found me. And then she let me go."

"But you're still interested."

"Doesn't matter. She's not."

Brenda blew a raspberry out the side of her mouth. "Are you that stupid? When a woman says, *I want you, I want you, but I can't have you,* it's up to you to go after her and show her that yes, she can."

Jesse had considered that. "I'm not in a position to be aggressive."

"All you have to do is knock on the door. Give her a chance."

Jesse looked for Tea, and found him leading the hotcake onto the dance floor, wearing a boyish grin. "You wouldn't say that if you knew what kind of guy I am." Bad joke, considering.

Brenda rested her hands on the table with a clunk of rings and bracelets. "Then tell me."

Jesse didn't know what happened then. Maybe it was the mood, the alcohol, or Brenda's been-there-cleaned-up-after-it air of experience, and of course her mysterious connection to Estrella didn't hurt. Or maybe it was just that he was ready to talk.

For whatever reason, he told her, Estrella's friend, in quick words and a soft voice, about the loneliness that had filled him with futility and anger as a boy, his fall into crime, the harshness and beauty of going to sea, even the stupid drunken night in a bar that had put him in prison. Brenda looked alarmed at the latter, but then she asked him about Estrella and he closed his eyes to answer—not being eloquent, although he sure as hell wished he could—and when he opened them she was nodding. Yes. He was approved, and that meant more to him than he'd expected.

Chapter Five

There was a chest at her peephole. Estrella knew instantly that the chest belonged to Jesse. But when he stepped back in the hallway, giving her a view of the rest of him, the air went out of her lungs. Her fingers and toes and tongue—even, seemingly, every hair on her body—curled.

His face tilted toward the peephole. "Estrella?"

"Yes. Give me a moment." All ten fingers were wound around the handle of a mop. She pried off five to unlock and open the door, looking over her shoulder at the apartment. She'd lapsed in her weekly chores and had spent the day catching up. Eve would expect the place to be perfect when she arrived home tomorrow.

Estrella absolutely could not invite Jesse inside.

She peered around the edge of the steel door. Clearly, he'd come straight from work. The orange vest was gone, but his blue T-shirt and jeans were ripe with the day's sweat and dirt. A damp stain around the collar testified that he'd washed up as best he could.

"Jesse." She widened the door. "Come in."

He hesitated, looking through to the shining apartment, an ice palace with white marble floors, spans of glass and mirror, and walls so pale, it was nearly impossible to discern they were blue. "No, thanks. I'm a mess. I only dropped by to—" He pulled an arm out from behind his back. "—give you these."

Flowers? Estrella's eyes widened. A half-dozen sunflowers, big and gaudy as Mexican dinner plates, wrapped in green tissue.

"I chose wrong," he said, frowning at the apartment.

"They're beautiful. They're perfect." She put every emotion into her voice as she took the paper cone and it seemed to her that the vastly unoriginal and inadequate words rose out of her to bob in the air like helium balloons. "I love them. Thank you."

"You're welcome." He smiled with one side of his mouth. The wry side. "I'm not really the kind of guy who brings flowers, but they seemed like ones you'd like." His eyes went again to the apartment.

She shoved the mop aside. "You caught me playing Cinderella. Are you sure you won't come in? I don't mind that you're di-dirty." Her tongue stumbled. She colored, certain that he remembered how she'd told him she wanted to get dirty with him. "I, um, owe you an apology for . . . you know. And I'd rather do it inside." Was that also suggestive? "I'd rather we sat down, I mean."

She walked away from the door, juggling the flowers as she wiped her hands on the back of her jeans. "Take a seat. I want to pop these in a vase."

The apartment was open concept, so she had no reprieve from his tracking gaze even in the kitchen area, which had been designed to disappear within the sleek modern decor. Estrella had never seen a less kitcheny kitchen. She'd taken days to learn the whereabouts of the few usable cabinets with their touch latches cleverly hidden in the seamless expanse of high-gloss surfaces.

While she filled a crystal vase at the tap, she smiled nervously at Jesse, perched uncomfortably on a low Barcelona chair made of bands of woven white leather and crisscrossed steel legs that looked like they might snap under his weight.

Why had he returned, and with flowers? The flowers were either a last shot at getting into her pants or a sign that he had actual feelings for her. Both options put her on guard.

She plunked the vase on the granite countertop. The sunflowers were glaringly out of place here, but they'd cheer her own drab place immensely once she got them home. Lavish arrangements of white lilies and roses were placed around Eve's apartment. As she'd instructed, they'd been freshly delivered that morning to be at their peak for her arrival.

Jesse had noticed. He rubbed a finger behind his ear, staring at the bowl of white roses on the glass coffee table. "I really got it wrong."

"No, you didn't." Estrella wondered if she should explain, but decided not to. Better to wait and see what he wanted.

She seated herself on the sofa, dread growing as she thought of the doorman downstairs. He was a friend, but she couldn't expect him to cover for her. Bad enough that he'd stopped her that morning and wordlessly, amusedly, handed over a small envelope that turned out to contain her ripped panties. "How did you, ah, find me?"

"The doorman wasn't too sure about letting me up," Jesse admitted. "I look disreputable, huh? He even tried to deny you live here, but I pointed out the mailbox label for E. Romero on the sixteenth floor."

Estrella blinked.

"That's you, right? I guessed it had to be."

"You found me." She knitted her fingers in her lap. Okay, what now? Her eyes went to his arms. The wave tattoo was covered by a short sleeve, but on the other arm were two marks, not even remotely threatening in the light of day. "About the other night," she started.

"Forget it. I understand. You changed your mind."

"Not exactly. It wasn't that I stopped wanting you." Oh God. She flushed. His face drew her eyes and she had to force them back to the tattoos that hardly seemed to matter anymore. "To be honest, I still want you. Just looking at you makes me—" *Sweat.*

"Makes me remember. How it was." She blew out a breath. "And then you bring flowers." Her head bowed. "It was just . . . I had a moment of panic. Because of your tattoos."

He nodded.

"Irrational, hm? But that was it." She lifted her hands, palms up, then dropped them back to her lap.

Jesse didn't speak until she looked at him and saw the patience in his face. "Let me show you," he said, getting up to sit beside her.

He reached for his sleeve. She held herself very still. "This one I got in Japan, on my first overseas job. Most of the guys had some nautical theme going. I went for the more artistic version."

"It's faded." The inked outlining was all in blue with a faint shadow of gray. With his tan, the tattoo might have been only a tracing of veins just beneath his skin. Her hand rose, then stopped midair.

"Go ahead," he said.

She put her palm over the wave drawing, like a child playing peekaboo, though there were no feelings of fear. That moment had passed. There was only a quickening desire. Her fingers played scales against the firm muscle, then drew down the inside of his arm, where the real veins rose to the surface. She wanted to take his hand, but he was pointing to his other tattoos.

"Here, a hula girl from a crazy weekend on Oahu."

She almost laughed. Could there be a less ominous tattoo?

His thumb rubbed against his forearm. "And this one."

A small blue star. And silence.

"No story?" she prompted.

"Prison," he said. "The guy used pen ink."

She pulled air through her teeth. "You're lucky you didn't wind up with hepatitis. Why did you get it?" Imagining gangs and threats.

"Boredom," he said first, then corrected himself. "I missed the sky at night."

She lifted his hand, pulled his arm into her lap. Outlined the star with one finger. "That's my name, you know. *Estrella* means 'star' in Spanish."

Jesse smiled.

Coincidence or not, the revelation seemed significant. She leaned toward his arm, her hair falling forward to veil her face as she closed her eyes and kissed the tattoo. *Tony's not here, he'll never be here, I got away and I will be safe,* she said in her head, a promise that had been repeated many times since her move and the painful break with her family, but that finally, finally seemed real.

She realized her lips were still pressed to Jesse's arm. And he was breathing hard. He stroked her hair, smoothing it away from her face. She let her gaze slip sideways. Wetly opening her lips until suction pulled his skin against her teeth, she kissed again, a slow dragging caress that plucked at the tattoo. His hand curved around her cheek, and although he applied no pressure, she couldn't have resisted the magnetic pull into his arms even if she'd wanted to.

She reached her face toward him. He dropped his forehead against hers and their mouths met. The first small peck became sensuous licks and searchings of his velvet tongue. Their hair interlaced, their fingers too. She smelled his earthiness, tasted his tickling breath, shared the sweetest desire, underlaid by coals that needed only a poke to flare to spark and hot flame.

A pressure—hot electric tension—had built in Estrella's chest. She pulled back, biting her lip. If she opened her mouth, more of the bright shiny balloons would appear, ones that might say absurd, romantic, far too hopeful things.

"I'll go," he said.

"No!"

"It's okay. I shouldn't have come by like this. We can see each other some other time."

She imagined him showing up unexpectedly, when she was in uniform. Or worse, Eve opening the door. Who would probably point him toward cleaning an air filter or unclogging a sink before he could get Estrella's name out. Impossible.

"What if it's now or never?" she asked.

"Is it?"

"It might be."

He raked his hands through his hair. "You're hard to resist."

Then why are you trying? she wanted to ask, but he stood to walk away and she felt a thudding defeat. She put her head in her hands, berating herself for the irrational fears that had let him go— *made* him go—earlier. But she had to follow her instincts, didn't she, even when they were reacting to remnants of the past? She had learned the hard way that listening to herself, believing in herself, saved many a mistake.

The sound of the sliding door to the balcony interrupted her reproach. He wasn't leaving!

Estrella stood, brushed back her hair. She gave herself orders not to be so artless. He would know soon enough just how plain and simple she really was.

Outside, the air was balmy, faintly redolent of the jasmine that grew on a neighboring trellis. Below was the geometry of walkways and gardens, the aquamarine rectangle of the pool. Beyond, the dazzling city lights.

Jesse stood at the balcony railing, breathing deeply as he looked up. She followed his lead, hoping to see stars, but the night wasn't clear. Only a few dulled lights showed through the clouds.

"It's an impressive view," he said. "I can almost hear the ocean."

"It's farther than it seems. But sometimes I think that too, hearing the waves."

"You should live in a house on the beach. Close to the earth, even if you are a star."

"I'd like that. The beach or the country, even the city if I had a cozy neighborhood, somewhere with room for a garden. Someday I wlll."

She moved closer, pressing her arm against his, her hand splayed, their fingers touching. But she didn't say anything more. Didn't make eyes, or brush her breast against him, or let out any of the hundred other ways she'd imagined coaxing him to try again. *Let him make up his mind.*

The lights of moving vehicles streamed along the thoroughfare where she had first seen Jesse. When she closed her eyes to a slit,

the lights blurred and melded into streaks of amber and red, loop-
ing like a pinwheel at the intersections.

"Estrella," Jesse said, and she knew he'd decided even before he
added, his night-dark eyes burning into hers, "My shining star."

A shiver shook over her skin like powdered sugar through a
sieve. She moved into his arms.

He held her away. "Wait. This shirt—I'm rank."

"Then take it off." She pulled the T-shirt from his waistband
and slid her hands beneath it, following the pleated hem as he
yanked it off overhead. She stretched on her toes to lock her fingers
at the back of his neck, her body elongated against his length. She
kissed him.

"You can have a shower if you want." A teasing giggle. "If I get
to watch. But it's not necessary. I like the way you smell." Luxuriat-
ing, she pressed a hot cheek to his chest and found that his skin was
even hotter. Her mouth opened; her tongue unfurled. She laved his
beautiful bronzed skin. "And I love the way you taste."

She felt the thudding of his heart. Then the stirring beneath his
zipper, which produced a similar heating and thickening in her. She
was so filled with longing, it oozed out of her. Longing and happiness and nervousness and the deep demanding need that had refused to go away.

Jesse's hands came up to grasp her waist, holding her still against
him while his mouth tracked a leisurely kiss over her bare shoulder,
into her neck. He nosed her chin up, nuzzled beneath it, his lips and
tongue working on her throat. She melted, blood humming in her
ears like honeybees. He reached her mouth and kissed her hungrily.

"Take me inside," she whispered.

He peeled her hands off his neck, kissed each pinkened palm

and clasped them together as he led her through the doorway, stepping backward so his eyes never left her. "Which way?"

She nodded toward the open archway to her right, where mirrored sconces lit a path like moonlight on the shining marble floor.

He let go of one of her hands to push open the double doors into the master bedroom. Even in the dark, the room shone with reflective surfaces and crisp cleanliness. The bed was immense and white, freshly made with lavender-scented linens that Estrella knew for a fact had a thread count higher than a perfect bowling score, two frames. Her conscience twinged. Eve would die if she knew . . . or she would see that Estrella did.

I don't care. I'm bad, I'm wild, I'm a dirty, dirty girl. I want Jesse—

Abruptly, she stopped thinking and spoke instead.

"I want you spread-eagled in the middle of the bed." Her lashes dipped, her insides fluttered, her lips curled. His face was deliciously dumbstruck. "Naked, of course."

"You want—what?"

She pointed. "You, on the bed, naked."

"It might be better if I wait until—"

She stripped off her tank top, dropped her jeans, then had to wrestle around to get them and her sandals off in one jumble. By the time she straightened, her breasts were falling out of her low-cut bra, so she got rid of that too, leaving her in nothing but a thong.

Jesse, oddly, was slow on the draw. She was able to drop him onto the bed with one firm push at his chest. "Shoes first," she said cheerfully, kneeling before him to tackle the laces of his work boots. The rawhide laces weren't difficult to undo, except that he'd double-knotted them, and then she had to tug at the boots. She did it with a particular zest, knowing that he was watching her breasts bobble and sway. The room was air-conditioned, but by the time she was finished, her skin was giving off a moist heat and she still had his jeans to do. The oozing jelly was practically bubbling between her thighs.

She reached for his zip, sending him a smoldering look beneath her lashes. "I had expected you to be more of the take-charge type."

He spread his hands, amused, then dropped them behind him and leaned back, turning his torso into a golden-bricked lane she very much wanted to follow. "This is your show."

Deliberately she studied his bulging package. "I'll show, you tell."

"Tell what?" His teeth met with a *click* when she gave the taut zip a wicked tug.

"Anything you want. About you, about me, about the man in the moon."

"I'm a doer, not a talker."

"These jeans are very tight." She'd had to stand to work them down his hips and once again his eyes were burning holes into her dangling breasts.

"Only going to get tighter," he said needlessly.

"I'm doing this," she said, and *Dios,* was she ever, as he lifted his hips a little to help her get the jeans down. "Showing you off," she added under her breath as she peeled back the clinging cotton of his briefs and his cock sprang out. Good thing she hadn't bent any closer or he would have put her eye out. She knelt again to slide the jeans and underwear off his legs, her hands working blindly. Once they were gone, she motioned for him to lie back on the bed, more toward the center. "And you're the teller," she finally remembered to say, stopping for a moment to marvel before she slithered up his body and cupped her hands between his legs.

He inhaled. "You think I can talk when you're touching me there?"

"I can stop, if you prefer."

That earned another of the wry, lopsided grins. And a quick, "Okay, I'll talk. About anything, right?"

She should have looked at him before she answered, but she was absorbed elsewhere. "Mm-hmm."

The springy hair on his thighs tickled her. "Spread 'em wider."

She should have wondered why he was compliant, but she was still absorbed elsewhere.

He jerked under her touch. Fascinating creatures, penises. So hard and yet soft. So alive and purposeful. She used the tip of one finger to follow a pulsing vein and when she reached the rim of the head, already engorged to the point where she wondered how he would ever fit inside her, it jerked again. Petting the creature wouldn't calm it, but she tried, grasping the shaft between her palms, stroking and cradling it. The thing insisted on pushing itself out of her grasp. Still growing. Perhaps she should attempt a soothing lullaby? She grinned. Or a kiss . . .

Estrella looked up. "Jesse?"

His eyes were squeezed shut. "Yeah? Oh, yeah." He shook his head. "I forgot what I was going to say."

She let go of his penis, put her hands on either side of his hips and got her legs up under her. Looked at him expectantly.

"Uh, right. I want to talk about you."

"I'd rather hear about you, but go ahead."

He paused. "You taste like cinnamon. And sugar."

"That was the churro I had for a snack. I was craving one, so I stopped at Pasquali's Bakery on my way back from the dry cleaner's."

"You had dry cleaning in the convertible on the day we met."

"Well, Eve—everyone with a white fetish has a lot of dry cleaning." She squeezed his balls.

Good distraction. His eyes rolled back in his head and he arched off the bed, forgetting all about dry cleaning. She wondered what would happen if she sucked them into her mouth.

Not yet. But if he continued to ask questions, she might resort to any number of illicit distractions. For now, she gentled her touch, rolling his warm sac around in her fingers. "You were saying?"

He got a determined look on his face. "I was saying you taste like cinnamon sugar. Sweet. But that's not all. You're spicy too. Hot and tangy."

"Um-hmm." She took the head of his cock between two fingers and bent her head. Said, "Keep talking," and then opened her mouth.

"Peppery."

Extended her tongue.

"Pungent," he blurted.

She stopped a fraction of an inch away from the pearled slit. "Pungent? Does that mean smelly?"

"No. It means, uh, well-seasoned."

She chuckled. "I'm not sure about that one, but go ahead."

"Got a thesaurus handy?"

She smiled. "You can always talk about another subject."

"No, I like this one." His eyes gleamed at her from the shadows at the silk-padded headboard, like a cat lurking in the bushes. "I could tell you about how it makes me crazy when your nipples get all hard and dark pink. The way they are now."

She resisted the urge to touch them. "Wait a minute. Is this all going to be dirty talk?"

"You disapprove?"

She worked her thighs against each together. The thong was drenched. "I guess it's okay."

"That's nice. Because I love your round little body, and seeing you turned on like this. It would be even better if you played with your nipples."

More of the hot honeyed flow, funneling down her center. She tried to sound blasé. "No, I'm busy. You go on without me."

"Ungh." His hips gave another involuntary jerk as she stroked his erection, putting more pressure into it. She pumped, released, then felt sorry for the frustration on his face and wrapped her hands around him again. "Tighter," he said, straining to speak. "That's right. Tight. Like that. How your body will be, squeezing down on me."

"Oh?"

"God, yesss. Your pussy will be tight. I know it."

She made a questioning sound as she puckered her lips and fitted them to the end of his penis, lightly sucking before she slipped the tip of her tongue along his opening.

"Ahh." Jesse shuddered. The coverlet wadded in big wrinkles as his hands clenched spasmodically. "So . . . damn . . . tight." At first, he forced the words out. Then they came faster. "The way I had you that first night. In the pool. Naked and sleek. Hot and tight. Clenched around my fingers so damn tight."

She pressed her hands flat to the bed. Went after him with only her mouth, jaw practically unhinged as she opened to suck him into the heat and wetness that she knew would drive him over the edge.

"You wanted it so bad. But you stopped." He breathed through his nose like a bull, lifting his hips to thrust until she made a small choking sound, gorged on the thickness filling her mouth. At once he drew back. "Tonight you won't stop." What should have been a statement carried an underlying questioning tone.

She looked at him with the eyes of a seductress, giving him a lollipop suck before she popped free. She licked her lips. "I won't stop. But you keep going." She crawled forward and lowered her body over his, filling his hollow with her curves, enclosing his jutting sex between her thighs. "Tell me more."

"I want to feel your skin, your beautiful skin."

Her body caressed his, moving like a wave across the sand.

"I want to taste you in my mouth."

Crooning, she freed her breasts and pillowed them against his face for him to nibble and kiss and suck.

He groaned. "I want to feel you on my cock this time. Riding me."

The words were a sweet shock, the last push she needed to tumble headlong into full-out abandon. She levered up higher, opening her legs and rocking into place. He was iron pressing against her softness. But she was strong too. Although her body would yield, she wouldn't be broken.

With his steady voice and patient ways, Jesse had made her know her own will. Already she was a little bit in love with him, if only for that.

He put a hand on her hip to stop her. "Get my jeans. My wallet."

"Ah." She twisted off him to reach for the floor where his clothing had been tossed aside. The position poked her rear end in the air and he took the opportunity to get his hands on her, dragging down the thong and squeezing her buns, together and then apart, the tips of his fingers delving into the hidden places where she was hot pink and succulent. A tremor followed each stroke, drawn through her in a shower of sparks like the tail of a comet. Her hands shook as she extracted the condom packet—*muy grande,* no surprise—and pushed it at him, not even thinking of trying to do it herself. Empowerment went only so far, at least their first time.

They hunched together, her hands hovering near his, both of them breathing hard. Once he was sheathed and she rose up on her knees astride him, ready to impale herself, he grabbed her face and kissed her, hard and deep. His fierceness had returned. She was exhilarated, outlandishly aroused. Her hands twined in his long dark hair as his mouth traveled over her face, her shoulders, her breasts. She clutched at him, dying over and over, wild new sensations coming one after the other until the pleasure was too much to keep hold of by herself. She had to have him or burst at the seams trying.

She reached for the wide stem of his cock, holding steady as she fitted him to her swollen opening. He was large, much larger than any other man she'd been with, and she had to force herself down, feeling her flesh slowly give way as he entered, a thick spike of steel and heat and raw passion.

I want him. Wild me, naughty me, sweet nice kind me. Brazen, she pushed at his shoulders, tilting her weight into him so they tipped over onto the mattress with a jounce. His hands remained at her hips, his cock wedged inside her. They were locked—the plunge onto the bed had given her another inch of him, and then more as she rocked her pelvis, opening, spreading with short panting downward thrusts. She was full, too full, and there was more of him to take.

"Slow," Jesse whispered. "Easy. Give yourself a minute to adjust."

She leaned into his chest, drained and weak. "I'm greedy. I want you all."

"You're small. But we'll get there."

His face was strained, every muscle in his abdomen rigid and quivering. He was trying to hold back and instead of understanding she gave him a hard biting kiss to incite him. *Nasty me.* "I want to be there *now.*" She grabbed his shoulders. "You have to fuck me."

"Damn it, Estrella." His head twisted away. "I was trying to be considerate."

"I know. And that's appreciated. But now I'm giving you *permission.*"

"Fuck," he said, and she thought, *yes, please,* as he clamped her body beneath his big hands and rolled her over. She barely had time to wind her legs around his lean hips to keep him close, but it turned out that didn't matter, because as soon as her butt hit the bed, he was pile-driving into her, forcing the air out of her lungs, the bones from her hip sockets, the "Sweet" from her cry of "Jesus!"

She loved it.

He slammed her. She asked for more, and faster, inflaming him with her willing body. Their mating wasn't pretty or graceful. It was about sweat and hunger and hard-core sex. They fed into each other and off each other, twisting and grinding, unwilling to slow until they came, together, crashing through to the point where they'd lost all contact with physical sensation except the white hot burn-out of a roaring climax.

"Oh man," Estrella said some time later—she wasn't sure how long—as the feeling came seeping back in through her fingers and toes. "I think I passed out."

Jesse was facedown on a pillow. "You okay?"

"I will be."

He put his hand between her legs. Like a homing pigeon, she thought, wincing a little as she straightened a knee. When had she bent that way? Better yet, how?

There was something nagging at her, but his fingers were more important. He caressed gently, easing the burn. Oh yeah. *Eve.*

"Listen." Estrella tried to raise up on her elbows, then gave up, flopping over into a slanted patch of moonlight. "Jesse." For a couple of seconds her fuzzy brain lingered on the satisfaction of saying his name, but then she flexed her tongue and refocused. This was Very Important. "You can stay, but we've got to be up early. I have work. Okay?"

"Sure. So do I."

"Don't forget." There was a clock to set and they had lots of time between now and then, but if he always screwed so hard, there was no telling what she'd lose track of—the time, her head, maybe even her heart.

Chapter Six

Estrella in the starlight.

She thought he'd forget any detail about this night? Never.

Jesse watched her for a long while, dozing with her peaceful face bathed in the silvery light from the wall of windows. She was deservedly exhausted. The first time, that raw, wild pounding, hadn't been enough for either of them. After an hour of recovery, she'd gone searching for condoms in the bathroom and had returned triumphant. Even surprised. If her body hadn't already told him, that reaction would have—she wasn't accustomed to this. He would have to be more gentle, no matter how wicked she got with her tongue or her provocative words.

He'd been surprised too. Gentleness had come easy to him. He'd thought he'd lost that capacity years ago. Maybe it was having a woman like her that did it. She gave him reason.

Jesse laid his head on the down pillow. He wasn't worried about sleeping too late. He never did. Prison had hardwired him to wake up at every sound.

Of course, there was no comfort in prison like Estrella to keep him in bed. He turned and pressed against the back of her curled body. She woke enough to snuggle her ass into his groin. The warmth of her spread through him. She was a sturdy little space heater, but soft, so very soft. . . .

His arm went around her, intending to hug, until his hand found her breasts and he cupped their sweet weight. Her nipples formed two hard points beneath his pattering fingers.

"Jesse," she murmured.

"Shhh." He forced his hand to go still.

"Okay. But that was nice."

He buried his nose into her hair. "You need to sleep."

"What about you?"

"I'm thinking too much."

She seemed to drift off for a minute, but then she shifted her butt against his wakened penis. "Talk to me."

He moaned. "Not again."

A small laugh burbled in her throat. "Tell me what you're thinking."

Such a girly request. But he found he wanted to. It was necessary. "I was thinking that I want you to know about—" He breathed, unashamedly taking his comfort in her fragrant skin and womanly curves. "—about my record. My crime."

"Oh, that."

"You don't think it's important?" For chrissakes, she was the woman who panicked at the sight of a tattoo. How could she just trust him?

According to Brenda Ventano, that was the way Estrella was— wary but naive. Sweet but tart. Slow to open up, but once given, her friendship was solid as a bar of gold.

Jesse wanted her to know that he could live up to her trust. "I told you about being in trouble when I was younger. I grew up with a single mom, but that's no excuse. She had no help from anyone, least of all my father. She had to work two jobs to make ends meet, but she did everything she could to raise me right." His hand began to move again, absently stroking Estrella's breasts. She felt so good. "I was just too stubborn and angry. I wouldn't listen."

Her arm reached back, her hand found his thigh. She patted it, saying nothing. The touch was enough.

"But I got older and smarter. At least I thought so. When I quit the ships, I had savings and a plan to make something of myself. Then a few shipmates took me out to get toasted their last night in port. There was this girl. . . ."

Estrella inhaled. "You loved her."

"Hell, no. I didn't even know her."

"Hmm. You don't know me either," she said lightly, sounding relieved that he wasn't mooning over a lost love.

He tugged a nipple. She wiggled her butt, aware of exactly how to get him back. "You're wrong about that. I know you, Star."

"You know my body," she said with a sigh, lazily trying to turn around.

He held her with one hand pressed flat to her belly. "Stay like this. Let me finish."

She made a sound of assent, burrowing deeper against him, again squirming her bottom more than strictly necessary.

"This woman was having a fight with her boyfriend. They were both drunk, and after a while they got to pushing and yelling. The other customers just watched. Me too, I'm sorry to say. A bouncer came to get rid of them, but the fight got worse. He tossed them out. Except . . . ," Jesse sighed. "I was near the exit. I saw the guy swing at her as the door shut. He'd split her lip open."

Estrella whispered, "I get it. You tried to rescue her."

"I didn't want her to be hurt. My mom had a boyfriend who—" He swallowed another sigh. "The thing was, the guy fought me and I lost my temper and beat him up. Then in court, his girlfriend testified for him. They made up a helluva story about me instigating the fight. Because of my record, I was given the maximum sentence." He let out a rusty chuckle. "Eventually commuted for good behavior. But by then I'd lost my savings to the lawyers."

Estrella was quiet for so long, he thought she'd fallen asleep. He had closed his eyes, waiting for the remaining tension to drain from him, when she spoke in a small tentative voice. "I know about women like that, so caught up in a destructive relationship that they can't break free. Do you blame her?"

"I don't know if blame is the word. I've wished a thousand times that I hadn't tried to help her."

"That's understandable."

He swallowed. "But I'd probably do it again. Except this time I've learned the tools to control my temper so maybe I could avoid the fight."

She patted him again. "Good."

"That's the story. I just wanted you to know."

"Thank you for telling me, Jesse."

He kissed the back of her shoulder. "Go to sleep now."

"I'll try," she said under her breath, twining her legs with his beneath the sheet. He let his hand move against her stomach, barely a caress, to settle her. Maybe to settle himself.

Before long, he knew that it hadn't helped. Her body had worked on him. The hot curve of her ass was the moon, pulling at his instincts, pooling his blood. He was semierect, fitted against her ripe slit. Temptation, succor and torture all in one.

But she was sleeping.

He clenched his teeth. Counted to a hundred.

She moved. Reached to a mirrored nightstand, flipped a packet at him. It fell among the sheets.

"Estrella?" he whispered.

A purring sound was her only response. Until she reached between her legs and rubbed his shaft in her hot slippery fluid. He found the condom, pulling free to slip it on. She whimpered, one imploring squeak, and searched further for him, lifting her thigh so the tangled sheet pulled taut.

They didn't speak again. He swept away the sheet. She rolled over onto her drawn-up knees, staying curled in on herself, head in the pillow, arm down between her legs where her fingers splayed to pull apart her pouting labia and offer him the glistening inner flesh and her budded clit. A dewdrop clung to it.

Estrella in the starlight.

The soles of her feet were white against the creamy gold of her ass. He covered her with his body. Hugging her. Holding her. Wanting to keep her whole even as his cock split and filled her, forcing a deep-throated grunt out of her. He kissed the bumps of her spine, the blades of her shoulders. She flattened beneath him and he held her tighter, higher, sliding his thighs under her, nudging her farther apart. They rocked back and forth, panting.

She turned her head, pressed her teeth against his forearm, sucking and biting. He pushed against her, driving deeper, losing his last shred of reason to the erotic slide and squelch of their flesh. Their fingers met over her clit. He rubbed it and she bolted beneath him but there was nowhere to go except surrender. With one short sharp cry, she came, gloriously liquid. He let go too, jetting into the velvet vise of her convulsing body. All the affection in him, all the love and caring that he'd sworn had dried up and blown away, came pouring out too. The warmth of it enveloped him. He didn't know if she felt the same, since he had no words to explain, but he thought that she might. She very well might.

They tumbled over onto their sides, finally replete, and dropped off into a blissfully entwined sleep.

Lassitude had sunk into Jesse bone-deep. He sprawled on sheets impossibly soft, smelling the outdoors—flowers nodding in the hot sun. The dream was so real, his eyelids squeezed shut against the screeching drench of light.

Sunlight?

Screeching?

He bolted upright, flinging aside the covers, ready to attack even though he could hardly see, the room was so bright.

There was a loud crash. A thud. Shattering glass.

A woman's voice rose to the ceiling. "Estrella! What is this?"

Jesse blinked. A woman stood at the end of the bed, staring horrified at his naked body. The remains of the vase of sunflowers were smashed against the stone floor, broken stems, shards of glass, a spattered puddle of water.

"Estrella!"

The screech sounded like rusty metal. Jesse grabbed a pillow off the bed to cover himself. Estrella was sitting up, pushing the hair out of her face. "Eve?" she quailed. "You're home?"

"Yes, I am. I caught an early plane." The woman spoke through zippered lips. "I cannot believe my eyes. You used my bed. My sheets! You dirtied my Porthault sheets!"

Estrella scrambled out of the precious sheets, crouching to gather their scattered clothing. She threw Jesse a panicky look, then his jeans. "I'm sorry. I'll wash the sheets, of course."

"You'll burn them, and buy me new ones." The woman's face darkened as she gaped at Jesse, who'd dropped the pillow and was pulling on his jeans. "My God. He's a brute. What were you thinking, letting a stranger into my house? I gave explicit instructions—"

Her house? Understanding socked Jesse in the gut.

"He's not a brute." Estrella cringed, holding his crumpled T-shirt over her breasts, but still she defended him. "He's—he's—"

"Her boyfriend," Jesse said, straightening. "I apologize, ma'am. We shouldn't have used your house." He looked a question at Estrella.

She bowed her head, dragging his shirt over it. "This is Eve Romero. My, um, my employer."

For few seconds there, he'd thought the woman might be an older sister, even Estrella's mother or aunt. She was a dark-haired Latina, but there the resemblance ended. Eve Romero had none of Estrella's wholesome goodness. Her slender body was rigid and angular inside an expensive white cashmere suit. The narrow face was squeezed of all compassion and joy.

"Eve, this is Jesse—"

"I don't want an introduction," the fury said, averting her eyes. "I want him out." She pointed to the door. "Out. Immediately."

Estrella's face had blenched. She nodded miserably, keeping herself away from Jesse when he moved past the bed to take her arm. She ducked, picking up the sheets, the tangled skein of her thong. "Yes, of course. I'll go too."

"Oh, no, you don't. You're staying, Estrella. After you strip the bed, I want this room cleaned from top to bottom. *Then* you'll go when I tell you."

Jesse glowered at the woman before trying again to reach Estrella. "You don't have to stay here and be treated like this. Come with me. It'll be all right. I'll take care of you."

Her eyes flickered. "Thank you all the same, but I can take care of myself." She thrust his boots at him and pushed him past Eve and out of the bedroom, speaking hurriedly in a whisper. "Please, Jesse. Just go. I'll take care of the situation here."

He resisted. "I don't want to leave you."

"Eve is only angry, not hurtful." Estrella shook her head, hushing him when he would have protested. "She has a right to be, don't you think? She's never mistreated me, and I've paid her back poorly for her trust."

The screech came again. "Estrella—I'm waiting."

Her eyes pleaded with Jesse. "Please. You have to go. I don't want any more trouble."

He let her hustle him out the door. "I'm sorry I didn't wake up early enough." He tried a grin, a squeeze of her hand. "I slept like a log."

Her answering smile was distracted, and still she wouldn't look into his eyes. Ashamed for her lies, he supposed, which he wanted sorted out, although that was not his chief concern.

"Go quickly." She stared at his bare chest in consternation, plucking at the front of the oversized T-shirt she'd put on. "I'll have to change. Wait in the hallway and I'll bring your shirt out to you."

"Never mind about that," he said as she started to close the door. "Just tell me where we can meet."

She winced. "I can't think about that right now."

"But—"

"I told you that we might be a now-or-never proposition."

Stunned, he stepped back from the door. Did she honestly mean that she never wanted to see him again? Could he have been that wrong about her intentions?

Estrella hesitated for a couple of seconds, her face bleak, then whipped her head around when Eve's voice started in again as she stalked into the living room.

"What's that disgusting dirty rag you're wearing? Get into your uniform at once and start—"

Estrella slammed the door shut.

Surging with anger and protectiveness, Jesse lifted a fist to beat on the steel door. But he stopped himself before the first slam. Losing his temper would lose him Estrella. Forever.

Chapter Seven

*I*n times of stress, Estrella needed the comforts of home. Home was a small house in a small town in New Mexico, where her parents and two of her siblings still lived, a place she hadn't seen for two years but that was more real to her than Eve's immaculate marble mausoleum or even her own threadbare apartment. Lately, the closest she'd come to finding the feel of home was at the Ventano's cheerful, chaotic household, but Brenda wasn't off work yet.

Besides, Estrella was determined to cope on her own.

She'd been fired. The shock had worn off after a couple of hours. Instead of taking the bus home, she'd walked into a department store and used up all of the cash in her purse on a deep-fat fryer.

Utterly ridiculous. But comforting.

Now it was dinnertime. She'd taken a long bath, put on shorts and a T-shirt and gathered her hair up in a ponytail. The oil sizzled as she squeezed another dollop of pastry into it. Watching the dough bob about and turn golden brown was as close to being in her mother's kitchen as she was going to get, hundreds of miles away, with no easy phone contact.

There was a knock at the door. Estrella's stomach gave a funny little spin, but she told herself it was Brenda, or one of the neighbor children, smelling the freshly made churros. She lifted the fresh batch out of the fryer and laid them on folded paper towels before answering the door, peeping through a crack with the safety chain on.

It was Jesse. With more sunflowers. Smiling and wearing long sleeves that covered his tattoos.

Estrella shut the door. She fussed with her hair, her shirt. Patted her flushed cheeks. Her heart tried to drum itself out of her chest, but she swallowed it down again and opened the door. "Hello, Jesse. How did you find me?"

"I remembered that Brenda had mentioned working on Alvarado. I went from café to café until I found her. She gave me your address."

"You know Brenda?"

"We met, a couple of nights ago. By chance." He extended the flowers. "To replace the ones your boss smashed."

"That was an accident. Eve was startled by the sight of us." Estrella accepted the flowers, widening the door so he could enter. "Come in. Um, it's nothing fancy. Watch your head."

He had to duck the doorframe, going into the living room. "This place looks more like you." He turned a slow circle, studying her secondhand furniture and the few homey touches she'd added to brighten the apartment—family photos, mosaic flower pots, a woven wall hanging. "Smells good."

"I was making churros." She hurried into the kitchen and thrust the flowers into the stained ceramic sink. "The oil is hot. . . ."

"Go ahead. I don't want to interrupt."

"Please sit." She nodded to the drop-leaf table with a pair of rickety chairs she'd painted emerald green and robin's-egg blue. "Have you ever had churros?"

"I'm not sure. What are they?"

"Fried pastry. Very simple, just flour and water and a few other ingredients." She piped several stripes of the dough into the oil. "When I'm homesick, I crave them."

Jesse sat, cautiously. "You're homesick?"

She poked at the pastries, making them swim in the bubbling oil. "I haven't seen my family in two years, since I moved here. We don't get to talk very often either."

"Why not?"

So many questions, but none of them about her charade pretending to be Eve Romero. The delay was making her nervous. Or it might have been the surreal experience of having Jesse in her house, filling the rooms with his very large presence. For a fantasy man, he'd become all too real.

The oil popped, stinging her as she transferred the churros to the paper towels. "I have to be careful about contacting my family. My ex-husband has tried to use them to find me. Even threatened them. We call and send letters through a neighbor, so there's no record of my address and phone number in their house."

She stole a look at Jesse. He'd lost some of the old poker face, and she could see him grimly absorbing the news. "Did Brenda already tell you about that?"

"No."

"Oh." Of course not. Brenda wouldn't, although she might hint, if she was convinced that Estrella wanted Jesse for more than the fantasy.

"What did she tell you? About Eve, or my job, maybe by accident?" A thought struck Estrella. Perhaps Jesse had known all along that she was not the sophisticated lady she'd pretended to be. Her faced heated, and she hurriedly bent over the fryer, adding more dough. Too many churros already, but she needed to keep busy.

"No, we talked about me. But she did tell me to try again with you. That you had your reasons for the phobia about tattoos."

"Tony, my ex-husband, had tattoos. I used to watch his hands and arms a lot, to be ready if he was . . . in a bad mood."

"He hurt you?" Jesse kept his tone neutral, though she could hear how doing that strained his throat.

"Some. Mostly it was about being in control of me. When I did something he didn't like, he might grab me, push me. Now and then I had bruises, but mainly there was a lot of yelling. He was threatened because I wanted to be more than his wife." The old feelings of humiliation swept over her. She hated to think of how long she'd stayed, making excuses for putting up with the bad treatment. "I was sixteen when we met, eighteen when we married. You know, young and stupid in love. It wasn't always so bad."

Jesse had put his head down. She saw him clench and unclench his hands beneath the table. "And you feel safe here?"

She rescued the well-browned churros. "Yes, finally. We think he's given up, and soon I may be able to have my family out to visit. Until we're sure, I'm using an old family name from my father's side—Ianesque."

"But you really are Estrella?"

"Oh yes."

"I'm glad of that. I couldn't think of you by another name."

There was caring in his voice. And something more. A question? Of their future.

She caught her breath. It was too much for her to believe that he could forgive her deception so easily. "Aren't you angry with me at all?"

His answer was measured. "That depends on why you did it."

Estrella took her time, pretending absorption in making another batch of churros. Finally she set down the emptied pastry bag and leaned her butt against the edge of the counter, making herself look into Jesse's eyes even though that only got her more antsy. "I did it because I wanted to know what it was like to be different from the real me. The truth is, as I'm sure you figured out, I work as Eve Romero's maid. I do many housekeeping and personal chores for her too, but mostly I clean. I ride the bus to work every day in my maid's uniform, and that was when I first noticed you on the road crew."

She took a breath. "So, well, I started fantasizing about you. Then I started thinking that maybe I could make you want me, if only I was different. When Eve went out of town on business, I took off my uniform and got into her convertible." She shrugged. "The rest of it, you already know."

He rubbed at his forehead. The chair creaked. "Why did you think you had to be different?"

"Because it was a fantasy. One night where I could be as wild as I secretly wanted to be, after all these years of always being cautious and good."

"Maybe I would have preferred the real you."

Do you? she wanted to ask, but she couldn't.

"What happens now?" Jesse asked.

"I don't know, except . . ." Suddenly she was shy.

His eyes searched her face. "What?"

"I know you only said it to help me out with Eve, but I liked it when you called yourself my boyfriend."

"I liked that too. But I'm not—" He frowned and wrenched the words out of himself. "I'm not your best bargain right now. Aside from my background, I don't have money, and no real prospects except what I can earn with my hands. If you want a better life . . ."

She ached to hug him, but she didn't dare that either, not yet. "Don't you know that it's not money alone that makes a better life?" He looked up at her and she quickly smiled encouragement. "Besides, I have plans of my own. I'm in night school, getting a degree. Someday I'll have a good job, one to build on."

"Really? What are you studying?"

"Don't laugh," she said, remembering that the last of the churros were still frying. She dipped her slotted spatula into the sizzling oil. They were a bit too crispy.

Aware of Jesse's gaze, she pushed a damp tendril behind her ear. "I'm going to be a pharmacist." She shot him a little grin. "Something about wearing a white coat and being clean and orderly appeals to the maid in me. Plus, it's helping people."

She rolled the hot churros in her sugar mixture and brought him three of them on a paper napkin. "Do you think that's odd, me wanting to be a pharmacist?"

"I think it's just fine."

She sat and leaned her elbows on the table, licking her sticky, sugary fingers. "What about you?"

He watched with gleaming eyes. "When I still had my savings, I thought of buying a small plot of land and trying organic farming. My grandpa had a farm. I spent a summer there, once." He picked up a churro.

"Go ahead. Try it." She nudged his hand toward his mouth. "You could start a new savings account."

"I already have." He bit into a hot crispy corner of the golden-brown pastry, where it was crusted with melted sugar and cinnamon. "Mmm. Tastes familiar. Tastes like you."

"I don't know about that." She leaned across the table, reaching for a kiss. A hot, sweet, melting kiss. "I'm thinking they taste more like you."

"Sweet woman," he said against her lips.

"Hot man."

"Not a bad combination."

"Could work."

"Want to give it a try?"

"Only until we succeed."

Wanted: One Hot-Blooded Man

Pamela Britton

Chapter One

He hadn't changed in years.

Breanna Miller peered out through the front windshield of her car, watching as Trent Walker stripped off his shirt, sinewy cords of muscle rippling along his rib cage as he bundled up his shirt and threw it aside. It had to be ninety degrees, the heat causing sweat to glisten in each crevice and valley that crossed his chest. He lifted a water jug that sat on the tailgate of his construction truck, the black one-ton backed up to an industrial building site, Trent unscrewing the lid of the jug and tossing water all over his blond head. It made him shiver, water droplets flying off his head, rivulets cascading down his tan body.

Bree almost went home right then.

What was she thinking? she asked herself for the thousandth time. What the hell had she been thinking, flying fifteen hundred miles to meet up with a man she hadn't seen in ten years, one who probably wouldn't remember her despite how close they'd been, much less remember her name?

He turned toward her car, his blue eyes homing in on her like he knew she watched him. Bree ducked down behind the steering wheel. Jeez-o-peets, that'd been close. Just what she needed, for Trent to spot her.

The knock on her window a moment later made her scream.

Trent stared down at her, his big body bent forward as he peered into the driver's-side window, gorgeous blue eyes curious.

"Bree Miller?" he asked, his voice clearly audible in the dead silence of the car.

Oh. My. God.

He'd recognized her.

"You are Bree, aren't you?"

How the hell had he recognized her? a voice screamed inside her head. Granted, her black hair was still the same, but she'd long since lost her glasses and twenty pounds.

Bree blindly fumbled at the window control, warm air hitting her face like she'd just stepped into a hothouse.

"Well, hi, Trent. Fancy meeting you here," she said.

Lame. Stupid. Beyond dumb. Now he was going to ask—

"What are you doing here?"

She almost closed her eyes, almost flopped her head back. Instead she forced herself to think.

Think, Bree.

"Well, um, actually. I just flew in." *And boy are my arms tired.* "I, ah, just happened to stop here to get my bearings."

Liar, liar, liar.

"No kidding?"

"No kidding," she echoed back.

Did he believe her? Bree searched those hazardous-to-your-health blue eyes and found no sign of mockery.

"So you're in town for the weekend?"

"I'm here on business."

True, though not the kind of business *he* had in mind. *Monkey business.*

"Wow. Well, we'll have to get together."

"How about tonight?" Bree asked, cursing herself immediately. Jeesh, could she sound any more desperate?

You are *desperate.*

"Well, I don't know—"

But it was too good an opening to miss. The whole way over, she'd wondered how to excuse her presence at his job site. She'd been sitting in front of the place contemplating that very problem when he'd begun his striptease and she'd become . . . distracted. Now she saw an answer.

"It's been so long, Trent," she said, giving him a wide smile, even though inside she quaked in her pointed-toe boots. "And just think what a huge coincidence it is that I stopped here. Right here," she repeated. "To, umm, look up directions." She absently reached for the map that she kept nearby, only to shove it away when she spotted the giant, black X, that marked his job site.

"Tonight?" he repeated.

She nodded.

But then his face cleared, his eyes doing some kind of smoky, sexy thing that made her nervous. "Okay. Sure."

She almost lifted her hands in victory. *Step one accomplished.*

"What time?" he asked.

"Why don't you meet me at my hotel—the Embassy Martinique—around six?"

"The Embassy Martinique," he said back. "That sounds great."

Now if she could just get through step two: having sex with him.

Bree told herself she had nothing to worry about. She'd just meet him for drinks. Nothing had to happen—not if she didn't want it to. He'd never have to know the truth behind her sudden appearance at his construction site. He never needed to know that she'd traveled all this way to see him again because of something they'd shared in their past.

But that didn't stop her from dressing the part, in something sexy, not slutty. After all, she didn't want to scare the man away—jeesh, she still couldn't believe he'd recognized her. But as she dressed in a little back dress, the tight halter top and long, flared skirt a perfect re-creation of Marilyn Monroe's famous white dress, she wondered if she'd gone off the deep end.

You haven't even finished dressing and already your hands are shaking.

"I can do this," she told the mirror. "It's going to work out."

But what if Trent had a girlfriend and he didn't want to sleep with her?

You're making excuses, Breanna girl.

It was true, because the truth of the matter was, the thought of having sex with Trent Walker scared her to death.

But you have to.

She'd come too far to back out now. And if she didn't push herself to do this now, she was desperately afraid all the therapy to put Humpty Dumpty back together again would be for nothing.

So she slipped on black, strappy heels, ran her hands up her long legs to ensure they were smooth as glass, and brushed her loose hair one last time. When she'd finished, she forced herself toward the door. Forced because there was a part of her that still balked.

She knew the moment she entered the crowded bar that the dress had worked. Male heads turned to stare appreciatively, more than one woman took one look at her, narrowed her eyes, then dipped her head to complain to a friend who would also turn and glare. It'd be kind of gratifying if she weren't shaking in her stiletto heels.

He was easy to find—right at the bar where he said he'd be, his blond head towering over the lesser mortals standing nearby. And as Bree got another look at him she felt her anxiety slip away as a surge of pure, feminine appreciation took over.

Oh my.

All he wore was a white T-shirt, the logo of the company he worked for branded across his chest. That T-shirt clung to every previously noted muscle, the ones that hardened his chest and lower abdomen. Arms the size of ham hocks flexed as he lifted a drink to his mouth, his head swinging around.

Bree pasted a smile on her face. Their eyes met. If she'd been any other woman, the look he gave her would have made steam emerge from her panties. Instead it made her throat tighten in fear, made her smile wobble a bit.

"Hey there," he said in a low voice as she came up to him.

"Hi," she said, slinging her purse off her shoulders and placing it on a bar stool he'd saved for her. She smiled up at him in a wide, I'm-So-Happy-To-Be-Here smile. *It's just Trent,* she reminded herself. The guy you used to pal around with. Your best friend from high school. Remember? Sure, you haven't seen him in years, but it's the same guy just the same.

Actually . . . it wasn't.

She couldn't believe how big he'd gotten. In a lot of places. She noted the blue jeans he wore clinging to his crotch. He looked like he worked hard for a living, his body honed, arms tan, fingers callused. He looked like a man, not the pubescent boy she remembered.

"God, Bree. It's been—what—almost ten years?"

"Yeah," she said.

"I can't believe we ran into each other like that."

"Actually," she said, forcing her throat to work so she could swallow. "It wasn't exactly an accident."

"No?" he asked, looking surprised.

"No. I, um, sort of planned it."

"Really?"

"Really." And then she forced a fake and hopefully sultry smile to her face. "Look. Do you want to get out of here?"

She saw his pupils dilate a bit, saw the flash of something close to surprise. "What do you mean?"

"I mean go up to my room."

The pupils flared again, so did his nostrils, the look on his face going from soft and friendly to hard and predatory.

"I mean, if you don't have a girlfriend or anything."

He didn't say anything. Music began to play, a throbbing beat that instantly made people straighten up and voices get louder.

He leaned toward her. Bree told herself not to draw back. "Are you propositioning me?"

"Ahh . . . yeah I guess I am," she admitted, telling herself not to look away.

But she did glance away, only to see him finger the rim of the drink he'd been sipping. "What's the matter? You nostalgic for the good ol' days?"

But she'd been expecting the question. "I'm a professional, Trent. I don't have time for relationships. Nowadays sex is just a release for me. I try to fit it in when I can." She gave him the practiced smile. "No pun intended. When I realized I was coming here on business, I thought I'd look you up to see if, you know, you might have some time for me."

"Really?" he asked.

"Really," she repeated, running her foot up his left leg. "We used to have some fun, you and I. I was hoping you'd want some more."

Actually, he'd been her first love, but that been a long time ago.

She thought he might refuse, thought he might laugh in her face. Lord, she'd envisioned so many different reactions to her words.

His, "Let's go," was the reaction she'd hoped for. What she didn't expect was the way hearing those words would make her feel.

Oh God, Bree thought, her palms going sweaty. She started to panic. Her heart pounded against her chest.

He took her hand, Bree sliding off her bar stool. *Trent,* she reminded herself, *it's just Trent.* But the reassurance didn't help.

"What floor?" he asked.

Bree realized they'd crossed the lobby and she hadn't even known. She blinked, trying to realign her mind. Floor? What floor?

"Fourth," she said.

A minute later the elevator closed. Trent pressed a button, then turned her toward him, his head moving to her lips before she could stop him.

"Trent—," she managed to say before those lips covered hers. Familiar lips. Lips that had kissed her intimately . . . once upon a time.

But he'd changed. He wasn't the soft-mouthed teenager she remembered. Oh, no. This man was hard. He nipped at her mouth, his tongue caressing the sensitive swell of her bottom lip in a way that should have had her moaning in pleasure.

"I can't believe you're here," he whispered.

The elevator doors opened. They pulled apart.

"What's your room number?" he asked, tugging her out the door.

"489," she said, letting him pull her along even as her ears began to ring.

"Key?" he asked.

Bree fumbled in her purse, handed him the white card. He inserted it in the card-lock, and with a loud click and a snick, the door opened, light flowing in from the row of windows directly opposite. The moment she stepped inside, he pulled her to him.

This was it then, a voice inside her said. This was what she wanted him to do. Amazing how easy it had been—

He kissed her, his tongue slipping past her lips before she could form another word, and the shock of that hot, masculine invasion made her gasp. But she didn't panic because he tasted . . . familiar. Safe. Sweet.

Yes, she silently hissed. *Yessss.* This was what she'd hoped for. What she'd prayed for. He might have changed on the outside, but she *knew* this man. He'd been her first lover. Her first boyfriend. Her first *friend.* She needed that gentle man back.

And for a moment or two it worked. Her body sank into his. Ripples of excitement moved down her body. She felt herself swell and moisten as hope sent her spirits soaring.

And then he picked her up.

Bree went stiff, reality returning like the bracing slap of subzero breeze.

Oh God.

He set her down on the bed, slipped his shoes off, his hands moving to the fly of his jeans.

She couldn't move.

He unzipped himself, slipping down his jeans and his boxers in one, smooth motion.

His penis sprang free, the head of it fully engorged. His top came off next. And when he stood over her naked, his eyes were as hot as a swallow of whiskey. "Get undressed."

She couldn't breathe.

No, that wasn't true. She panted. Fear gave everything a crystal clarity. His erection, the veins swollen and engorged. The goose bumps just above his blond pubic hair. The fitness of his body, every muscle pumped and at the ready.

"Bree?" he asked again.

She looked up, her vision having narrowed so that all she saw was his blue eyes. "I can't," she said.

"You can't?" he asked, his voice so low, she couldn't hear him at first.

"I just can't," she said, looking away and then darting to the edge of the bed.

Chapter Two

Trent stared into the eyes of the only woman he'd ever loved, his mind refusing to comprehend her words.

He blinked, and it was as if by doing so he'd washed away a lust-induced haze.

"I'm sorry," she said, sitting up. She turned on the king-sized bed so she faced the other direction. "I know you think I'm a tease, but I just can't."

He saw it then, saw the tenseness in her shoulders, the way her rib cage expanded and contracted with each panicked breath. Because that's what she was . . . panicked.

"Bree, what's wrong?" he asked, the high he'd felt since spying her sitting in front of his job site fading away in a cloud of concern. She was back, yes, but obviously there was more to her reappearance than she'd let on.

"It's nothing. I just can't do this."

But it was more than nothing. He knew by the way she wouldn't look at him. The woman he remembered was one who'd never have had a problem facing her troubles. It was one of the things he'd most admired about her—and the reason she'd ultimately left town. San Jose had held no challenges for Breanna Miller. So she'd struck out for college with a vague promise of returning. Only she never had.

She'd broken his heart.

Trent bent and recovered his clothes. When he'd finished dressing, he went around to her side of the bed. She hadn't moved, her face pale, her black brows shielding her eyes. Amazing how little she'd changed. Well, she'd dropped a bit of weight but the black hair and blue eyes were exactly the same.

"Hey," he said, touching her shoulder.

She jumped about a foot.

Their gazes locked. Trent saw fear.

"God, Bree. Are you okay?"

Stupid question. Obviously, she wasn't. He stared down at her, unsure what to do next.

"What happened?" he asked.

"Nothing," she said in a monotone. "I just need to be alone."

"Fuck that," he said. "Something happened to make you like this. What was it?"

She didn't answer. Trent almost gave up. But she held him there, Breanna Miller and the past they shared.

"Somebody hurt you?"

Still no answer, but he saw the shoulders twitch, almost as if they'd flinched.

"My God . . . rape you?"

Her head ducked even more. Bile rose in his throat. It shocked him, the rage. He hadn't seen her in years. Hell, she hadn't even bothered to call. But the past melted away as remnants of his long-forgotten feelings for her resurfaced. God, he hadn't ever thought twice about jumping into bed with her.

Someone had raped her.

God *damn* it.

"Who?" he asked, trying to keep his voice calm.

He thought she wouldn't answer again, had decided he'd cross over to the armchair in the corner of the room, sit down and wait it out. But then she slowly looked up, and when their gazes met, it felt as if the walls of the room closed in.

She was crying.

"You don't know him," she said softly, sorrow, pain and a world of regret in her eyes. "But he was my fiancé."

Her fucking *fiancé* had done this to her?

He sat down in the armchair. Actually, he just sort of fell into it.

"When?"

"A little over a year ago."

"Ah, hell, Bree."

She went silent again.

"Did you press charges?"

She nodded. "He denied it. Told the cops it was consensual. I couldn't prove anything. He got away with it."

"Is that why you came back home? To get away from him?"

She shook her head, her upper teeth coming out to worry her bottom ones. And at least a bit of the fear faded. Thank God for that.

"Actually, I came back to have sex with you."

Shock. She could see the way his eyes widened. *Well, what did you expect, Bree? A whoop of joy?*

"Sex with me?"

She nodded. "You were the last man I remember feeling safe with."

"Shit, Bree. I thought you'd forgotten me."

"No, Trent, I've never forgotten you."

Something passed between them, something that made Bree feel regret.

"Look, I'm sorry for dragging you into all this. I've tried everything I can to get better. God, if you only knew how hard I've tried. Nothing's worked so far and so I got this crazy idea that maybe you could help me, you know, help me get over my—" What should she call it? Anxiety? It was a whole lot worse than that. Phobia? That was closer to the truth. "My fear of men," she finally finished, although that was probably a poor choice of words, too. She didn't actually *fear* men. She just didn't want them touching her.

When she met his gaze again, it was to see his expression turn to disbelief.

"Guess I better go buy myself a year's supply of batteries, huh?"

Trent stared at her, and she wouldn't have been surprised if he got up and walked out. Instead he surprised her by saying, "You're afraid of having sex?"

It sounded so pathetic when he repeated it to her that way.

It is *pathetic, Bree.*

"Let's just say the only kind of sexual stimulation I can tolerate nowadays is of the mechanical kind," she admitted, reminding herself that this was Trent. Once upon a time they'd been very close. She could have told him anything. "I have a whole drawer of gadgets back home."

"Are you afraid of me right now?"

No. She couldn't be afraid of him, not after how close they'd been. Jeesh. She'd almost married the man. And yet . . .

"A part of me is, yes, even though I know it's you and I really shouldn't be."

"Actually, given the fact that we haven't seen each other in years, you're right to be concerned."

But Bree shook her head. "You're a good man, Trent. I don't think that's changed in recent years."

"But you don't know that for sure."

Her heart had started to pound. "No, but I'm pretty certain I'm right."

"Oh, yeah?" he came toward her.

Bree edged away from him, her back coming to rest against the headboard.

"Don't play games with me, Trent. Not now."

"You took a big risk inviting me up to your room, Bree. A *huge* risk."

And he was right, damn it. She knew that. It'd been a stupid idea. But he'd stopped advancing.

She looked away from him, tears burning the edges of her eyes. What the hell was wrong with her? She'd never been prone to foolish acts before.

You're desperate, that's what happened.

A hand reached out and gently touched her arm. Bree flinched, but he only did it again.

"The truth is, Bree, you *can* trust me," he said softly. "And if you give me the address of the bastard who did this to you, I'll hunt him down and kill him for you."

She looked into his eyes, realizing he was absolutely serious. How had it happened? she wondered. How had all the years dissolved? And what was that look in his eyes? It was the same look as before, the one that made her feel . . . odd.

"I don't know what to do," she said, a part of her realizing the words had more to do with the look in his eyes than her state of mind.

"Let me hold you."

"I don't know if I can," she said, the tears falling down her cheek.

"Let's try."

She almost waved him away, but instead she forced herself to nod. He shifted, slowing scooting closer to her—like she was a wild animal about to flee. And maybe she was.

"I won't hurt you, Bree," he said softly, taking her into his arms.

Everything inside her froze, and then went wild, her pulse, her breathing, the adrenaline in her veins. She almost wrenched away from him, almost told him to let her go. But instead she made herself stay still, to try and relax, and eventually, slowly, she was able to do that.

He held her. She listened as he murmured soothing words—nonsense things that helped calm her down.

"Do you remember the first night we met?"

She nodded.

"I chased you up and down that cruise strip what must have been a hundred times, but I never caught you. And then, when I pulled into that convenience store, there you were." He rubbed her back. "My lucky night."

"I should have never left you."

"Nah," he said softly. "You had bigger and better things to do. I understood that. But I never forgot you. You were my first real girlfriend, the first love of my life. When I looked up and saw you in front of my job site, I thought I must be seeing things."

"I was afraid you wouldn't recognize me."

"How could I ever forget you?"

She shrugged.

"I still can't believe you came all the way back to make love with me. What am I? A stud service?"

Which made her smile. His voice was so familiar. And so very, very dear. She'd forgotten that. It also made her remember something else. Something she might be able to do.

"Do you remember what we used to do before we had the courage to actually make love?" she asked.

"Yeah, I remember," he finally said. Then he laughed. "We were so afraid of getting you pregnant."

They had been. And though she hadn't thought about it in years, it all came back to her: the empty pool house, their near silent whispers, their nervous laughter.

"I'll never forget it."

"Me neither," she found herself saying as she slowly regained some semblance of calm. She took a deep breath and said softly, "Do you think we could . . . do that again?" She looked up at him and saw the stunned surprise in his eyes, as well as a question: "Are you sure?"

"I'm sure, Trent," she told him. She licked her lips. "I need to do this. Please?"

He didn't smile, didn't nod—didn't do anything other than stand, release her hand so he could sit in the chair across the room.

With another deep breath she turned toward a drawer and the vibrator she'd stashed there. She'd brought it along in hopes of using it with him. And okay, when she reached in to grab the thing, there was another moment's hesitation. It looked like a penis, one fully engorged, and the thought of dragging the thing out and letting Trent see it . . .

You just saw the real thing a few minutes ago. Get over it, Bree. Now. Time to throw your inhibitions out the door.

So she grabbed the thing, desperation making her flip her skirt up. She peeked at Trent. He hadn't moved, but just the sight of him sitting there . . .

She closed her eyes, fear, trepidation, a healthy dose of embarrassment and yes even excitement causing her skin to heat as she slid her underwear down. She wore a thong, one with tiny straps that caressed her hip bones. And as she removed the tiny piece of silk, she caught the smell of herself, the salty-sweet scent warmer than the air around her.

Was she aroused?

Her eyes sprang open when she realized a part of her was. She wanted release. She craved release. Sex had been good before . . . before John.

You're safe now. Nothing to worry about. It's Trent. He's never hurt you.

So she slid her underwear off her ankles and out of lay back. She still wore her heels, she realized, but she didn't care. She grabbed the damn vibrator and turned it on. She could do this, she told herself, turning on her back and spreading her legs. She could.

And, God help her, the moment she touched herself her body reacted out of reflex. She might not want Trent in the room with her, but she sure wanted sexual satisfaction. It felt sooo good when she pressed that vibrator against herself.

So good.

Trent faded away as she ran the dildo up and down her valley.

Her body's instinctive reaction was to heat and moisten. She even dipped the thing inside her a bit, enjoying the feel of it stimulating her hole.

With each passing second she grew more and more aroused. Something about Trent watching her, something about the way he sat there—objective—and yet not. It did something to Bree.

She leaned her head back, working herself more. She was slick now. And hot. She loved the way her juices felt against her own hand. So she stroked herself, sweet release beginning to build, which was why she spread her legs farther.

Trent didn't move.

Her rib cage began to expand and contract as her breathing became irregular. God, she wanted to come. She wanted to cream all over her fingers, she found herself thinking, and to do it in front of Trent because he deserved to sit there and watch. He couldn't have her. No man could have her. They didn't deserve her.

She moaned, moving on the bed so that her open valley faced him. She thought she heard him moan, too, opened her eyes.

He was hard.

"Take it out."

He did exactly as she asked and began to stroke himself. He threw his head against the back of the chair, watching her through eyelids that were slits as he ran his hand up and down his cock.

He liked her fucking herself, did he? Well good. He probably wanted some of her come juices, too. Probably wanted to taste her. She stuck a finger in her mouth, sucking her own juices off.

He groaned again.

Her vagina pulsed in pleasure. Just knowing what she did to him, knowing that with every caress, every touch, she drove him nuts—it made her pleasure grow and multiply. She went back for more, loving the wet feel of herself, oh God, she was going to come. She wanted to let it go, wanted to throw her head back and scream her release. But it was too good, watching him stoke himself, hearing his moans as he moved his hand up and down—just like old times—it was all too good.

She moved the vibrator around and took pleasure in taunting him. A brief second of stimulation there, right there, against her clit, then a shallow dip into her vagina. Over and over again she did it to herself, wanting to climax. But she wouldn't let herself. She had to torment him more. He worked himself faster and faster.

Can't have me, she whispered to herself.

She ran the dildo around her opening, sucking on a finger at the same time.

She climaxed.

She hadn't meant to. Damn it. She didn't want to. But her whole sex organ throbbed in hard climax that flooded her fingers. Her neck arched, her labia pulsed outward, then inward in a series of exquisite contractions that made Bree throw back her head and moan.

Trent moaned, too, and when she looked over at him, it was just in time to see him ejaculate, white fluid surging all over his hand and lap.

Suddenly, their harsh breaths were the only sounds in the room, that and the sound of water running somewhere, and the low hum of the vibrator.

And it was good.

Lord, she could still feel the pleasure ripples flow through her.

She closed her eyes and lay there, her slick valley a yummy reminder of what she'd just done. She wished she could lie there like that all night. Instead she opened her eyes.

Trent gave her a small smile.

She shoved her dress down, pleased and yet . . . not. She'd done it. And he hadn't touched her while she did it. Even though she'd taunted him, even though she'd all but invited him to stick it inside her, he hadn't—and that went a long way toward reassuring her. And yet what she really wanted, what she wished she could have was the real thing.

He got up, and her hope that she was cured fled as quickly as it had come. She was still afraid, damn it. The moment he'd moved . . .

He headed toward the bathroom. The sound of running water filled the room.

Shit, what was wrong with her? Obviously she could trust him.

He came out, apparently all cleaned up. Unlike her. She felt like an oil slick, the smell of herself still clinging to her pores.

He'd brought her a towel, one that was slightly damp so she could clean herself up.

Just like old times.

"You still don't trust me, do you?" he asked after handing her the thing.

"No," she admitted in a small voice, suddenly unable to move as he hovered over her. He sat down on the edge of the bed again. She could smell him, the scent of his release combining with her own.

"Bree, you know you can."

"I do know that."

"But that doesn't make it better," he surmised.

She shook her head. "Maybe we should do it again?"

"No," he said emphatically. "That's enough for one night. I think we need to take this slow."

He was going to help her.

Gratitude made tears rise in her eyes once more.

"Why don't you meet me in the lobby tomorrow night at six."

"Okay."

He looked like he might bend down and kiss her, but he must have seen the warning in her eyes because what he did instead was say good-bye before walking away.

"Trent?" she called out to him, shocked that he was so quick to leave.

He turned back to her.

"Thank you," she said.

He gave her that look again, the one that made her breath catch.

"Don't thank me yet," he said gently.

Chapter Three

Five minutes later, Trent leaned his head against the steering wheel and groaned.

What the hell was that?

But as Trent turned on the ignition, he realized he would do anything to help her. Damn it. He still cared.

And so the next night, Trent showed up exactly at six. One look in her eyes as she said, "Hi," and he realized he might care for her a lot more than he realized. Damn it, what was it about the woman that made him nuts?

"Hi, Bree," he said, stopping in front of her, even though what he wanted to do was tip his head down and kiss her. In tight jeans and a peasant blouse, she looked hot. "You look great."

"Thanks," she said softly. "You look great, too."

Did he? To be honest, he hated wearing dress shirts and slacks. Give him a pair of worn-out work jeans and an old T-shirt any day.

"Thanks," he said, catching some guy looking at Bree, the man's eyes sweeping her lithe body up and down.

Mine, Trent wanted to growl.

"What are we doing tonight?"

"We're going to a dinner party at a friend's house," he explained, taking her arm and guiding her out of the hotel. She didn't seem to have a problem with him touching her in public, but he'd seen the momentary flash of relief that'd crossed into her eyes when he'd told her they were going out, not up to her hotel room. "I thought it might help you to relax if you weren't alone with me. After the party, we'll do whatever you want." He looked into her eyes. "*Whatever* you want."

The gratitude he saw was unmistakable. "Thanks, Trent."

"No problem."

But he *was* having a problem because his body reacted to the sight and smell of her. As he opened his car door, he could have sworn he caught a whiff of her femininity, the salty-sweet scent unmistakable, especially after last night.

"Nice car," she said, referring to his black, E class Mercedes.

"Thanks," he said, having gone instantly erect, memories of how she'd looked last night with her legs spread, her cum juices glistening on the inside of her thighs—

Oh, man.

If she'd been any other woman, he would have dragged her upstairs right there. But this was Breanna, and no matter how much he wanted to spread her legs and taste her for himself, he couldn't. Not yet.

"I feel kind of bad," she said as she slid in next to him, "because I never even asked how you've been doing?"

"I've been good," he said, a fantasy of what she'd looked like with her legs open making him want to moan.

Get control.

He was trying. Damn it, he was trying.

"What about you?" he asked. Too late he realized he shouldn't be delving into her past. Obviously, it was pretty painful.

"I've been," she looked away for a second. The sun had started to set, a sudden flash of yellow-gold light painting her face so that her blue eyes turned the color of ice—or maybe that was just a glimpse of her damaged soul. "Good," she finished, meeting his gaze again, her jaw set in something he'd describe as determination.

He decided to take the plunge. "What happened?" he asked. "How'd you find yourself with a man who," raped you, he silently finished. "Did that to you?"

She shrugged, looked away again. "He was nice in the beginning," she said, giving him a self-deprecating smile. "But I've learned that's what most victims say. A guy steps in, sweeps you off your feet. Everything's wonderful, except . . . except there are little niggling signs that something's off. A sudden flare of temper here, a fit of rage there. The first time he pushes you, you think it's just an aberration, and you're so into the whole 'I'm in love' thing that you find yourself forgiving it. The second time you're a little more upset, but then he gets mad at you because you're scared and before you know it that little shove turns into a fist. I tried to find a way out right after the first time it happened. He didn't like that."

She dropped into silence, her face in profile as she stared out the window, and as she sat there, she didn't move, didn't blink, didn't seem to do anything other than get lost in her thoughts.

Goddam sick bastard.

"Did *you* ever come close to marrying?" she asked.

He felt his brow wrinkle at the unexpected question, but then recognized it for what it was—a ploy to change the subject. And as he put his mind to the question, it was strange, because he remembered back when they were teenagers all they'd talked about was marrying each other. Now here they were, years later, and in so many ways they were perfect strangers.

"No. Not really," he admitted. "At first I was too busy trying to make something of myself." But now that my business has taken off, I don't have time."

He saw her nose wrinkle. Funny, he'd forgotten she used to do that when perplexed. He remembered teasing her about it right before a math test.

"Wait a minute," she said, eyes narrowing. "Are you telling me you're the owner of Horizon Construction?"

"I am."

Her brows lifted. "Wow, Trent. I'd heard what you did for a living, but I thought you worked for someone else." And then she smiled, and it was like sunlight breaking the plane of the horizon— a beautiful flash of yellow gold.

"And here I thought you might have rented this car."

The approval he saw in her eyes did things to him. Strange things. Like make him feel proud. Maybe even want to gloat a little. Instead he said, "I was lucky," a part of him wondering what would have happened if she'd never left town. "I hit the Bay Area construction boom just right. Made a lot of money, invested some, put away even more. I work when I want to work now."

"And so here you are," she said. "Mr. Successful."

"Somebody told me you haven't done too badly yourself."

She shrugged. "I have a degree in law." And then clouds rolled over her smile. "Obviously, it didn't do me a lot of good."

"One day, the guy will pay," Trent found himself saying. "I promise you that."

She nodded, still not looking at him.

Trent almost asked her for a name right then, but he decided to let the matter drop. He'd find out on his own—even if he had to hire someone. He started his car instead. And since he was staring at her right as he turned the key, he had a perfect view of the way her eyes glistened with tears.

He drove to the dinner party in a fit of rage.

He'd turned quiet, but that was okay with Bree. She needed time to think, time to reassure herself that she was doing the right thing by involving Trent.

He didn't seem to mind being involved last night.

Yes, that was true. But it wasn't really him she was worried about—it was *herself.*

She felt guilty. From the moment she'd looked into his eyes tonight, she'd begun to suspect he still had feelings for her.

So?

He's a big boy, Bree. He knows you're messed up. Don't let guilt stop you from letting him help you. Damn it, you need the help.

"What are you thinking about?" Trent broke the silence by asking.

"Us," she admitted, tempted to flat-out ask him if he still cared for her. She didn't have the guts to do that.

"You know—about us in high school," she improvised.

"I've put on sixty pounds."

In hard muscle. "You look good . . . so good, it makes me wonder what one of the campus queens would think of you now."

"Actually, I dated Crystal Gallager a few years back. She was crap in bed."

Bree laughed a little. "She *looked* like she was crap in bed."

Their gaze met, locked, each of them remembering how they'd stumbled across Crystal and her boyfriend having sex in the high school's equipment room. Of how they'd been about to back out when Trent had stopped her, the couple having sex on blue athletic mats too far gone to notice them. Trent had put his hand under her shirt. . . .

"I'd forgotten all about that," he said in a low voice.

Not her. It was the one sexual encounter she remembered with absolute clarity.

But she lied and said, "Me, too."

His eyes grew dark, just the way they had that day at high school. Now they were traveling toward the hills surrounding the Bay Area, headlights flicking in and out of the cab, but she could still see the way the memories of that night aroused him. She had a sudden longing to be normal, to not have incessant fear beating at the back of her throat, to be, if only for a moment, taken by him—by Trent, her high school sweetheart.

But she didn't think she was ready for that yet and so she appreciated the fact that he didn't delve into the subject further. She realized then that he was building her trust. Little by little, showing her that he wasn't going to hurt her.

"Nice house," she said as they pulled to a stop.

He didn't say anything, just hopped out. Bree wondered if it would prove too much for him. Maybe he regretted offering to help her. Maybe he would ditch her at the party for some hot babe who'd put out.

No. Not Trent. She might not have seen him in years, but he hadn't changed that much.

He guided her to the home's elegant front door, leaded glass allowing a faint hint of music to come through. Behind them a view of the Bay Area looked like fireplace embers on the ground, yellow streetlights twinkling around the perimeter of the bay.

"Stan Miller is a client of mine. He's a bit on the eccentric side, but I hear he throws a good party."

"You've never been here before?"

"No. He's invited me over a few times but tonight's the first time I've accepted the invitation. I should know a few people though. Everyone seems to travel in the same circles."

Bree nodded and soon they were shaking the infamous Stan's hand.

"Make yourself at home," their host said. *"Mi casa es su casa,"* he quipped, giving them a smile.

"Thanks, Stan," Trent said.

"Glad you could make it," Stan said, eyeing Bree up and down. And something about that gaze made Bree shiver, made her sidle up next to Trent.

"Bar's out back."

Trent nodded, his arm going around her shoulder as if sensing her discomfort.

"Maybe this wasn't such a good idea after all," he whispered as they walked away.

Gratitude had her smiling up at him. "No. It's okay. He obviously considers himself a player, despite his age."

"Then he must own stock in Viagra," Trent said.

Which made Bree laugh and feel better. It was a gorgeous home, and music poured out of hidden speakers. Trent seemed to know more than a few people, but he stayed by her side. She saw a few women eyeballing them, or more specifically, Trent. Not surprising. One of them, a stunning blonde, even lifted her champagne glass as if saluting Bree on snagging Trent as her escort. Bree looked away in embarrassment. If she only knew.

They mingled, they talked. Trent brought her drinks, and she had to admit, being out among a crowd was good for her. She hadn't been out in a long time. Trent helped a lot by keeping her amused as they nibbled on finger food.

"Tired?" he asked a couple of hours later.

"A little."

"Why don't we take a breather?"

She nodded, having forgotten how conscientious an escort he could be. He led her upstairs and to a game room that had a private balcony off the back, a small porch overlooking the pool.

Bree stared down at the water that glowed like a white neon sign, glad to be away from the noise of the crowd. The drinks had relaxed her so much that she didn't want to leave, Trent's pressure-free evening was exactly what she needed after last night. She scanned the people milling around below, thinking they all looked like they didn't have a care in the world.

"Why don't I get you another drink?" he asked.

Bree said, "Thanks," and handed him the glass. But she didn't really like being alone, she realized. Her eyes caught on a couple groping each other on a lounge chair. *Jeesh, they should get a room.*

"I saw you with Trent Walker earlier."

Bree jumped, a rap song's *boom-boom-bum* having masked the

woman's entrance. The stunning blonde from earlier stared back at her, blue eyes friendly as she joined Bree out on the balcony.

"Are you two seeing each other?"

The question surprised her, though Bree supposed it shouldn't. Trent was a good-looking man. It was only natural that women would be interested in him.

"No," she said.

The woman handed her one of two champagne flutes that she held, silver bubbles clinging to the glass's side. "Here. He asked me to give this to you."

"Trent?"

The woman nodded. "Told me he needed to use the little boy's room."

Bree said, "Thanks," taking a sip of the drink as she went back to staring at the pool. "He was my boyfriend a very long time ago," Bree found herself saying, wondering why she felt the need to insert that little bit of information. "But we—" What? Use each other for sex? That wasn't true. "Broke up years ago," Bree finished.

The woman nodded, a smile coming to her eyes. "I see," she said, taking a sip of her own drink.

Bree suddenly felt uncomfortable, but like a moth drawn to a flame, she found herself gazing at the couple below. The guy spread the woman's legs apart, and since she wore a bikini, it looked like they were having sex.

"That's Stan," the woman said, having followed her gaze. "He does that at every party. Everyone's used to it."

Obviously, Bree wanted to say, taking another sip.

"I'm Tina, by the way," she said, holding out her hand.

"Hi, Tina. I'm Bree." And Bree could have sworn there was more to her touch than just a simple handshake. It lingered just a little too long, her soft fingers brushing Bree's knuckles as she let her go.

"Nice to meet you, Bree," Tina said, moving in close.

Bree tensed, but Tina stared at the people down below. "Look over there," she said.

Bree looked, then felt her brows lift. Two women made out against the side of a pool house, their tongues flicking in and out, breasts and butts barely contained by tiny triangles of brightly colored fabric. Not that the bathing suits would be covering them for much longer by the looks of things.

"That's Lila and Tory."

"I see," Bree said, feeling suddenly uncomfortable.

"They like fucking each other."

Maybe it was her drink, maybe it was the woman's words, but suddenly Bree felt a little odd. Stan's near-naked friend had wrapped her legs around him. She saw Stan reach between their bodies and lower his trunks.

"Look," Bree said, dumping the last of her champagne out. "I'm going to go find Trent."

"No, don't do that," Tina said, and was it her imagination, or had she stepped even closer? "Not yet."

What the heck was going on? And why was Bree suddenly hesitant to move?

Below, the woman cried out in pleasure, and despite telling herself not to, Bree glanced down. The man had shifted down the woman's body, his tongue lapping at her. The woman moaned again, her hard nipples thrust high into the air as she rode an obvious wave of pleasure. Stan's tongue came out, and Bree saw him stick it inside her.

Heat tingled along Bree's thighs.

Jeez, she was turned on.

"Isn't she beautiful?"

Bree's mind had gone numb. It took her a moment to realize Tina meant Stan's friend.

"I think I need to leave," Bree said, turning away.

Her companion stepped in front of her.

"Do you want to be kissed like her, Bree?"

Chapter Four

Bree froze.

Did she? She'd often wondered what it'd be like to be with another woman. Lord, in recent months she'd even wondered if she should give it a try.

"Do you want to be touched?" the woman asked.

"What?" Bree asked, the instant jolt that hit her—a jolt of sexual arousal—was such a shock that she couldn't move.

"I want to kiss you."

"No."

The woman stepped forward. "Please," she asked.

Move, Bree. Move now.

"I don't think—"

"*Don't* think," Tina said, sticking out her tongue and dragging it along Bree's lower lip.

Good Lord.

"Let me kiss you," Tina said, swiping her tongue along Bree's lower lip again. "All over," she said, moving closer, and then closer still, her tongue and teeth working Bree's mouth.

Move, Bree.

But that sweet mouth had captured Bree's bottom lip, tugged on it, made Bree feel things, *want* things she shouldn't want.

Oh, Jeez.

It'd been long, so damn long, since anyone had kissed her.

They were body to body now, just like the two women downstairs, Tina dragging the edge of Bree's peasant blouse down and then finding her nipple, squeezing it, working the tip that hardened beneath her expert touch. She bent and took Bree's breast in her mouth, and the sight of Tina tugging on her nipple, of her mouthing it, flicking her tongue over the tip, Jeez, it turned her on.

And that was so strange, a part of Bree realized. She'd always been very firmly heterosexual.

"Let me kiss you between your legs," Tina begged.

The words made Bree pulse in pleasure.

The woman slid her hand down to Bree's waistband. Bree felt it, told herself to move away. But suddenly Tina's fingers were there—right there—her hand caressing Bree's wet valley. Bree moaned. It'd been so long, so damn long since someone had touched her there. And she wanted that touch, damn it! Tina kissed her again—harder this time, only to draw back, her tongue lapping at Bree's lips as her finger stroked her clit.

Pleasure.

Oh, Jeez, it felt *so* good to be touched by someone.

Tina's hand lifted, tugging the other side of her shirt down and working Bree's nipple, her teeth gently nipping the hard end, the pressure sending darts of excitement down her body.

What am I doing? screamed a voice.

But then Bree gave up. It happened just like that. One minute she was resisting and the next she wanted to be fucked by Tina, by anyone, by anything.

Tina lifted her head, her mouth moving closer and closer.

Bree kissed her, opening her mouth and giving Tina her tongue, loving the flush of excitement that zinged down her body as she sucked on the woman's hot flesh, loved mimicking the motions of Tina's finger as she glided her hand along Bree's slick, hot valley.

And then Tina was gone.

Bree opened eyes she hadn't even known she'd closed, about to protest, only to realize Tina had gone down on her knees, her hands peeling Bree's jeans down.

Where was Trent?

She shouldn't . . .

But Bree had been so expertly aroused, so thoroughly turned on that when Tina encouraged her to pull one leg out of her jeans, she did as she asked. She wanted that hot mouth on her. Wanted Tina to suck her off, wanted so many erotic, naughty things that when she felt the first brush of the woman's tongue, she nearly came undone. And she wanted Trent here with her.

"Oh, shit," Bree thought she groaned, but she couldn't be sure, because she was so busy spreading her legs, she could barely concentrate.

"Mmm," Tina moaned.

Lights flashed behind Bree's eyes.

The woman tongued her again.

"Oh, Jeez." Bree panted.

The woman used her mouth to fuck her deep and Bree was beyond caring that it was a woman who gave her such exquisite pleasure. She spread her legs as far as they would go, angling herself to give Tina better access. The blonde was an expert. She knew exactly when Bree was on the verge of orgasm, drawing away at just the right moment, then coming back for more. But Bree wanted it all. Now.

Tina must have sensed that because she stood suddenly, Bree meeting her kiss with an open mouth.

She almost climaxed right then. God, the taste of herself, Tina's face so slick with Bree's own cum, the smell was everywhere. She wanted to lick it all off. She kept lapping at the sticky wetness, wrapped her lips around Tina's tongue and worked it like it was a hard cock, wanting to get every last drop of her juices off. Shit, she even tried to undo Tina's pants so they could rub their clits together.

"No," Tina said, dropping down her body. "I want *you* to go first."

"Yes," Bree said breathlessly. "Oh, yes."

Tina went in deep—over and over and over again, then going deeper still. She pulled back with a gasp, saying, "Give it all to me, Bree."

All of what?

"Please," the woman begged.

And then she knew—she knew what Tina wanted. And it would feel so good. So fucking good. . . .

Pleasure, such incredible pleasure. Spasms contracted her vagina as an orgasm began to build.

"More," Tina ordered, and sucking sounds filled Bree's ears.

Bree moaned, clutching at the balcony railing, wondering when she'd put her foot up on a planter so she could spread herself further. And then she climaxed, hard. Bree tossed her head back. *God. Dear God.*

"What the—?"

Bree's eyes snapped open, her body still pulsing.

"Trent," Tina said, a self-satisfied smile on her face. "Just the man I've been waiting for. Come here and fuck me while I make out with your friend."

"What are you doing?" Trent said, his face slack with shock.

"I don't know," Bree moaned. All she knew was that she was still spasming in pleasure, her orgasm going on and on and on.

"Did you give her something?" Trent asked Tina.

"Just another drink. But she didn't drink it all."

"Fucking-A," Bree heard Trent say. An arm wrapped around her. Bree collapsed. "Maybe somebody else slipped her something."

"Calm down. I just sucked her off."

"You're a fucking slut."

"She could have told me to stop. I didn't force her."

"Trent, no." Bree said. "She's right, this was my choice. I could have stopped her."

"See," she heard Tina say.

"No. You didn't want her, Bree. It was the alcohol or . . . whatever."

"No, I wanted it. I liked it."

She looked over at the blonde. "Tina . . . I don't know what to say. I'm not usually attracted to other women." Bree closed her eyes, then opened them again. "And it's been so damn long since someone's kissed me."

Trent wanted to lash out. Not at Bree. She'd been through enough. At Tina. At Stan. At the whole damn world.

Instead he found Bree's clothes, helped her slip them on, then spirited her away. She was still woozy. Maybe drunk. He didn't know.

He'd call Stan first thing in the morning, he vowed. Tell him what happened. And that he'd never do business with the bastard again.

"You're upset," Bree said as they drove home.

"Damn right, I'm upset. We were supposed to hang out together. No pressure. I wanted you to have a good time. Instead—"

"I *did* have a good time," Bree said, her eyes wide. "I enjoyed it—even if all the time she was touching me I wished it was you."

"Ah, Jeez, Bree."

She looked out her window. "I must be more messed up than I thought."

A tear slid down her cheek. Trent's heart broke for her. He drove. He hadn't even known where he was going until he pulled up in front of his house.

"Whose place is this?" she asked, monotone.

"It's mine."

"I want to go back to the hotel." And she showed no emotion. No anger. No curiosity. Nothing.

"I'm not letting you sleep alone tonight."

"Why? You afraid the realization that I'm a lesbian might send me over the edge?"

His stomach clenched. "You're not a lesbian."

"I sure enjoyed myself like one."

He got out of the car, quickly moving to her side. She stared straight ahead as he opened the door.

"Bree, come on out."

"Take me back to the hotel, Trent."

"No."

"Then call me a cab."

"No," he said.

"Trent—"

He bent down and took her in his arms.

"Don't," she said, starting to struggle. "Don't. I'm okay."

And his heart broke all the more, because it was apparent she wasn't okay. Tears stung his eyes as he tugged her into his arms. He didn't care that he was out in front of his house, his neighbors probably watching. He didn't care that she really didn't want to go into his arms. He held her anyway and he didn't let her go. He *wouldn't* let her go.

She began to cry, huge, gasping sobs that seemed torn from her body.

"Fucking bastard," he thought he heard her murmur. "How could he mess me up so much?"

Trent held her, and a second or two later guided her into his house stroking her hair the whole way, rubbing his thumb up and down her bare arms, just held her and told her he was there for her.

She stopped crying.

He would have been hard-pressed to say when, but suddenly she was quiet, his grandfather clock tick-tick-ticking in the background.

"Do you remember the Mitchell boys?" he asked her softly.

He felt her stir, felt rather than saw, her head nod.

"Do you remember how they used to beat the crap out of me?"

She didn't answer, but he knew she did.

"I hated those jerks. Every day they'd lie in wait for me. I was only . . . what? Nine? Ten? They were at least five years older than me, but that didn't stop them from hassling me."

"They stole your skateboard."

Aha. She did remember. He almost smiled. "I think my mom knew I was at the end of my rope. She never said anything to me about it, but she knew what was going on. And then one day she took me into our garage. It was just me and her, if you remember. I didn't have a dad, which is part of the reason why I think the

Mitchell boys picked on me. 'Mama's boy' they used to call me, and they were right. But you know what that mama of mine did?"

She shook her head, Trent resting his chin atop her head.

"She bought me a punching bag and taped a picture of the Mitchell boys right in the middle of it. Told me to beat the crap out of it."

She shifted, leaned back and looked up at him. "She did?"

"Yup." And Trent's heart broke at the sight of her tear-ravaged face. He forced himself to finish his story. "And because of that, I was able to kick the shit out of those boys a few weeks later. They didn't know what hit them. Two months working with a punching bag and I was able to stomp all over them."

She smiled. Just a tiny little thing, but it made Trent's spirits rise. And then he gentled his words, reached around and lightly stroked her cheek with his thumb. "I would give you a thousand punching bags if I could, Bree. A thousand and one, if that's what it'd take to make you feel better."

She burrowed herself in his arms.

"Will you let me keep on holding you?"

"Yes," he heard her whisper.

And to his amazement, she did.

Chapter Five

Bree fell asleep in his arms. She woke up as he placed her on a bed. And it was a sign of how emotionally drained she was that she didn't even ask where she was as he crept in next to her. If she were honest, she wanted him there.

She went out like a light. And when she woke the next morning, Bree realized that crying in his arms had helped.

She rolled over, Trent's arms falling from her sides, which was where they'd stayed all night. And as Bree turned to face him, she realized how much she'd missed this—missed a man's company. And though she never would have thought it was possible, she actually felt relaxed in Trent's company, likely because he'd proved himself trustworthy in more ways that one.

She reached out a hand, gently wiping a lock of hair off his forehead. He looked both familiar and unfamiliar. The nose was the same, as was the jaw—but there the similarities ended. There were lines around his mouth and eyes, wrinkles that hadn't been there before. His lashes were still long, especially while he was sleeping, but the mouth had changed. No longer boyishly thin, it had matured, appearing almost sensual now.

Who was this man? she found herself wondering. Who was this stranger who tried to help her even though he hadn't seen her in years?

She leaned forward and kissed him.

His eyes sprang open.

Bree drew back in alarm.

He smiled.

And she reminded herself there was nothing to be afraid of—not from him.

"Good morning," he said.

"Good morning," she answered.

"Sleep okay?" he asked.

"Mmm-hmm."

"Good." He sat up. Bree felt that momentary stab of panic, but it faded when he turned away from her, dangling his feet over the edge of the bed. "There's towels in the bathroom and a robe hanging on the back of the door." He went over to a huge chest of drawers, opening first one and then another. "Here's a T-shirt and an old pair of sweats you can change into." He didn't turn and hand them to her, just tossed them in an armchair. "I'll go make us some coffee."

And then he left, Bree feeling her brows lift at the suddenness of his departure. He hadn't even asked how she was feeling. And if she was doing better. How odd.

But it wasn't until after her shower, when Bree was sitting on the edge of his bed admiring his bedroom, that she understood the problem. He still wouldn't look at her when he said, "My turn to take a shower." And then, so low that she probably wouldn't have heard him if his spacious house wasn't so quiet, he said, "A *cold* one," under his breath.

Bree froze.

Stupid, Bree. Of course that's what the problem is. He is a man after all—not a saint.

Yes, but he'd been so gentle.

And had probably woken up with a woody, which was why he'd left the bed so quickly.

"Thanks for the clothes," she called out to him.

He didn't even acknowledge the words, just went into the bathroom without a backward glance. Bree stared at the closed door, certain Trent was trying to hide from her. What would he do if she walked in on him? she wondered. What would *she* do?

One thing she did know: after today, she doubted she'd ever see him again. She was scheduled to fly out tonight, which meant if she wanted to give it one more try . . .

No, she told herself with a firm shake of her head. She couldn't ask that of him. He'd done so much already.

Yes, another voice urged.

Because after waking up in his arms, there was one thing she did know: she wanted to be normal again. She wanted it with a fierceness that made her stiffen in resolve. She didn't need a woman to turn her on. That had been a mistake. Trent wasn't a mistake. He was an honest, caring man.

She got up from the bed, her nails digging into her palms.

Now or never.

She could see Trent through the glass of the shower, his head resting against the tile wall, eyes closed.

He was stroking himself.

Bree froze. His butt cheeks clenched as he pushed against his hand, water dripping down his head and onto his fingers.

Let him be, Bree. Obviously he's busy.

Because of *you,* she admitted to herself.

He started to move his hand faster now, and for a second she remembered that first night. Remembered the pleasure she'd experienced just from watching him. And though anxiety made her stomach tighten, the sight of him working himself made her warm and swell.

She wanted sex.

"Trent."

He didn't hear her at first, just continued to work himself, his knees bending as he pressed himself into his hand.

"Trent," she said again.

He turned his head, peered out at her from beneath a stream of water.

"Let me do that for you."

He slowly straightened, his head coming out of the stream of water so that he looked sweaty and flushed. Bree had a moment of hesitation.

I can't do it. God help her, she knew by now Trent wouldn't hurt her, but a part of her still didn't trust.

And then she saw the cord. It hung around a shower curtain that decorated one side of the stall. It was gold, and braided and obviously sturdy enough to tie a man's hands.

Would it help? Would it make her feel better?

Regain your power, a voice sounded in her head—something she'd read in a self-help book not too long ago. That same book had prompted her to get on a plane and find Trent.

"Turn around," Bree said, stepping toward the shower.

"Bree—"

"Please," Bree begged. God help her, she didn't need him protesting. She needed him to keep quiet. To just let her *do* this.

He turned around.

She unhooked the cord, then opened the glass door. Hot air made heavy by steam instantly clung to her face. Trent didn't say a word as she grabbed one arm, pulled it behind him, then grabbed the other, wrapping the cord around him as tight as she dared.

"Oh, man, Bree," she thought she heard him moan.

She took the robe off quickly, before she could change her mind, though to be honest, knowing his hands were tied helped. She felt more confident, and more important, in control.

"Turn around," she said.

He faced her, a golden god glistening with moisture, his dick rosy red and fully engorged from his manhandling.

"What are you going to do to me?" he asked.

Her eyes shot to his, the words giving her another jolt of power. She stepped back, sitting down on the vanity behind her.

"Make me ready for you," she said, spreading her legs.

"Bree."

"Please," she asked.

He stared at her for a long second, then slowly sank down. Bree tingled, one of those delicious, pre-coitus tingles such as she hadn't felt in a long, long time. She scooted forward and watched as his tongue flicked out to work her. If he tried anything, she'd use her feet to knock him back on his ass.

But he wasn't going to try anything, and the realization gave her power. He was dipping his tongue in her now, his eyes looking up at her. Watching him mouth her, feeling his teeth nip at that tiny ball of pleasure—the one that sent hot tingles through her labia. She used one of her hands to spread for him, encouraging him to take her button into his mouth. He did, sucking on it like it gave out the sweetest nectar.

"That's it, baby. Fuck me with your mouth," she ordered, hearing herself use the crass language and liking it. The words excited her, just like pushing out some of her essence turned her on—He suckled her and she threw her head back, clutching the counter.

They started a rhythm, one that began with his tongue flicking inside her, then swiping up her hot, swollen valley. And she could smell the tangy sweet essence of herself, liked the scent so much she dragged a finger up her valley so she could taste herself. He watched, his mouth sucking her harder. Jeez, her tits were so hard, she couldn't resist touching them. She squeezed one, pinching her nipples as she pulsed out more of her juices for him to taste.

It was just like last night, only better, because what she really wanted—what she suddenly realized she would always want more than any woman's hot tongue—was his cock.

"Put it inside me," she said, opening her eyes in time to see his own go smoky with desire. "Do it."

Somehow he stood, and she saw his cock pointing in her direction, his rod swollen from lack of satiation. God, she wanted it. There. Right there, she thought, guiding it to her.

Trent's lips were tight as his dick entered her, stretching her to the point that she gasped. "Fuck me," she panted.

He bent down to kiss her.

She pushed him away. "No," she ordered. "Just fuck me."

He thrust. Bree just about screamed. Pleasure. Oh, Lord, the pleasure. She'd forgotten because no amount of manual stimulation, no amount of female manipulation ever felt as good as a man. Never.

He drew out and pushed into her again. Bree watched his chest rise and fall, his veins standing out along the line of his shoulder and into his arms. She angled her hips, leaning back a bit as he pumped, her clit so coated with sex juices that she could hear each slap of his body against her own. The veins of his neck had started to bulge, Bree knowing he was about to come.

She tightened her vagina around him.

He groaned. She did it again, enjoying the sense of power it gave her to watch him come unglued.

"Bree," he groaned, his thrusts so hard, she had to clutch the counter to keep from moving. He was there, right there—that spot that made her want to squirt all over him. He wanted to come inside her, too. She felt him swell as he prepared to fire off his load.

Maybe that's why she did what she did next.

Without thought she pushed him away. He staggered back, his dick slick and wet, a tiny stream of cum dribbling out of the end.

She tensed, waiting for him to say something, to get mad, to yell at her.

He didn't say a word.

Bree felt something shift inside her, something that made her shoulders straighten in determination, that made her feel ashamed and relieved and grateful all at the same time.

He still hadn't moved.

She went down on her knees and took him in her mouth, ignoring her own need for release. She wrapped her mouth around his head and gobbled down all her salty essence. He gasped, bent his knees. Her vagina pulsed in sexual satisfaction as she suckled on the sticky taste of herself. She knew he was going to come—and quickly—took the first squirt down her throat, swallowed, then drew back and worked his staff for more, satisfaction filling her as another hot stream shot out and landed on her chest.

"Jeez," she heard him moan, and looked up to see him staring down at her. His dick hadn't softened one bit and so she knew she wouldn't have any problem when she turned around, giving him her ass.

"My turn."

He didn't need to be told twice, just pushed into her as she rested her upper body against the cold counter, spreading herself wider and wider as he pumped and pumped and pumped.

She screamed, wanting release, craving release. He worked her harder and harder.

She didn't come.

She changed positions, letting him pound into her from the front, her legs wrapping around his middle. He was grunting now, thrusting and thrusting, their thighs slapping and slapping.

She wasn't going to come and the more she tried, the further and further it slipped away until she was just a shell, tears streaming down her face.

"Stop," she gasped.

Trent kept working her.

"Stop," she ordered, hitting him on the shoulder. That got his attention. He froze. Bree pushed him away, tears of anger and disappointment falling from her eyes.

"Bree, what's wrong?"

But she didn't answer, *couldn't* answer because she knew if she did, she'd lose complete control.

Trent watched her walk away, shock holding him immobile. But then he bent down and picked up the robe she'd discarded, throwing it on as he ran out the bathroom door.

"Bree. What's the matter?"

"Nothing," she said, her hand wiping at her eyes as she went to his armchair and grabbed the shirt and sweats he'd left for her.

She was getting dressed?

"What are you doing?"

"Leaving."

"Leaving?" he all but shouted. "What are you leaving for?"

"I'm giving up," she said, tugging on his shirt. It hung past mid-thigh. "Throwing in the towel," she added, bending to pull on the sweats. They were too small for him, but they absolutely hung on her tiny frame. She didn't seem to mind. "Calling it a day."

"Throwing in the towel on what?"

She turned to face him, and the sadness in her eyes, the dismay and, yes, the anger, made Trent want to go to her, to pull her into his arms, to hold her like he had last night. "On me," she said softly.

But he knew if he tried to touch her she'd only run away. Hell, it looked like she was doing that anyway.

"Bree, don't go. We're making progress—"

"Progress?" she said. "You call what I just did to you progress?"

"You're not afraid of me."

"I *tied you up.*"

"Which gave you confidence."

"Fat lot of good that does me when I can't have an orgasm."

His brows lifted. "Is that what you're upset about? You didn't come?"

"No, Trent, I *couldn't* come."

"Probably because you're emotionally wrung out—"

"Stop it, Trent," she shouted, stomping her foot. "Just stop it. Quit making excuses for how messed up I am."

"You have a *right* be be messed up. What you went through would mess *anyone* up."

"And so I guess I have a right to tie you up too?"

"I don't mind."

"And why is that, Trent? Why do you let me do whatever I want?"

He took a step toward her, wanting her to see the answer in his eyes. "Because I've always cared for you. We go back way too many years for me to turn my back on you now."

"Then there's something wrong with you," she snapped. "A normal man would have told me where to go that first night."

"Why? So you could seek out some other man you felt 'comfortable' with? You might have broken my heart all those years ago, Bree, but I wasn't about to let you do that."

And he could see the anger drain away, see the sadness that once again entered her eyes. "Well you don't have to worry about that anymore, Trent. I won't be trying this again for a very long time."

"No, Bree. That's not the solution. You should keep working at it."

"With you?"

"Yes, with me."

"So I could leave you once again?"

"It might not end up that way."

"Yes, Trent, it would," she said softly, her eyes brimming with tears.

Damn it, he hated to see her cry. Hated to see the pain in her eyes. It made *him* want to pound his fists. "Please, don't go."

But she closed the distance between them, lifting up on bare toes to kiss his cheek. "Good-bye, Trent. I can't thank you enough for putting up with my nonsense the last couple of days."

"No," he said, reaching for her shoulders. "Don't go."

"I have to," she said, turning and scooping up her clothes and shoes before walking away.

Chapter Six

*A*nd that was how she left him, the image of Trent standing there burned into Bree's mind. He'd tried to talk her out of it while she'd waited for a cab, but she'd put him off. She'd just wanted to leave California behind . . . and Trent.

So she ignored his calls. If anything, the longer she was away from him, the more she realized she had been right to take off. It had been a stupid idea to go and see him, and while she appreciated all he'd done, it was better she'd ended it where she had. Obviously, she was beyond repair.

So she sank into routine. Work during the days. Sleep at night. A troubled sleep, one that kept her awake most of the night.

And eventually he stopped calling.

How screwed up was that? All she'd wanted him to do was stop calling her, and yet when he did, she sank into an even worse depression. That depression forced her to seek out professional help . . . again. Only this time she chose a different type of therapist, a woman whom Bree immediately liked. And as the days passed, she began to have hope.

She was just returning from one of those sessions when she saw the envelope. Actually, she almost missed it, only noticing the thing when she went to push on her door, her hand landing right smack in the middle of it.

How odd.

She took the thing down, the thumbtack that'd held it in place falling to the ground. She didn't notice. She was too busy looking at the handwriting on the front. Years of going to school together allowed her to recognize who'd written her name.

Trent.

Her heart began to pound.

She unsealed it, her brow furrowing because there was a picture inside.

John's picture, she realized, her pulse skittering off. And it wasn't just any picture; it was a mug shot.

"Oh my gosh," she gasped.

"Bree?"

The envelope fell. Bree turned.

Trent smiled down at her.

"Hi," he said softly.

Bree held up the picture she still clutched. "Did you send me this?"

He nodded, running his hand through his hair. "I thought you'd like to know."

"How?"

Obviously, she didn't need to clarify what she meant by the question because he said, "I did some calling around, spoke to a friend of mine who does private security for the very wealthy. He gave me a name—a woman's name, one who's made it her mission in life to put sex offenders away."

Holy shit.

He nodded. "She's good, Bree. She went poking around in his past, got some other women to come forward. The guy is scum, Bree. Once the DA realized that, he went ahead and indicted him.

"Thank God," she breathed.

"Glad you're happy, Bree, because the DA is taking a second look at the charges you filed. If he's convicted on all counts, he's going to go away for a long, long time."

Her hands had started to shake, Bree's mind trying to absorb the fact that it was done. John was now behind bars. All the pain, all the anger was still there—but tempered by her realization that he was going to be made to pay.

Trent stepped forward, his hand cupping the right side of her face. "I told you I'd take care of him."

"You did."

"I'm a man of my word, Bree. You should know that by now."

"Yeah, but I never thought . . ."

"Anything is possible if you know the right people and have the right amount of money."

"I don't know what to say."

He smiled. "You could invite me inside."

Bree didn't hesitate as she stepped aside.

Trent wanted to take her into his arms. God, he'd missed her. Incredible how often he'd had to fight the urge to hop on a plane and find her. But he hadn't been able to do that, not until he took care of her ex for her.

He walked into her modest-sized apartment, thinking she looked gorgeous in a black turtleneck, the color nearly the same as her hair. Blue eyes were wide as he walked past her and looked around the bright, airy rooms. It seemed like an apartment Bree would own—the old Bree—with its floral prints and light yellow walls. He stopped near her kitchen, fresh cut daisies on a small side table reminding him that they were her favorite flower.

"Bree," he started to say.

"No," she said, interrupting him. "Let me start." She was quiet for a moment and Trent watched the play of emotions across her face—gratitude, happiness, regret.

"Thank you," she finally said, looking him square in the eyes. "Thank you," she said again. "You've given me *so* much, a shoulder to cry on," she smiled a bit, "a body to use. And now *this*." She came forward, reached up on tiptoe and kissed him. "Thank you."

"You're welcome," he said.

And then she wrapped her arms around him and Trent didn't need a second invitation. He hugged her back, inhaling the smell of her. She smelled like cotton candy and flowers and it was a scent he'd missed in recent weeks.

She drew back and Trent worried she'd boot him out again.

"So how have you been?" he asked.

She didn't push him away, just nodded her head once and said, "Good. I'm seeing a new therapist."

"Oh?"

"A sex therapist."

And that almost made Trent smile. "Oh really?" he asked with a wiggle of his brows, trying to make light of the matter.

She smiled a bit, looking away for a second almost as if in embarrassment before meeting his eyes. "I always thought sex therapists were crackpots. You know, secret nymphomaniacs who got their rocks off listening to other people's problems. But then I met Dorien."

"Hmm . . . a woman, eh? I know how fond you are of women."

She hit him in the arm. Trent felt hope. She seemed different with him. Almost happy to see him. "Don't remind me of *that*."

"Sorry," he said with a teasing grin.

She shook her head. "Anyway, Dorien's been a big help."

"Did she prescribe some more sex toys?"

"Trent," Bree scolded. "Of course not."

"Just checking."

And then she smiled—a real smile, one that tugged the corners of her mouth up and made dimples appear in her cheeks. Lord help him, he loved those dimples.

"Actually, she gave me some very good advice. Advice that I've been dying to try."

And suddenly Trent went on alert. He didn't know why, but he suspected that "advice" had to do with *him*.

"She told me to have sex with you."

He couldn't help it. He laughed. "Wait. Isn't that how this all started?"

"Yes," she said, not cracking a smile. "But this time I need you to be the aggressor."

"Excuse me?"

She took a step toward him. "You need to tie *me* up."

"*Excuse me?*"

"I know that sounds strange, but when Dorien explained it to me it made perfect sense. I think I need to give *you* control. All this time I've been calling the shots, telling you what to do. But that's not what I should do to try to help myself. I need to relinquish control in order to regain it, if that makes sense."

No, actually, it didn't. "Bree, that's a crazy idea. Obviously, you haven't given this much thought—"

She kissed him. And, damn, but he hadn't even seen her move. One minute she was standing there and the next she kissed him in a way that made his fantasies seem like sawdust.

How the hell did she do it?

"Tie me up, Trent," she said against his lips. "I need you to."

He shouldn't do it. He knew he shouldn't. But he didn't have the willpower to say no.

"What do you want me to use?"

She kissed him again. "Thank you, Trent. I can always count on you."

Yeah. Good old, Trent. Whoopie.

Now or never, Bree thought, going into her closet to find a scarf. Her hands shook as she dug through a drawer, pulling out a blue one.

Oh, Jeez, she didn't think she could do it.

Trent waited for her in her bedroom, the blinds already drawn as he stood by the edge of the bed. She tossed the scarf down on her white down comforter, then tugged her shirt out of her jeans.

"Whoa, whoa, whoa," Trent said. "Maybe we should try and tie you up first."

"No," Bree said, jerking the turtleneck over her head. "I want to be naked."

"Bree, c'mon."

But she continued to undress, knowing the sight of her body

would arouse him. It always did. His protests would stop soon enough.

They did.

"Tie my hands behind my back."

"Bree," he protested again.

"Do it."

He still didn't move.

"If you don't, I swear I'll get some other guy to do it for me."

"Like hell you will," he said. He gave her one last look before picking up the blue scarf, wrapping it around her wrist then gently tugging it behind her back. It was a long scarf, the kind you could wrap around your neck and drape down your back. She'd never, not in her wildest dreams thought of using it for this.

He reached for her other hand. She almost panicked then, told herself to take slow, deep breaths.

It's Trent, she reminded herself. *Just Trent.*

She felt him wrap the scarf around her wrist.

Shit.

She closed her eyes.

Don't panic, Bree. It's okay. He's not going to hurt you.

"There," he said.

"There's a condom in the side drawer, go get it."

"Bree—"

"Damn it, Trent, do as I ask."

"But—"

"Just go get it," she all but yelled, trying not to panic because she'd tested the scarf around her wrists and it was tight, almost too tight.

Oh, Jeez.

She heard, rather than saw, him go to the side table. Heard because she'd closed her eyes, taking deep breaths, reminding herself over and over that his was Trent, not John, and that she wasn't going to be thrown down to the bed, her legs spread apart, and then stabbed at—

No, she mentally screamed. *No.* That was in the past. This . . . this was now.

"Got it," he said, sounding grim.

"Good, now get behind me," she ordered.

"Bree—," he tried again.

She shook her head, emphatically shook her head. He hadn't yet grasped that she *needed* to do this. It didn't matter that that one horrible night was coming back to her. That Trent was about the same height and size as John. That John had come around behind her . . .

Oh God.

"Give it to me in the ass."

"What?" he asked, one minute behind her, the next in front. "I don't know what you think I am, but I can't screw you like this. I'm not even hard."

She let him see it then, let him see the fear, the determination, the absolute terror she felt. "You have to," she said. "Don't you see, Trent? I have to give it up. I have to give you control. If I don't, I'll never get over this. Never."

"I can't," he said.

"Let me get you ready."

"Bree—"

"Take down your pants."

He didn't move.

"Please, Trent," she implored. "I have to at least see if this will work."

Still, he didn't budge.

"Please," she added again.

He looked to the side, his hand coming up to his hair. "I can't believe this." But then he turned back to her, his eyes never meeting her own as he stripped out of his pants.

She went down on her knees. He was flaccid, just as he'd said, and for some reason that made Bree feel better. She took the tip of his cock inside her mouth.

"Shit," she heard him gasp.

Her lips encircled him, her tongue sheltering his sensitive flesh as she gave him one long suck.

He grew less flaccid.

She worked him again, taking the whole thing in her mouth.

"Shit," she heard him curse again. "Jeez, Bree."

His dick began to grow hard, her juices leaving a slick trail as she worked his head, rolling her tongue around the underside, tasting the pre-cum that surged from the tip.

It got her hot.

She was just slut enough to love the taste of him, to love the way he moaned as she began to work his cock, taking the thing as far as it would go, then mouthing the tip when he drew back. And with each long pull, she herself grew slick, felt that lovely buzz of sexual excitement that made her swell. It didn't matter that her hands were tied; she lived in the moment, loving what she did to him, her mind acknowledging that she'd gone back to taking control.

No.

She was supposed to give *him* the power.

But he wasn't ready yet. He needed to want to come. And she was getting him there, his hips thrusting into her mouth now, his head thrown back as she sucked him, the blue veins of his penis swollen from pleasure. He was fully engorged now, his head reddish purple from the pressure of her mouth working him.

"Jeez," he was saying. "Jeez. How do you do it?"

She worked him harder, taking him deep, sucking him down. His legs flexed, so did his butt, his hips working faster and faster.

Close, she had him close.

She let him slip from her mouth.

He froze.

"Don't move," she ordered.

You're controlling him, Bree.

No. *He* was about to control *her,* and her desire cooled as quickly as it warmed when she stood, gave him her ass and said, "Put the condom on and take me."

And still he hesitated.

"Damn it, Trent. Fuck me right *now.*"

He grabbed her by the hips and pushed into her. But not in her ass, in her cunt, her slick pussy taking him all the way.

Oh, Jeez.

"Is this what you want, Bree?" he panted

"No," she cried out, trying to turn but he wouldn't let her. "Do me in the ass."

"You can't have it there," he said, wrapping his arms around her, one of his hands cupping her pussy, dipping his finger into her valley until he found her pleasure knot, pressing it until it caused that odd mixture of pleasure-pain, working it, making her body come alive, despite it all.

"Damn it."

He drew out only to ram her again, his arms holding her in place. No good. This wasn't what she wanted.

But it felt good.

His fingers fondled her and it felt so good. He had her bent over, his cock ramming her again and again and again.

"Is this what you want?" he gasped.

She didn't answer.

"Is it?" he asked, taking his hand away.

"Yes," she finally answered, wishing she could move. She'd strangle him if her hands were free. "Yes."

He gave it to her again, fucking her to the hilt and she threw her head back and took it—took it all. He found her G-spot. She gasped again.

"Trent."

Yes, she thought, her pleasure building as he worked her. Damn it, he was going to make her come. No, wait—that was a good thing. She wanted to come. Had been afraid . . .

He fucked her even deeper. She cried out.

And that was it for her, that was all it took, one hard slide of his dick and she slipped over the edge, his big body holding her as she gave herself up to pleasure, each contraction more beautiful than the last, each wave of pleasure building on the other until she had nothing left to give. Nothing.

She began to sob. He released her hands, turned her around . . . and held her.

She'd done it. She'd had an orgasm.

She held him, too, crying out all her emotions: relief, joy, bitterness. Bitter because it'd taken so damn much to get her to this point, joy because she knew John had lost his power over her. She had Trent now. Just Trent.

She looked up at him. He had tears in his eyes too.

"You okay?" he asked gently.

"I think I am," she said, wiping her eyes. "I think I'm going to be."

"Good," he said, his hands moving to frame her face. "Because I wouldn't do this for just any woman."

"I know." Her smile became misty then, misty and full of joy. He bent and kissed her, Bree realizing then that he still had an erection. And why wouldn't he—the man was a stallion, one who knew how to hold back so he wouldn't come. She reached down and tugged off the condom, then pulled him down onto the bed with her.

"Make love to me," she told him. "Make love to me, Trent, and show me how much you care."

"I do care, Bree," he said softly. "I do."

And then he kissed her. Bree spread her legs for him, loving how huge he felt when he entered her. He filled her up completely, her legs wrapping around his waist as he began to thrust. And it was a different type of lovemaking this time, as different from the first as number one was to three. He kissed her, Bree giving him total access to her mouth as he slid his tongue in and out of her, his dick doing the same thing. She clutched his ass, feeling his butt flex with every deep thrust. His shoulders tensed and she knew he was about to lose control.

"Come," she said softly, wanting to feel him spurt inside. She needed him to do that—needed him to fill her up. "Come," she asked again.

"Bree," he cried out, thrusting into her. "Bree." And then he stiffened, his whole body going—if possible—harder. She felt it then, felt the deeply satisfying pulses deep inside her. He thrust once more, each push deeper and harder than the last as he spilled his cum inside her.

Yes, she silently cried. *Yes.*

And then she too felt an orgasm build. She opened herself wide, pushed herself up on his cock.

And came.

Oh God—it rolled through her, made her whole body arch in pleasure, a deep orgasm, spasms of ecstasy that rolled over her one after another. She gasped, felt her eyes tear up in wonder.

Perfection, she found herself thinking. Absolute perfection.

"Bree?" a gentle voice asked.

Bree wiped at her eyes. Damn, she probably scared him off now with all her stupid tears.

"You okay?"

"I'm okay," she said, something pitching and shifting inside her as she looked into his eyes.

"You don't look okay."

But she couldn't stop the tears of joy that fell from her eyes. "I feel as if I've come home," she said, her voice thick with tears.

"You have come home, Bree. You'll always be at home in my arms."

And Bree knew that was true. The past was forgotten. In Trent's arms she might have found her future again, and maybe love.

Epilogue

The phone rang at 1:08 P.M.

"Convicted of four counts of rape," the DA told Bree. "He'll be serving three consecutive sentences totaling ten years."

Bree sank to the bed, her hand so tight around the cordless phone, she accidentally switched the channel.

"You there?" the woman asked.

"I'm here," Bree said softly, her lids tightly closed as words repeated themselves over and over in her head.

Finally. *Finally* he was going to pay.

"You happy?"

Was she? Bree didn't know. Relieved, yes. Thrilled he was going to jail, yes. But she'd long since moved on with her life. It had taken nearly two years to bring John to trial, and in that time she'd done a lot of healing—both emotionally and mentally.

"I'm happy," she answered at last, but she referred to her new life, not John's conviction.

They hung up, a gentle hand landing on her shoulder. Bree turned into Trent's arms, his big hands resting flat against her back as she laid her head against his heart.

"Well?" he asked.

"Ten years," she said.

He tightened his grip. "He should have gotten twenty."

"He didn't have a record."

"And the electric chair."

Which made Bree smile. She'd long since gotten over her rage. She couldn't be angry when what had happened had ultimately brought her and Trent together.

"I'm just happy he'll never be able to do that to someone again."

"You want to go out and celebrate?" Trent asked.

Bree leaned back. "Actually, I was thinking of another kind of celebration."

He smiled, tipped down his head and kissed her, and as Bree felt his lips gently nudge apart her own, she marveled at how lucky she'd been. Things could have turned out so differently. Instead she was whole again.

"I love you," she said, pulling back to stare up at him.

"I love you too," he answered, grabbing her hand and kissing the engagement ring he'd placed there a few months back. "And I'll love you even more when we're finally married."

"Oh?" she teased. "Does that mean I don't have all your love now?"

He scooped her up in his arms. "I'll give you all my love, baby."

Which made her laugh, the teasing glint in his eyes causing her spirit to soar. And a few minutes later he did give her all his love, that and so much more, because while sex with Trent was always great, it was what he gave her emotionally that most mattered. He gave her love and hope and a joy she'd never had before. He gave of himself—and Bree would go on taking that for the rest of her life.

Have Mercy
Susan Donovan

Chapter One

Winifred Mackland's kidskin pumps made quick work of Fifth Avenue, but the brisk pace and straight back were all bluff. The truth was, the screenplay tucked inside her Gucci briefcase was fifty percent written and one hundred percent crap, and this was not her usual triumphant stroll to her agent's office, guaranteed hit in hand. This was a march of defeat. This was a trudge. This was bad news, and possibly the end of her career.

Win knew what happened to screenwriters who couldn't write. They became Hollywood pariahs. Shopping-cart ladies. They went home to live with their mothers in Dothan, Alabama, where they could sleep in their middle-school-era beds adorned with matching pink quilt and pillow sham. These has-beens eventually came to be tried in literary court, where a judge could sentence them to death by frustration, death by ignominy, death by failure, death by—

"Good morning, Miss Mackland." The security guard smiled politely as she signed in as one of Artie Jacobs's clients. She tried to smile back, making an effort to shake off all the negative thinking. Win hated how her brain could find certain doom in a run of writer's block. She knew she should be pouring that creative lava into the mold of her latest screenplay, the final installment of the *Lethal Mercy* trilogy. It was supposed to be the hottest, the best, the sexiest adventure yet for big screen bad-ass Maximillion Mercy. But for many weeks now, her thoughts had spun night and day, fuzzy, random, spiraling into nothing discernible.

With a shock, Win caught her reflection in the slick marble walls by the elevators, and realized her hair could be described in those exact terms. She hated August in Manhattan. She hated her curls. She hated that her perfectionism had sent yet another fairly serviceable boyfriend packing.

And most of all, she hated her most embarrassing dirty secret: that she couldn't write unless she had a man in her life.

"Win! Baby!" Artie met her at the entrance to his office suite as he always did, standing up on tiptoe to kiss her cheek, guiding her through the mahogany doors and sending Betsy for decaf lattes. "Come on in, sweets. How've you been? How come you didn't return my calls from the Berkshires?"

Win cocooned herself in Artie's creamy white leather sofa and tried to find a place to hide her briefcase. She gave up, propping the leather-encased, half-written pile of crap against the coffee-table leg in full view. There was no escaping the inevitable. "I don't like to bother you on vacation."

Artie sniffed and waved his hand. "I wouldn't call you if I didn't want to talk, now, would I?" He smiled at her, his mischievous old eyes narrowing into wrinkly slits behind his glasses. He laughed. "You're *that* unhappy with the script? You know, we can always send it directly to the studio and they'll assign a rewrite team."

Win's head snapped to attention. "I'd rather be eaten by a pack of rabid dingos, and you know it."

"Same difference." Artie often amused himself, and this morning was no exception. After a few moments he stopped chortling and patted Win's stocking-clad knee. "Let's have it. Let's see the script, babycakes."

"It's not done."

Artie's pleasant expression evaporated, and he glowered at her over the top of his thick-rimmed glasses. She could see the lamplight reflecting dead center on his bald little head. "This is not good, dear," he said.

"You've already read it?"

Artie shook his head with disappointment. "You can't be late on this one, sweetheart. They're nearly pissing themselves waiting for this script. Production budgeting is done. It's in the pipeline. I promised them one more month, doll—four weeks, I said, and Marla would have it in her greedy little manicured hand."

Win swallowed hard. If Artie Jacobs told executive producer Marla Chen that something would happen, it would happen. That's what made Artie what he was—the most powerful literary agent on the East Coast and Win's own personal fairy-freakin'-godfather. Nine years ago, the man lifted one of her action adventure scripts from the slush pile and made her a very happy—and financially solvent—girl. If it weren't for Artie, she'd still be mixing cosmos at Lower-The-Bar in Chelsea.

"*Four weeks?*" The outburst sounded whiny even to Win's own ears.

"Hand it over."

Win unzipped the Gucci case, loving the feel of well-crafted steel and soft-as-butter leather, knowing she'd soon be toting

Land's End canvas if she didn't get her act together. She handed him the severely deficient pile of paper.

Artie flipped through it, his expert eye grazing over dialogue and stage directions, devouring what she'd spent nearly six months ripping out of her brain and soul.

"So where's the sex?" Artie flipped through the pages like Evelyn Wood on poppers. "I see no sex here, doll."

Win scrunched up her nose and shrugged. "Yeah. About that. I haven't felt motivated lately."

Artie placed the half-script on the glass coffee table between then. "You know, Winifred, you have the worst love life of any single woman I have ever had the pleasure to meet."

"How sweet of you to say."

"Look at you—you are stunning. Bright and charming and what—? What are you now, thirty-five or something?"

"I'm thirty-three." *God.*

"You go through men faster than Barbara goes through hundreds at Barney's." Artie sighed. "How many suitors have you deemed unworthy so far this calendar year? Five? Six? *Seven,* for God's sake? I've lost count."

Win didn't appreciate that comment, though, truthfully, she'd lost count, too. But aside from Carly, she didn't let other people talk to her with such bluntness. A girl expected that from her best friend, but not necessarily from her agent.

"You need a change of scenery." Artie got up and headed for his speaker phone. "Betsy, bring in the lattes and get my sister on the line if you please."

Win was relieved to hear the lattes were coming, but a bit confused about what Artie's sister could possibly have to do with their current dilemma.

Betsy came in, smiling, and placed two big white stoneware mugs and saucers on the glass-top table. She winked at Win and headed toward the door. "Your sister is on line two," she said to Artie in passing.

Win half listened to Artie on the phone as she sipped the hot, sweet froth, letting her eyes stray to the coffee table. The stark white pages of the screenplay mocked her, cursed at her, reminded her that she was washed up. Her stomach twisted and her heart tripped. Her left eyelid twitched. *Four weeks. Four insanely short weeks made up of seven days each.*

"We're all set, sweets." Artie came back to his leather chair. "Day after tomorrow, I'll have a car pick you up at your place. All you need to bring is your laptop and an extra battery, and some comfy clothes. Oh, and I'd throw in a couple of sweaters because it gets chilly at night."

Win held the latte an inch from her lips, too stunned to either sip or put it down. None of this was registering in her brain as information she would need to know, for any reason. "Exactly where does it get chilly?"

"The Berkshires."

"Why would I need to know about the weather in the Berkshires?"

"Winifred. I'm sending you to my place for three weeks. You'll be comfortable. You can concentrate. You can immerse yourself in the story, let it flow out of you."

"No, thank you."

Artie patted the pile of pages and gave her a malignant grin. "I'm afraid I must insist."

Winifred didn't like the tone he'd just used, or that menacing smile. It reminded her of something one of Maximillion Mercy's evil antagonists might do while holding a gun to the hero's temple.

She placed the latte mug back on its saucer. "Let me see if I understand this correctly, Artie. I am being kidnapped by my seventy-two-year-old agent?"

He howled. He hooted. He wiped his eyes and sighed contentedly. "No, darling. You'll be going alone. Trust me when I tell you that there is nothing you'll want for up there. The place is Park Avenue meets Paul Bunyn. If Barbara can stand it, you know you won't exactly be roughing it. As you know, my wife does everything first class."

"Uh-huh."

"It's settled then."

"Excuse me?"

Artie patted her knee again. "Do you honestly think you're going to get back in a taxi, head back to your nice little home office and whip this out in twenty-eight days?"

Win gulped. Of course not. "Yes," she lied.

"Fibber. Dirty rotten fibber."

Win snatched the screenplay, briefly noting the large black letters that she'd carefully printed out dead-center, halfway down the cover page: *Have Mercy*. She shoved it inside the briefcase and decided she'd simply complain her way out of Artie's offer. He couldn't exactly drag her bodily to the car, right?

"I've lived in Manhattan for fifteen years, Artie. I don't *do* the woods anymore. I have nothing to wear to the woods, and I don't like to be alone like that. I like people around me. Noise in the streets. Activity in the night." With that, she stood up, now towering over her agent. "I will feel vulnerable. I don't like to feel vulnerable. Vulnerable is not a good vibe for me."

Artie grinned up at her. "Activity in the night, eh?"

"I'm not going."

Artie stood up and put his hands on his hips. "Come now, Win. It'll get your juices flowing. How about this—if you don't absolutely love it in three days, I'll send the car back for you. Fair enough?"

Win was about to say something testy but noted the sincere look in Artie's eyes. He really did want to help her. More precisely, he really wanted this script turned in on time. And could she blame him?

"I don't see how pine trees will get my juices flowing."

Artie shrugged. "You might be surprised, doll."

She nodded. She suddenly understood. "Is this about the sex scenes, Artie? Are you sending me to the hills to sit around and daydream about sex?" She grabbed her briefcase. "Because if so, then let me assure you I'm capable of obsessing about sex in the comfort of my own apartment. Trust me on that."

"You have four weeks to finish this script, Winifred. As your agent, I must tell you that if you don't, your stock will plummet. You cannot afford to miss this deadline."

Win squeezed her eyes tight. Of course he was right. "Oh, hell," she whispered.

Artie guided her toward the door. "I want you to take this one over the top, babes. Give Max Mercy exactly what the fans want for him. Make the men want to *be* Max and the ladies want to screw his brains out."

"More of the usual, then."

"Oh. And if you should have any problems with anything—the electricity or the heat or what have you, my nearest neighbor will help you out. His name is Mr. MacBeth."

She swung around, mouth ajar. "I thought you said the place

was Uptown all the way? Why should I have trouble with any of that stuff? Does this guy have a first name?"

A corner of Artie's lips twitched. He shrugged. "Just call him Mac. He's a good guy. I've known him all his life. I'll fax you all the particulars about the house."

"Fine. Whatever." Win was about to open the door but paused. She frowned at Artie. "Do you suppose I could get my hands on a rental dog?"

"Huh?"

"Can people rent dogs? You know, for protection? Is there a dog-rental place in Manhattan?"

Artie hooted with laughter again. "Why don't you find out, then let me know, sweets?"

Winifred bit her lip. This could be the solution. The rental dog would sit at her feet while she wrote. It would sleep by the door, ears attuned to any potential danger. It would accompany her on long walks. They'd bond. She'd get one of those elegant retriever types. She wondered how much a three-week retriever rental would set her back.

She narrowed her eyes at Artie. "If I don't like it in three days, you'll send the car? You promise?"

"I promise. Have fun, Win. Relax. Loosen up. Flow. Write, baby, write!"

Artie watched his favorite client click her way across the parquet floors to the elevators. He might be old, but his eyes worked just fine, and that was one nice caboose Winifred Mackland had squeezed into that Michael Kors suit.

Betsy made a *tsk*ing sound and Artie glanced toward the reception desk.

"What?"

"I've never seen you interfere in a client's life like this, Art. You could be doing more harm than good."

Artie smiled and shrugged. "Win Mackland is too picky."

"She has a right to pick her own boyfriends."

Artie waved his hand through the air. "What she has a right to is a little surprise in her life. She needs to be shaken up, knocked on her tush. You know what they say, no surprise in the writer, no surprise in the screenplay." Artie laughed at that. "It's about joy, Betsy. I'm just trying to find some joy for that young lady."

Betsy rolled her eyes.

"My sister says young Mac is still there, cleaning out his dad's cabin. How perfect is that?"

"Yes, Artie, I know, but Judy also said he's as antisocial as ever. He's refused every invitation anyone on the mountain has extended to him. I don't see how your plan is going to work."

Artie smiled to himself. With Judy's help, the plan would work just fine. She'd agreed to send some handymen up to the house to do a little handy loosening of fuses, stopping up of shower spigots, and unplugging of one or two vital household appliances.

"Your sister also told me that Mac Senior is doing better, making the transition to the assisted living home like a trouper."

"I'm glad to hear that." Artie sighed heavily. One by one, his old friends both in the city and in the country were croaking, stroking, or crumbling like stale saltines. Life was short.

He watched the dark-haired youthful beauty of Winifred Mackland vanish behind the closing elevator doors. She had a scowl on her face.

Without joy, life was just too damn short.

His shoulder was giving him hell, and Vincent MacBeth stood on the wooden porch of the cabin and raised his left arm over his head, wincing at the pull of the staples on skin, the tight burn of the healing muscle. He was already going stir crazy, but old Mac was such a pack rat that it would be several more weeks before he could ever consider listing his dad's property with a Realtor.

Mac had to admit there was a charm to this place, but not enough to lure him to take it off his dad's hands. His life was unpredictable as hell, and this past week had been proof that he didn't have the time or patience to deal with the headaches of homeownership, even in residence. He couldn't imagine trying to arrange for gutter cleaning from the underbelly of Saudi Arabia, Yemen, Pakistan, Egypt or wherever the team went next. Second only to a woman, property stewardship was the most unappealing commitment he could imagine.

Mac moaned as he lowered his left arm to his side and slowly circled the shoulder. He'd been shot six times in fifteen years, but this last one was a doozy. He knew the longer recovery period had more to do with the twenty-foot fall he'd taken after he'd been hit, and less with the wound itself. That, or he was just plain getting old.

He'd rather not think about it.

Mac sat on a wooden front porch step and took a breath of the cool, spicy mountain air. His dad had inherited this old place from his own father, along with what was now considered an astounding five hundred acres of forest, and they both knew developers were circling like wolves, waiting to sink their teeth into the land. Within a few years, there were bound to be scores of vacation mansions packed in here, leaving just enough space in between to give the illusion of seclusion.

He sighed, stretching his neck and looking down the ridge toward the Jacobs place, its renovated splendor hidden by a half-mile of blue spruce, oak, maple and sycamore. Old Artie Jacobs had just spent a couple weeks up here with his wife—now that had been a mind fuck. He hadn't seen the Jacobses since he graduated from college. Artie was the same as Mac remembered him, only a lot richer and a little more stooped. Barb was well preserved. And their house—good God—they'd turned that old cabin into a sleek two-story spread of glass and pine that made his dad's place look like an outhouse.

Mac smiled to himself. He supposed that as a rule, hotshot literary agents pulled down a little more green than retired firefighters.

The kitchen phone rang and he hopped up from the steps, maybe a little too fast, because pain shot all the way down to his fingertips. He hated being less than a hundred percent. It could make you an easy mark.

Mac smiled to himself as he opened the squeaky old screen door. Like there was anyone or anything up here that presented a danger?

"Come, Lulu!"

The toy poodle stared out the opened limousine door and blinked, then looked at Win like she was insane for even making the suggestion.

"That dog don't look too interested in coming out, miss."

Win looked at the limo driver and huffed. "I realize that. Let me get you the key." She rooted around in her purse until she pulled it out. "Would you please take my bags inside to the—" She unfolded the fax. "—first bedroom on the right, second floor. Thank you very much."

The driver shrugged and went around the back of the car to retrieve her bags, and Win glared at the dog. How was she supposed to know you couldn't rent dogs? In retrospect, she couldn't blame the Humane Society people for laughing at her when she asked about a loaner. But still, it was *rude*.

Carly had been hesitant to let Win borrow her dog for three weeks, pointing out that Win knew close to nothing about caring for pets. Carly relented, but only after giving Win an all-day training course, which included how to mix dry with canned food, how to use a tiny toothbrush on Lulu's teeth and gums, and how the dog needed her bed moved into a patch of sunshine for her afternoon nap.

Carly also insisted that Lulu not have contact with wild forest creatures or be allowed to wander off-leash; then she'd actually cried when the car came to her apartment that morning, handing over Lulu like she was her firstborn child.

Win looked at the dog's soulful brown eyes now, and grabbed the little puffball out of the backseat, tucking her under her arm. She turned around toward the house and—"No way!"

The limo driver was just coming out the front door. "Is there a problem, miss?"

"This house! Oh my Gawd!"

"Wait till you get a load of the inside. Is there anything else I can do for you?"

Win dragged her eyes from the towering modern structure and blinked at the driver. "What? Oh! No thanks." She dug around in her bag with her free arm and pulled out a wrinkled twenty. "Thank you for everything. See you in three days."

"Only if I get a call from Mr. Jacobs."

"Of course."

"I put the dog supplies in the kitchen."

"Fabulous."

The long black limo swept around the circular gravel drive, and once the tires cleared the stones it became shockingly quiet. Win stood where she was, taking in the dramatic pitch of the shingled roof, the angled glass wall that stretched from the foundation to the sky, the straight extension of the trees, and the crisp blue heaven overhead.

Lulu began to squirm, and Win put her down in the gravel. She peed immediately, leaving a little rivulet in the rocks. Win hoped that was all right, because she'd forgotten to ask Artie about that little detail.

Win pulled the leash, a bit too energetically perhaps, as Lulu momentarily became airborne. "Sorry, doggie." Win scratched the little curly white head and the dog's eyes looked up at her with accusation. "I'll get better at this, I promise."

The two of them strolled up the stone walkway and across the crescent-shaped porch, and into the open front door. Win gasped. The house was dominated by one massive, sunny great room, decorated in earth tones with a smattering of jewel colors for accent. Antique pottery sat next to modern blown glass. A rustic farm table was topped with a sleek aluminum sculpture. A Calder-like mobile hung from the very highest point of the pitched ceiling. A bouquet of dried wildflowers was tucked into an old metal coffeepot.

Somehow it all worked, and Win had to say it was dazzling.

An hour later, she'd unpacked, finished the wholly unappealing task of preparing the dog's lunch and had toured the entire house. She'd chosen the farm table in the great room as her work space and unpacked her laptop. She'd chosen a set of pale yellow four-hundred-thread-count sheets for her bed. She'd poured herself a glass of Shiraz and was enjoying the sweeping view from the back deck.

Win glanced over at the hot tub, then the Swedish sauna built into the side of the house, and decided that maybe a few weeks here might not be so bad after all.

She had no idea how long she slept. She awoke with Lulu's leash clutched in her hand and her stomach growling. Win cut into a nice wheel of Brie, ate two slices of fresh pumpernickel and decided to do some exploring. She put on her Reebok trail runners and a pair of Ann Taylor jeans, and went outside.

In the fax, Artie had said there was a nature trail that went about a half mile up the ridge. He said it was clearly marked and went past a small waterfall. That sounded like the perfect introduction to her surroundings, and Win located the trail without difficulty. Soon, she and Lulu were off on their adventure.

The walk itself was soothing, but Win found the silence unnerving. The only sounds she heard were their footfalls—two of Lulu's quick little taps to one of Win's deeper beats—and the wind in the treetops, the sound of birds for which she had no names, and the occasional invisible little animal skittering across the forest floor. She held Lulu's leash tight, mindful of Carly's warning about contact with wild creatures.

The trail eventually became steeper, and Win found herself seeking out tree roots and rocks to use as footholds as she climbed. Lulu panted a bit but seemed to enjoy the challenge. They reached a leveling off, then it was back down, this time into a cool hollow, where a waterfall trickled into a brook.

Win sat on a moss-covered rock and closed her eyes, breathing deeply. She thought of Maximillion Mercy, his dark and foreboding beauty, the two-inch scar directly under his left cheekbone, his knack for being at the right place at exactly the right time, with all the right tools.

Maybe she could put a moss-covered rock in the chase scene. Maybe just a slick rock would do. Yes—the woman double-agent— Win still couldn't decide between the names Eva or Zoe—would slip on a craggy rock jutting out over a raging waterfall, inches from plummeting to her death, when Max would arrive. He'd dive into the air, grab a lock of her long black hair and yank her to safety. Eva—or Zoe—would cry out in alarm and smack him across the face. Max would grab her by the upper arms and kiss her.

Or not.

Win sighed in creative despair and rose from the mossy rock, noting that if she fell off, the worst she'd get would be a pair of damp sneakers. "C'mon, Lulu."

She turned and froze. Lulu made a strange vibrating noise Win thought might be a growl. And she had no idea what to do next.

The animal—it looked like some kind of skinny wild dog— shook all over, holding its position in the middle of the trail, teeth clenched. Blood streamed down its left front leg and dripped onto the dirt. Its eyes were crazy with pain and terror. White foam collected around its snarling mouth.

Win wasn't proud of her ignorance, but she was wholly unprepared for a close encounter with nature and so scared she thought she would pee her pants. Why didn't she know more about the natural world? Why hadn't she watched more *Wild Kingdom* as a kid? What the hell were you supposed to do when facing a rabid wolf, or fox, or whatever this was? Were sudden moves a good thing or a bad thing? Did you run for a tree? Escape to the creek? Lie down in the dirt and pretend you were dead?

And how do you protect a toy poodle in this situation?

Win instinctively stepped backward, but her foot hit the rock. The animal let out a horrible rumbling sound from deep in its throat and took a step toward them. Well, that didn't work. And there was nowhere to go.

This was ridiculous, Win thought. She's out of the Upper West Side for less than *one day* and she's mauled by a rabid mountain lion—or lynx or dingo—whatever it was.

Crack!

The animal fell to the dirt in a lifeless lump of fur, a small red hole in its forehead. From the opposite bank of the creek came the sound of rocks tumbling downhill and crashing into the creek. Win spun around in time to see a man—a very big dark-haired man— come flying over the water. He landed with a thud by the animal's side, peered closely at the creature, then stood upright.

The wild mountain man had to be six-four. His back was wide, and all Win could see was a wall of burgundy and cream plaid, breathing heavily. She went ahead and took that step backward, even if it meant she was standing on the moss-covered rock. Then she took two more to her left, picked up Lulu, and started running through the thicket as though her life depended on it.

"Wait. Please."

The voice was low, contained, and shockingly polite. Win turned to find the mountain man facing her, a half-smile on his un- shaven face. His dark eyes were wide and he held his hands out, palms up, to show her he wasn't a threat. *Yeah, right.*

"It's the damn traps. People can be so stupid."

Win stood with her mouth hanging open and her heart beating so hard, she worried it would explode. *"You killed it!"*

"The animal was suffering and scared and just about to go for you and your little dog."

Win scrambled over downed trees, ferns and bushes and made it back to the trail. Then she walked backward, keeping her eyes on the mountain man. "Do not come any closer to us," she said. "We are leaving. I have a cell phone and I'll call the police if you come near us."

The man smiled at her, and something in that face caused Win's entire being to go on alert. "You'll find cell reception really sucks up here."

Oh, God. Oh, dear God! How bizarre! Win had to blink several times to make sure she wasn't imagining this—because the man standing in front of her was Maximillion Mercy in the flesh. No, he looked nothing like Hollywood superstar Tony Cardone, who was now synonymous throughout the world with the *Lethal Mercy* hero. But the man standing in front of her was the embodiment of how *she* had written Maximillion. How she'd seen him in her mind's eye. The man had Max Mercy's magnetism, his quiet strength, his dominant sensuality. The man was fiction come to life, her fantasy made real.

That ugly lumberjack shirt, however, had to go.

"I didn't mean to frighten you."

"I'm leaving now." Win swallowed. She turned to walk away, but spun around again. "How could you kill that animal! How could you shoot that poor thing?"

With that, she turned and ran. The sexy, intelligent, gun nut of a mountain man didn't come after her, which relieved her and disappointed her in equal measure. She made it back to the clearing around Artie's house in no time, and put Lulu down in the grass.

The stupid shower spigot in the guest bath didn't work, so Win settled for a soak in the master bathtub. Then, after double-checking the security system and all door and window locks, she sat down to write.

And for some reason, Maximillion was alive in her imagination like he hadn't been in months. He had it going *on*—hot but level-headed, suave but raw, in the way only Max Mercy could be.

Win's fingers flew across the keyboard until two in the morning.

Chapter Two

Winifred woke up the next morning and attempted to write. She went about the same rituals that had brought her such success the night before, such as positioning the chair at a slight angle to the fireplace, which had apparently been kick-ass feng shui. She played the same smooth jazz CD as the night before. She drank the same mint herbal tea in the same earthenwave coffee mug, which she placed in the exact same spot to the right of the laptop keyboard.

Last night, this delicate balance had allowed the words and images to fly from her brain so fast, her fingers had trouble keeping up.

But today—zilch. Nada. Not a damn thing. And she'd planned on spending the day adding *oomph* to the budding relationship between Max and Eva. (She'd decided the exotically beautiful Lebanese-British spy was definitely an Eva, not a Zoe.)

Win shook her wrists and took a deep breath, then positioned her fingers on the keys. What she needed was some red-hot sexual tension, a handful of racy double entendres, and a few scenes where

Max and Eva were forced into confined spaces, their lives in danger and their endorphins raging.

Win sensed Lulu staring at her, and looked up to see the dog lying in a pool of sunshine, pity and disdain written all over her curly face.

"I'd like to see you write a red-hot script," Win said to the dog. "I bet you can't even type."

Lulu sniffed the air and turned away, as if she'd been embarrassed by the outburst and was too ladylike to respond.

Win groaned. She jumped up from the straightback chair and began to pace. She rubbed her own shoulders and her own lower back as she let her eyes wander over the huge room. She did some stretches, some wall push-ups, some toe raises. She stood next to the towering window at the front of the house and ran in place for what seemed like seven hours but turned out to be two minutes and thirteen seconds, according to the stopwatch feature on her Rolex.

Her mind wandered to the mountain man, all the subtle sexuality that simmered in his dark eyes. The astounding ledge of his shoulders, the deep rumble of his voice. Where did that guy *come* from? Could she have imagined him? The idea frightened her—was her stress level so high, she was seeing things? Was she so sex-starved that she was having arousing encounters with pretend men?

Win ran to her laptop, took out the Boney James CD and put in The Black Eyed Peas, then danced around the room singing "Let's Get It Started" At some point during the chorus, Lulu left the room, obviously needing more dignified environs.

And so it was that at about noon, Win found herself standing at the kitchen sink eating a huge Mrs. Field's Macadamia Nut Chocolate Chip cookie and drinking skim milk directly from its half-gallon jug, wishing she had chosen to be a kindergarten teacher or a computer chip designer or an elephant trainer—anything but a screenwriter.

Win brushed the crumbs off her shirt and decided that if she wasn't able to write, then she should do something useful, so she made her bed and rounded up a few dirty clothes—including the jeans she'd muddied running away from the make-believe mountain man—and headed to the washer. She threw them in, poured in the soap and turned the knob. *Click*.

"What the—?"

Win pushed and turned the damn knob a dozen times and even resorted to reading the operating instructions on the inside of the Maytag lid before she decided the appliance was broken.

When she called Artie's office, Betsy informed her that her agent was having lunch with a client, and suggested she try the neighbor, Mr. MacBeth. No, Betsy didn't have a telephone number for him, but the directions to his place were on the fax. Yes, she'd tell Artie to call. Yes, she'd tell him to get the car ready for the next day.

Win put on a pair of hiking shorts and, as a last-minute precaution, she grabbed a paring knife from the kitchen butcher block. She wrapped the knife inside a thick cotton tea towel and shoved it under her belt. Win supposed it was ridiculous to walk into the wilderness prepared to peel an apple, but after that encounter with the animal—and the imaginary mountain stud—she wanted to have something in the form of protection. She left Lulu in the house and headed out.

Win walked across slippery creek stones and climbed the same embankment from which the mountain man had leaped to her rescue the day before. About ten minutes up the trail, she saw a little cabin tucked in the trees. If Artie's place was Park Avenue, then this place was Possom Holler. It was tidy, but just a simple log structure with a small front porch. And out front sat a big, shiny, black Chevy truck with Virginia plates, which Win found strange. She walked to the front door, worrying that she would be interrupting Mr. Mac-Beth's visit from a friend. She knocked and heard a rustling inside.

"Who is it?" asked a male voice.

She cleared her throat and announced loudly, "Mr. MacBeth? I am so sorry to disturb you, but my name is Winifred Mackland and I'm staying at the Jacobs place and Artie said that if I should have any problems, you'd—"

The thick pine door opened, leaving just an old screen between herself and Mr. MacBeth, who, it turned out, was the mountain man, and who had, in fact, ditched the flannel shirt and now stood bare from the waist up. He opened the screen door, and that's when Win saw that the half-naked man was sporting the most fabulous upper body she'd ever seen, decorated with an angry red welt at the left shoulder in the shape of a small scythe blade, held together with staples.

Win felt woozy. She opened her mouth to say something, but her eyes settled once again on the painful, crimson pucker of his flesh.

If she were writing this scene, Win would not have awakened the instant her face slammed to the floorboards. Instead, there would have been a dramatic moment when she recovered from her faint only to find Max Mercy—or the mountain man—hovering over her, looking concerned. But no. As it turned out, Win hit the floor, woke up, staggered to her feet and leaned over the porch railing, where she puked into the bushes.

"Expecting someone else, Miss Mackland?" He handed her a damp paper towel.

"Uh. Thanks." She wiped her mouth. "How do you know my name?"

He shrugged. "The usual way. You just told me."

"Right."

"Let me get a shirt on."

"Perhaps that would be best."

"Care to come in and freshen up?"

Win followed him into the cabin, stunned by the buns of titanium he packed in those jeans. She'd never seen a physique like the mountain man's, except in her mind, every time she pictured Maximillion Mercy.

The place was torn apart, boxes everywhere, furniture stacked into piles, plastic storage crates full of books and papers.

"My dad's stuff. I'm getting ready to put the cabin on the market for him."

"Oh."

He directed her toward the bathroom, where Win threw cool water on her face, rinsed her mouth and checked out her hair. She gave up.

He waited for her in the hallway, leaning up against a knotty pine wall. "Mississipi?"

"Excuse me?"

"Arkansas, then? Louisiana?"

Win huffed and crossed her arms over her chest. She'd done remarkably well in masking her southern accent in the last fifteen years, to the point that hardly anyone ever noticed the underlying slow drawl of home.

She noticed that Mr. MacBeth now wore a heather green corduroy shirt. He smiled down at her, and suddenly the narrow hall seemed like one of those endorphin-charged confined spaces she should have been writing about. "Alabama. But I'm a New Yorker now."

"Never would have guessed. So where's Fifi today?"

She realized that he was making fun of her, and walked past him toward the main room, seething. How dare some card-carrying NRA member who'd been sliced up in a roadside tavern brawl make fun of her because she lived in the largest city in North America and was accompanied by a borrowed poodle?

"Her name is Lulu."

"My bad."

"I came here for a reason, Mr. MacBeth." She turned to him, trying not to be too snarky, because she needed him to fix the washer. He clearly had no manners, because he hadn't even asked her to have a seat. A quick look around showed her there weren't any seats.

"You mentioned you needed help with something at the house?"

"The washer. Seems the water isn't making it into the machine, and I hate to impose, but could you take a look?"

Mountain Man MacBeth frowned, those remarkable black eyebrows coming to a vee above those rich, deep, sexy eyes. "Is the water turned on at the main?"

"The main what?"

"The water main in the wall behind the washer."

"I have no idea what you're talking about."

He nodded slowly. "I can see that, Miss Mackland. Let's go have a look."

She watched him walk toward the door and grab a set of keys off a hook. She gasped. The idea that she'd get in a moving vehicle with a known animal killer was preposterous.

"I think I'll walk."

"Takes three minutes by car, Miss Mackland. Twenty by foot."

How did he know how long it took to reach the Jacobs place? Had he been stalking her? Peering in the windows as she wrote? Observing her breasts move under her thin tank top with each breath?

"I lived here every summer of my life till I turned eighteen. I've probably walked the path to the Jacobses' a thousand times."

Now Win felt foolish. This was his home. If anyone was stalking, it was her, just showing up unannounced like this.

"Of course," she said.

"I won't bite." His voice betrayed his amusement. "My name is Vincent MacBeth. People call me Mac."

He reached in his pocket and Win took a step backward, propelled by the memory of the gun.

"It's always tucked into the back of my pants. Never my pocket." He slowly reached toward her, his eyes clearly gauging her level of discomfort. "This is my wallet. Look at my ID so we can zoom on over and check out the water line, all right?"

She accepted the worn brown leather with trembling fingers. Holding this stranger's wallet seemed like such an intimate act, almost a brazen suggestion on his part. Wallets were a man's most personal possession, and handing it to her like that implied a great deal of trust. It felt like they were skipping several "get to know you" steps and heading right to the good stuff.

Win looked up and he was smiling at her. *Holy shit,* he was beautiful. Those eyes were authoritative and wise, his mouth a delicious collection of thick lips and white teeth surrounded by un-shaven stubble. She wondered about all the textures she might en-counter if she put her lips on his. He would be smooth but rough, wet and warm, gentle yet self-possessed and—

"Aren't you going to look at my ID?"

"Right."

Win opened the wallet. She encountered two forms of photo identification under clear plastic. A Virginia driver's license and a U.S. Navy active duty badge with a rank of lieutenant, both with the name Vincent J. MacBeth. In one of the wallet slots was a con-cealed weapon permit. This would explain so many things.

"Yes, my injury is work-related."

She handed the wallet back to him and his fingers grazed her own. That simple contact, combined with his seeming ability to hear her unspoken thoughts, wreaked havoc with Win's nervous system. She felt exposed. She felt vulnerable in his presence. She felt the heat of total body awareness spread through her, culminat-ing deep in her belly, her core, the command center for her personal juice flow.

"Let's go turn on some pipes," Vincent J. MacBeth said.

"Amen to that," Win said, and got into the truck.

It took Mac about ten seconds to find the water valve and turn it to the "on" position. He smiled to himself quickly before he stood up.

"Next crisis?"

"I am so embarrassed. Can I get you anything? Maybe some lunch?"

He rested his left hip against the happily purring washing ma-chine and pondered her generosity. It was the best offer he'd had in a long time, from the prettiest woman he'd seen in ages, and he'd be a fool to turn it down. But he didn't want to appear overeager.

"You don't need to go out of your way."

The lovely lady tossed her curls and laughed. "It's no trouble at all, Vincent. Have you had lunch?"

Vincent? No one had called him that since his mom died. She was the only person he'd ever allowed to use his full name and walk away with two functioning legs. His displeasure must have shown on his face.

A little scowl appeared on the woman's flawless brow. "You don't like to be called Vincent?"

"Just not used to it."

"Would you prefer that I call you Mac?"

Mac smiled, thinking to himself that he'd prefer she called him a badass muthafucka or any number of other out-of-her-head obscenities, at the top of her lungs, while she lay underneath him.

"Vincent works for me."

He could have sworn he saw a little seductive twitch on her lips, but it could have been the light. "And you prefer Win over Winifred, I assume?"

"Wouldn't you?"

Mac laughed. Contrary to what he'd first assumed, this woman was no brainless tart. She'd clearly been out of her comfort zone in the woods yesterday—okay, and with the scar and the washer today—but apparently she was not used to rabid coyotes, gunshot wounds or malfunctioning appliances. She seemed more at ease in the comfort of Artie's home, and Mac figured she was some hotshot New York producer Artie was trying to soften up for the kill. A few days up here could get anyone to relax their guard, even high-strung city women like Win Mackland.

"So what's on the menu?" he asked.

Win sent him a flirty grin and gestured for him to follow her from the laundry room into the big, open kitchen. Following her was no great sacrifice—he'd follow a round, firm booty like that to hell and back.

"I was thinking a little salad and maybe some grilled teriyaki salmon. What do you usually have for lunch?"

Mac laughed. "A can of pork and beans. If I'm feeling frisky, I heat it up."

"Yummy." She blinked at him with a pair of stunning blue eyes. "But not exactly my style."

Women with her coloring—such pale, pale skin, light eyes and dark hair—had always been his weakness. He'd never been a fan of blondes—too washed out for his tastes. He liked contrast in his women, and Win Mackland packed quite a few contrasts on her small frame. Like the way her breasts jutted out in contrast to her narrow shoulders and small waist; the way her hips swelled in contrast to her slim, long legs. When God put a woman together like this one, He had only one thing planned for her—a lifetime of fending off men.

"So you're in the entertainment business?" He'd apparently spent too many months on assignment, where the only women around were the kind who'd enjoy stabbing him in the back, because he was having a viscerally sexual reaction to this pretty city girl. Though their conversation had been nothing but polite, Mac needed to change the subject in his own head. His mother had raised him better than to behave like a pig.

"Sort of. I'm a screenwriter." She opened the refrigerator door. It was such a no-frills movement, but the turn of her torso, the slight bend at the waist—it was like she now had a big red bull's-eyes drawn on all her female parts. Mac began to sweat. He told himself it was the result of the discomfort in his shoulder, not the hard-on in his pants.

"So you're one of Artie's clients?" He didn't know how much longer he could keep up with the chitchat, when his hands were itching to feel that remarkable hair. He'd known women before with outrageously sexy hair like Win's, and for every one of them it had been a source of consternation. He never understood why women fought to tame something so beautiful, keep it under control. Win had pulled hers back in a big clip, twisted up along the back of her head, leaving curls cascading down the sides like little black springs. He wondered how far the curls would reach down her back once he yanked out its restraint.

"Yes, I am one of Artie's clients. I'm the one who's going to single-handedly ruin his reputation if I don't get my new script written." Win unwrapped a large salmon fillet and turned on the kitchen grill. "He sent me here to live in exile for three weeks. My orders are to write, or not bother coming back."

Mac's head began to pound. This woman was going to be here three *weeks?* He was thinking he'd have to fight off his attraction to her for a weekend. This made things infinitely more difficult, and interesting.

Win got out the lettuce, an orange pepper, tomatoes and cucumbers, and Mac offered to make the salad. Win smiled at him, got him a knife and a cutting board, and put him to work.

"Can't we just use the one in your belt?"

Her eyes widened. "What?"

"Your belt. The knife you've got tucked in your belt."

Win giggled in relief, clearly embarrassed, then reached for the small knife, unwrapped it and placed it in the sink. "It was for protection," she said.

"Of course."

"You never know when some mountain man will force you at gunpoint to julienne vegetables."

Mac smiled at her as he worked on the salad. "You're a funny lady, Win. Do you write comedies?"

"Not really. I'm best known for the *Lethal Mercy* movies."

Mac nearly sliced off his thumb. He tossed the knife down and stared at her, and the look on his face must have been a little too intense for Win, because she took a step back.

"Sorry. It's just—are you *kidding?*" He laughed. "*You* wrote the Max Mercy movies?"

She huffed and turned away. He hadn't meant to offend her, but he couldn't fucking believe that this hot little piece of ass had dreamed up the action hero that his team relentlessly teased him about. When the first movie came out four years ago, everyone on his team—from the computer geeks to the sharpshooters to the language specialists—began calling him "Mac Mercy" behind his back. Then to his face. Which took a lot of nerve, considering he was their commanding officer.

Mac couldn't stop smiling.

"I take it you're amused," she said, flipping the fish and brushing it with a coat of teriyaki sauce.

"I'm fascinated. I'm astounded. I'm . . ." Mac didn't know how to put this without scaring her away. He did not want to scare away this remarkable woman. "I know your work well. I'm a fan of yours, and I'm becoming a bigger fan by the second."

Win slowly turned her head. In her eyes he could see amusement, doubt, and something more—something hot and blatantly sexual. She gave him a pensive smile.

"This is going to sound strange and I hope you don't flip out when I say this, Vincent." She leaned up against the counter and crossed her arms over what he estimated to be C-cups. "But you remind me . . . well . . . you are so much like—"

"Yeah," he said. "Let's have lunch."

They sat at the table on the back deck and ate and talked and talked some more. By three in the afternoon, they were sprawled out on lounge chairs with a bottle of Artie's 1994 Opus One Cabernet Sauvignon and two glasses for company. Win supposed she should feel guilty about raiding her agent's top-notch wine cellar, but she rationalized it by noting that her creative juices were flowing.

In fact, her juices were flowing so much, her panties were damp.

Vincent had just told her he couldn't remember the last time he'd had an afternoon so relaxing. He said life had been hectic with work and then his dad had a stroke six weeks before. Mac Senior had already moved from the cabin to an assisted-living facility, where he could be independent and have medical care right at home.

Vincent also talked about his childhood in Brooklyn, how his mother died when he was sixteen, and how his father had a hard time controlling his wild teenage son. "I was a one-boy wrecking crew," he said. He glanced her way with a crooked, stubble-framed grin, "I still am, but now I get paid for it."

At that moment, Win noticed that the wine—and the man—had stunted her ability to think straight. Her fingers began to tingle, her chest was warm, and she let her head loll back against the chaise cushion.

Suddenly, she emerged from her wine- and celibacy-induced fog to see it all clearly—she'd been set up! Artie *wanted* her to meet Vincent! He *arranged* this encounter to get her out of her writing slump!

She giggled, realizing she was so relaxed, it didn't even piss her off, and let out a big sigh.

"Did Artie tell you I was coming up here?"

Vincent frowned a little and gave it a moment's thought. "No."

Win took a sip of the rich, dark wine. "The script I'm working on is supposed to be Max Mercy's love story, did I mention that? Max meets his match—a beautiful and dangerous babe in serious trouble, of course—and the two of them go around kicking a lot of ass in exotic foreign locales and having a lot of sex."

One corner of Vincent's mouth twitched. "Sex and violence. It's a Max Mercy movie all right."

"Ah, but this time it's the real deal." Win smiled at him. "He falls in love."

Vincent's right eyebrow arched high in disbelief. "Max drops the L-bomb in this movie?"

Win laughed. "Hey, the bigger they are, the harder they fall."

"So they say."

Win watched him take a swig from his wineglass and settle comfortably in the chair. She decided to tell him of her dilemma. "The problem is, I've been suffering from a little writer's block lately, so the story isn't really where it should be."

Vincent pondered that for a moment. "Are you blocked with the ass-kicking or the sex-having?"

"Both."

He turned his big body in the chair toward her, his interest in both topics plain to see. When his shoulder touched the cushion, he grimaced in pain.

"Does it hurt?"

"Not as much as it did two weeks ago."

"What happened to you?"

Vincent smiled and said, "A buddy of mine in an exotic foreign locale was having some serious trouble, so I had to go kick a lot of ass."

"I see. Did you have any sex while you were out and about?"

"None whatsoever. But I did manage to take a bullet and fall from a second-story window ledge, which can screw up your life almost as much as sex."

Win gasped. "Oh my God!"

"It's getting better every day."

She sat up and swung her legs over the side of the chair, leaning closer to Vincent. Her head was spinning and she quickly glanced at the wine bottle—empty. No wonder she was dizzy. She leaned forward on her elbows.

"Do you know how funny our names sound together—Winifred and Vincent? We sound like an old British couple with bad teeth and a country house."

Vincent chuckled. "We both have excellent teeth, the country houses aren't ours, and I love your imagination." He adjusted his position and hissed in pain.

Win walked over to his chair, and sat right next to him. "Can I do anything for you?" she whispered.

All right. She knew that was stupid—she had no business flirting with a powerful stranger at a remote wilderness retreat. Any woman who did something that dumb got exactly what she deserved. At least that's what she was hoping.

"As a matter of fact, you can." Vincent put his wine down, and studied her carefully. His face was serene, strong and sexy as hell.

"Take off all your clothes, Winifred, and sit that incredible ass of yours down in that hot tub over there and wait for me to join you." He flashed his white teeth at her. "I'm going to get another bottle of wine."

Win gulped audibly. He hadn't even touched her—not even a handshake—and he was telling her to get naked and wait for him in a hot tub? That smile still lingered on his face, and it did little to temper the glint in his eye. This man was dangerous. This man was hot. This man was the answer to her prayers.

"Okay," Win said, standing up. She began by taking off her hiking boots and socks.

Vincent laughed and got up from the chair, hissing in pain again. As he headed into the house he turned. "Uh, Win? Did you bring condoms, by any chance?"

Win's hand froze on the buttons of her shirt. *Of course she didn't bring condoms!* "No! I came up here to *write* about sex, not actually *have* it."

Vincent laughed and shook his head. "If I'm not mistaken, Artie probably planned for every contingency. Be right back."

Win was having an out-of-body experience. Someone's hands—they looked a lot like her own—began to unbutton every last button on her shirt, then undid her belt buckle, removed her hiking shorts, pulled off her French-cut panties and underwire bra, and removed the clip from her hair. Somehow, she found herself walking toward the hot tub. That familiar-looking hand found the control panel on the wall, flipped the switch, and pulled off the thick padded cover. Then the hand held on to the railing as she stepped in.

So hot, so hot, so hot . . . and her skin tingled and her nipples drew up and tightened and she heard a little voice sing out in her head, *"Let's get it started in here. . . ."*

Win eased down until the water lapped at her shoulders and her bottom rested comfortably on the ledge, massaged by conveniently placed water jets. And then it hit her—deadline stress must have weakened her mores! She didn't even *know* this man! This was not like her. She had a three-date rule from which she never deviated. All right, just that once, but that was one hell of a first date and it was in *Montreal,* for God's sake, and it was a private jet, not a commercial carrier.

And this? Win's heart bounced around in her chest with the force of a jackhammer. She felt herself smile. This was better than Montreal and the private jet. Hell—this was better than anything she could cook up in her imagination, which was definitely saying something.

There were condoms everywhere—condoms in the bedside table in the guest room, condoms in the medicine cabinets, condoms in the cookie jar in the kitchen. As Mac went around the house on condom patrol, he figured Artie must've arranged for someone to take care of all these little details, including turning off the laundry room water main.

Poor Win never had a chance. And now, neither did he.

"Thank you, Artie," Mac whispered, selecting a nice 2001 La Tache French Burgundy from the cellar, deciding they should stick with red.

He exited the doors to the deck and stopped in his tracks. Win's delicious dark curls tumbled out behind her, spread out on the redwood rim of the hot tub. Her eyes were closed, and her dramatic lashes lay thick upon her pale cheeks. Her lips were stained red from the wine and were slightly parted. And bobbing in the bubbles were two stupendous breasts, hard dark pink nipples just visible under the roiling surface.

Mac couldn't seem to catch his breath. This beautiful woman was game. It was almost unbelievable. He knew it had been so long that if he didn't exercise caution, he'd pop his own cork before he could open the second bottle of wine.

He walked stealthily toward the sunken tub and stared down at her. She opened her eyes and smiled; then he watched her gaze travel to the plastic grocery bag dangling from his hand. Mac set down the wine bottle and corkscrew, then held the bag open for her inspection.

"Damn," she breathed.

"I fear Artie may overestimate me."

Win sat up a little, her eyes wide. "There have got to be two hundred condoms in there!" She leaned her head back and laughed quite hard, and Mac loved the sound. It was loud and raucous and oh yes, he could hear the Alabama in it. Plus he could see all of her nipples now. He began ripping off his clothes and was down to his boxers when her laughing abruptly ended.

He gazed down to see Win's open mouth and wide eyes. "Do you need to see additional forms of ID before we go any further?"

She shook her head in silence.

"Good." Mac hooked his fingers into the elastic waistband of his shorts and pushed down. Win let out a cute little squeak as his cock jumped free, and she kept squeaking the whole time he lowered himself into the tub. The water felt so damn good, he released a roar of satisfaction.

"Is your shoulder going to be okay?"

"I don't plan on swimming in here, so I'll be fine."

That was when he felt a small, soft hand land on his good shoulder, then run down to his bicep, stop, stroke down his forearm, stop again, and run back up to his bicep. She made that squeaking sound again.

"What exactly *do* you plan on doing in here, Lieutenant Mac-Beth?"

He liked her directness. He liked it a lot. Though really, what option was there in this situation? They were adults. Naked adults. Half-drunk naked adults alone in the woods—in a hot tub. Directness was almost called for.

He smiled at her. "I plan on using a lot of those condoms, and not for water balloons."

She laughed again and moved her soft little hand to the back of his neck, where she rubbed. The pleasure was off the chart, and all she'd done was caress him above the waist. He hadn't had a woman touch him like that—with desire and real affection—in years. Three years, to be precise. He hadn't realized how much he'd missed that combination until right this moment.

"Would you like some more wine, Vincent?"

He let his head roll around as she kneaded the tight tendons on the back of his neck. "Absolutely."

"Unfortunately, we left the glasses over by the chairs."

He groaned. "Be right back."

"No." She stopped massaging. "Please allow me."

Fuck, fuck, fuck, fuck . . . she was up out of the water and climbing over him to get to the steps and that's when he put his hand right on the sweet swell of her ass. He marveled at the fact that it was the very first time he'd reached out and made contact with her. There had been no handshake. No kiss. No gentlemanly palm to her lower back as he opened the door for her. Nope—the first time he intentionally touched Win Mackland it was big palm to sweet, wet, creamy-skinned ass.

He wasn't going to last five minutes at this rate.

She rose from the hot tub, and he stared at her like a man who'd never seen a naked woman in his life. Perhaps he'd never seen one like this. All those womanly curves he'd noticed under her clothes were jaw-dropping in their unadorned state. Her breasts were round and soft and jutted out at this amazing little upward tilt that made him want to suck like a newborn. Her ass was a goddamn work of art, with fleshy but firm globes decorated with two little dimples at her spine. She bent over for the glasses and he got his first flash of dark pink, pouting pussy surrounded by a little patch of dark curls and he had to bite down hard on the inside of his mouth to keep from shouting.

Then she turned around, wineglasses in hand, her face lit up with a knowing smile that he could easily get used to, and she took her time coming back. He watched her thick hair bounce, her hips sway. He watched rivulets of water trickle down her taut tummy. He watched her lush thighs move back and forth, framing that delicate little pussy of hers. Suddenly, he realized there was a real risk that they'd run out of condoms. Three weeks was twenty-one days. If they fucked ten times a day, they'd be cutting it close. He'd have to pace himself.

Win eased herself back into the water and opened the wine, which she set aside to breathe.

"You know, this is not the norm for me."

Mac was relieved to hear it and gave her a smile she apparently liked.

"But you are one incredibly sexy man, Vincent MacBeth." Her voice was a whisper. "And I have a very big favor to ask you."

He wasn't sure where she was going with this, but he figured he might as well get his only concern out of the way. He hoped she'd take it well.

"No, you may not call me Maximillion," he said.

She laughed again, loud and deep, running a hand through her damp curls. "As a rule, I keep a decent grip on reality, Vincent. And besides, I know you're not Max, because you're . . . well, you're *real*."

He liked that answer and smiled at her. "I am indeed. So what can this very real man do for you, Winifred?"

She batted her eyelashes at him, bit her bottom lip, then said, "I need you to be my muse for a few weeks. Think you're up to the job?"

Chapter Three

Mac had to laugh. This beautiful, nude woman had just asked if he was up to the challenge of being her temporary boy toy! She'd just asked the United States Navy's most versatile covert operative to be her plaything! The woman had a lot of nerve. He liked that about her.

"I'm up for anything at the moment, as you can see."

Their gazes fell to the water, where they watched the periscope of Mac's big cock head come up for a look around.

"Hell-o," she whispered.

"So how big is Max Mercy?"

Win's eyes flashed. "That detail has never made it into a script, but I always pictured him bigger than average. Everything about him is larger than life, you know."

"And how does Max like his sex?" Mac reached out and brushed a finger down the side of her face, along her jawline, down into the hollow of her collarbone. He could see Win's pulse bang away under the pale skin of her throat. She seemed to be enjoying the line of questioning, but she hadn't answered him yet. "Aren't you going to tell me? Is Maximillion Mercy a soft and romantic guy or a little rough around the edges?"

Win wrapped her sweet little hand around his cock, or at least tried to. She gulped. "Uh. Max has very strong opinions about sex."

"Of course he does. Go on."

Win's voice was husky and barely audible over the hot tub jets. Her hand began to stroke him. "He's a demanding lover, but there are rewards for meeting his demands."

"Hmm. Define *demanding,* please."

The corner of Win's little red mouth hitched up and her eyes sparkled. "Oh, he demands total concentration, Vincent. A Zen-like devotion to living in the moment. A one-hundred-and-ten-percent effort. But he gives as good as he gets."

He chuckled. "The man's got a solid game plan." Win chose that moment to lick her lips and slide her cute little hand up and down his shaft in concert with the roiling water. Mac thought he'd die.

"Extremely solid," she whispered.

"Oh fuck, Win. This feels so wonderful—"

She offered up her luscious lips to him, and he leaned down and took them. She was so hot and willing and wet and her hand had found a perfect rhythm on his dick and before he knew it, she was up and over his legs, straddling him, her hands still at their blissful work, her mouth moving on his, taking his tongue, urging him into the hidden world of something so deep and powerful, it made him tremble.

Eventually, she pulled away, and Mac wondered if his own face showed a similar shocked expression.

"That was certainly an interesting kiss," she said, licking her lips again.

Mac laughed. "*Interesting* isn't the word I'd use."

Win began to move her hips, and he could feel the brush of her mound against his balls and the base of his shaft, all while her hands kept up with their erotic ministrations.

Her breasts were right in front of his face, little rivers of water running down the pink flesh, dripping off her hard nipples. He licked at them, one at a time. She tasted salty and sweet and he adored how her nipples grew tighter as he flicked his tongue across their surfaces.

She sucked in air. "So how would you describe that kiss, Vincent?"

He put his fingers where his tongue had been and decided he could get used to hearing his name again, as long as it was her voice saying it. He also could get used to her hands wrapped around his dick, her delicate weight pressed into the top of his thighs. He could get used to her kisses and her breasts and the way she made him laugh.

"That kiss was burning-up hot, Winifred."

"And it was only a warm-up."

"In that case, I've decided I'll be your muse."

"Excellent."

"In fact, I'm ready to muse the hell out of you right now."

She let her head fall back and erupted in a big, rowdy laugh. Then she looked him in the eye and said, "Do it, sailor."

Mac reached up over his head and fumbled around until he pulled a string of condoms out of the plastic grocery sack. He used his teeth to yank off a packet, then used his good arm to raise himself onto the ledge of the tub with Win attached to his lap, ignoring the discomfort in his injured shoulder in favor of the pleasure to come. He handed Win the condom.

"Put this on me. And just so we're clear, this first time won't be very fuckin' Zen."

Win laughed again. Her cheeks were flushed from the hot water. She was so pink and soft and beautiful that she was making him nuts. Mac couldn't recall ever being this hard in his life. She ripped open the condom and had him covered in a jiffy.

"I want to watch you put me in."

"Are you being demanding?"

He cupped her bottom in his hands, raised her up, looking down at the sweetest little pussy he'd ever seen, watching with reverence as she wrapped her fingers around him and began to rub his cock up and down her wet slit.

"You are so beautiful, Win," he breathed. "I can't wait. I can't—"

Mac thrust his hips and was instantly submerged in her heat and her grip. Her squeaking resumed, this time punctuated by husky grunts and moans, and he grabbed on to her ass and was glad he was born a male.

"Oh, my *Gawd,*" she groaned. "This feels amazing."

"You are so tight. Ride me, Win. Give it to me."

"Uhm, Vincent?" She'd stopped moving on him.

"More ID?"

"*No.* But I'm going to get splinters in my knees if I keep this up."

"We can't have that. Wrap your legs around me."

Mac swung his feet toward the hot tub steps, grabbed the bag of condoms and walked up and out, his good arm supporting Win's soft ass.

She sighed contentedly, snuggled down into the crook of his neck and kissed him there. They made it into the house and up the staircase, Win squeezing him with her inner muscles all the while, making him see spots. Mac lowered her down on the guest bed, one of those high four-poster things that made it possible to fuck from a standing position. She stretched her arms up over her head and gave him a lazy, mischievous smile.

It was the strangest moment for Mac—a rush of animal need and sweet tenderness that left him a little off balance. He had to stop a moment and just look at her. So lovely. So female. So willing. He studied how her pussy lips stretched to accommodate him, and it was a shockingly carnal image. Too good. Too damn good. And he wanted to fuck the breath from her and protect her forever all in the same instant. It was an unexpected combination. He couldn't stay still another second.

Mac placed his palms on the front of her hips, spread his fingers over her taut, pale belly and entered her over and over, his mind homing in on the only thing that mattered—his cock in her pussy, her moans of pleasure, his building release.

Mac brought her feet to his shoulders, yelping when her heel came down on his scar.

"I'm so sorry!" Win tried to escape his grasp but he shook his head and held her steady.

"I'm fine, baby. I've got this all under control." Mac moved her foot so that it was against his neck and away from his wound, and smiled down at her. "So you like having that pussy mused, Win?"

She cried out.

He lifted Win's bottom off the bed and held her close to his body, loving the way her head lolled and her curls fell in a dark mess around her face, how her breasts moved with each of his thrusts. Without warning, she opened her eyes and her gaze landed right on his. There was a flash of sadness and wonder in those baby blues, then she came—so hard—and his world was narrowed to the feel of her inner walls milking him, squeezing him, as she screamed out his name.

"Vincent!"

"Oh, sweet Win. Give it to me."

She screamed some more, returned her gaze to his, and smiled in wonder as he continued to ravage her with his cock. That smile of hers—so open and sweet in the middle of such intense sex—sent him right to the edge. Then he went over, hanging in the thin air of deep, dark oblivion, and Win was whispering to him . . . whispering words that clung to the corners of his about-to-explode brain . . . *"Fuck me, Mac!"*

He'd definitely heard the *c* at the end of that name. He was almost sure of it. And he detonated, fell on top of Win, and gasped for breath.

It was far from Zen and Mac promised himself he'd make it up to her, but there was another concern that had to be dealt with immediately. Someone was licking his left ankle.

Even in her blissed-out, boneless state of awe, Win sensed something was wrong with Vincent, and she stroked his back. "Is it your shoulder?"

"It's my ankle, baby."

"You got shot in your ankle too?"

She felt the deep rumble of Vincent's laugh move through her own body. He kissed her cheek softly. "No, but Fifi is going to town on it as we speak."

"What?" Win pushed up and Vincent slid off her and onto the bed and Win saw the little poodle staring up at her with desperation.

"The name's Lulu, and I think I forgot to let her out today." Win was then hit with a horrible realization. "My God, I think I forgot to feed her, too."

She jumped off the bed, opened a drawer and grabbed the first thing she found to cover her top—a cherry red cashmere cardigan she buttoned twice between chest and belly button. Her jeans were still in the wash and her hiking shorts were on the deck, so she grabbed a pair of cotton pajama bottoms decorated with a scattering of little pink, high-heeled kitten slippers, which she tied at the drawstring waist.

"Is that what they're wearing in Manhattan this season?" Vincent pushed up on his elbows and smiled at her, and Win stopped in her tracks. In all her thirty-three years on the planet, the only place she'd ever seen a man that beautiful was in her imagination. Vincent MacBeth was all hard flesh and long bone and warm skin, covered in patches of dark, dark hair. His muscles rippled when he moved. He was as graceful as he was big. And his smile was broad and disarming and went all the way up into those wily brown eyes.

"Actually, it's what I'm wearing to walk the dog. I doubt I'll run into any beautiful people in the backyard." She picked up Lulu and rubbed the poodle's head. "Sorry about that, girlfriend," she whispered.

As she headed for the door, Vincent said, "Come back to me, Win."

She spun around. The change in his tone of voice startled her. He sat just as he had, propped up, sprawled out and gloriously naked, but his smile had become tender.

"I will." She tipped her head to the side and smiled at him. "Want anything while I'm downstairs?"

"Much more Miss Mackland is all I need."

The dialogue began to bubble up in her mind. . . .

Max and Eva would barely escape with their lives. They'd find an empty hunting cabin in the wilderness, where Max would light a roaring fire. They'd fall into each other's arms on the rug in front of the fireplace. Eva would eventually stand to search for a blanket. *Come back to me, Eva,* Max would whisper. Then the beautiful Lebanese-British spy would tip her head to the side and give Max a Mona Lisa smile and say, *Is there anything I can get you while I'm up?* And Max would answer, *Just every inch of Eva.*

Or not.

"Win? I think the dog really needs to go."

"Huh?" If Lulu could cross her legs and hop around, she'd be doing it at that moment, Win realized. "Oh. Sure. Be right back."

As Lulu did her business, Win stared out into the woods, letting her mind race ahead, knowing she'd catch up as soon as her fingers could hit the keyboard. Eva would be nothing like what Max assumed her to be at first. Yes, she looked delicate but inside she was tough and crafty. Yes, she could use her beauty to seduce, but it was her intellect that ruled her world. She intrigued Max. She challenged him. She left him unsure for the first time in his life—that was *it!* Eva would leave Max off balance. Love would be his Achilles heel! The irrepressible Max Mercy would drop his guard just long enough to let Eva into his inner sanctum, and what would it get him?

Trouble—nothing but trouble!

"Hey Win?"

Somehow, Win found herself at the big farm table, her fingers racing along the plastic keys of her laptop, the *click click click,* suddenly disturbed by the sound of a man's voice.

She looked up to the second story railing and gasped. It was

Max. No. It was Vincent—and he was leaning on his elbows and he was still naked, grinning at her.

"Are you hungry? Want me to open a can of beans or something?"

Win laughed, leaned back in the chair and for the life of her couldn't remember coming inside and sitting down in front of her computer. She noted that the sun had set. The big open room was cast in shadows and she looked down at her hideous clothing ensemble, the little pink kitten slippers flooded in the blue light of her laptop screen.

"How long have I been working, Vincent?"

"A couple hours."

"My God."

"Get anything done?"

"Yes!" Win laughed with surprise. "Yes, I did!"

Vincent tapped the stair railing and nodded in satisfaction. She watched him float down the stairs to the first landing, turn, and float down the next set of steps. Win thought he moved with such grace that he could have been a dancer. But he was some kind of specialized soldier it seemed, and in the dusk he was big and dangerous and stealthy.

She'd always been of the opinion that men, as a rule, looked kind of goofy walking around the house naked, their parts flopping around. But Vincent MacBeth looked powerful and tightly wound and there wasn't a single thing on his body that seemed to be flopping.

"Oh, my *Gawd,*" she exhaled, watching as he walked right toward her. His face was cast in shadow but that smile cut through the darkness. He moved with a slight swagger. Then he braced his hands on the tabletop, leaned forward, and brought his face close to hers.

"Your muse needs more, baby."

Win gulped.

Vincent lifted his hands from the tabletop and that's when she saw he'd been hiding a little stack of condoms in his grip. He walked around the edge of the table and took her hand, gently assisting her to her feet. He reached down and in seconds had inserted the jazz CD into her laptop and hit "play." He did it so quickly, it stunned her.

"Dance with me, Win?"

"I—"

"I demand that you dance with me."

"Okay, then."

His hands roamed up the back of her cashmere sweater and a treasure trove of sensations rolled over her flesh—his hot and rough palms, the brush of his fingers, the caress of cashmere. As Vincent's lips came down and fastened onto hers, it occurred to Win that she'd never danced with a naked man before. It also occurred to her that before Vincent, she'd never been in the arms of a man so large and powerful. She'd always gone for the metrosexual urban intellectual types—art directors, photographers, editors, and even a few brokers and lawyers. But never a big, smart soldier like the one now kissing her with tenderness, pulling her close to his spectacular body, using his hands on her back and in her hair to take control.

Win shuddered, seeing with clarity that all these years her subconscious had lusted after Max Mercy but her reality had been more David Bowie! Something was so very wrong with that picture. . . .

Vincent ended the kiss and gazed down into her eyes. His smile was faint and gentle and he seemed to be assessing her, measuring her. When his fingers brushed the curls away from her face, she closed her eyes and sighed.

"Your mind seems to be somewhere else, Win. Should I let you work?"

His question shocked her. He was naked and aroused and kissing her and asking if she wanted to *work?* She blinked. The truth was, she did want to work. Her mind was on Max and Eva. There was something just at the surface of her awareness that she had to get into words.

"If you wouldn't mind. Maybe just for a little while?"

Vincent nodded, then gently pinched her chin between his thumb and forefinger. "Sure, baby. I guess this is the part they don't tell you about in the muse recruiting office."

She laughed. She liked Vincent. He had a sly sense of humor. He was extremely sexual. He was observant. He walked out the doors to the deck and returned fully dressed in his jeans and moss green corduroy shirt and headed into the kitchen, flipping on the occasional light as he went.

He opened the fridge and looked around. Then opened the cabinets. Vincent turned to look at her. "Since there doesn't appear to be a can of beans in the whole house, how does beef stroganoff sound to you?"

Win wondered if this was a trick question. "It sounds delicious. Are you teasing me?"

Vincent laughed. "I make a mean beef stroganoff, and it looks like we got what I need. You work and I'll cook. Then we can muse some more after dinner." His mouth hitched up into a crooked smile. "And look, since I've never done this before, I have to ask— do muses spend the night? Do they get overtime? Vacation pay? Are they allowed to watch Monday Night Football during the season? I really should have asked more questions before I signed on for this cruise."

Win remained standing by the table in her jammy pants and cardigan. She hadn't moved. She stared at this fine, funny, sweet man who was going to make her beef stroganoff while she wrote, and realized her heart was melting and her chin was trembling and she was near tears at the improbable wonder of it all. She hoped Vincent couldn't tell what was going on inside her head.

"Football is cool," she said cheerfully. "Spending the night is completely up to the muse himself. Benefits are negotiable."

Vincent crooked his head and crossed his arms over his chest. He studied her a long, serious moment, and then grinned. "Write, Win. I'll be here if you need anything."

So it was that Win came to write twenty-five pages in an hour, her head and heart full of the joyful mystery of the first throes of love. Max and Eva walked in big circles around each other like cautious animals of prey, and when they came together it was fiery and all-consuming and caused such a disturbance in their worlds that they retreated to their secure positions, where'd they circle again and start the cycle anew.

As Win wrote, she'd occasionally glance toward the kitchen to admire the way Vincent moved, to watch him frown in concentration at his task, to wonder if he'd ever really loved a woman and been loved by her in return. She wondered if he'd even had the time. She decided she'd do a little digging during dinner.

He described his work as "damage control," and Win inferred it had something to do with the country's antiterrorism efforts, but Vincent was short on details and long on the use of vague terms like *cleanup* and *facilitate*. The dead-serious look on his face told her that whatever he did for a living, it was grueling, dangerous and messy.

In the candlelight, he looked smoother, softer. His voice was mellow and deep, and she felt mesmerized by him, the way his lips formed words, the way his eyes looked so far away at times, the tiny crease of a frown on his brow. There were many contrasts within this one man—he was playful but somber, giving yet cautious. He'd served her a delicious dinner, and it had served to convince her that she wanted to know more about him—she wanted to know it all.

She told him about her life, which seemed small and inconsequential in comparison. But he listened with rapt fascination about how Artie had discovered her when she was a junior at NYU and working as a bartender, what her southern childhood had been like, her best friend, Carly, and her condo in SoHo. As an afterthought, she mentioned her recent list of not-quite-right men in her life.

"Well, it's not like you're an old maid, Win," Vincent reassured her over coffee. "There is no reason you have to be on a manhunt, is there? Take your time. See what's out there."

Win fiddled with her cup and pondered his word choice: *manhunt*. That term had an air of desperation to it, one she really didn't feel. It was simply that a man came in handy—someone talk to, take along to cocktail parties, spend Saturday nights with, someone to keep her enthusiasm up, to inspire her.

Win laughed out loud and looked up at Vincent, smiling amiably at her from across the table.

"What's so funny?" he asked.

She shrugged. "It's just that I think I've been going about this all wrong," she said, the amazement obvious in her voice.

"Wrong? You mean you've been dating wrong?"

She shook her head. "Not exactly. See, I've convinced myself that I will have trouble writing if there isn't a man in my life, someone I consider my 'boyfriend du jour.' I bet that sounds pathetic, but it's true." She gauged Vincent's expression but his face remained open and attentive. "It just dawned on me that maybe I'd be better off with no man at all instead of the kind who doesn't inspire much passion in me, and therefore my writing. I think I've been barking up the wrong tree, so to speak."

That last comment got a faint smile out of him, and Vincent chuckled into his coffee cup. "So you go through muses at a rapid rate, is that what you're telling me?"

"I go through *men* at a rapid rate. You're the first man I pegged as an official muse. You're a first for me, Vincent."

"I like that," he said. "Is it working?"

"Hell yes it is!" Win laughed with gusto. "I've written more stuff—good stuff—in the last two days than in the last two months!" She got up to clear the table. "Hey—where are you going to be at the beginning of next month, when I'm in revision hell? Do you think you'll be free to marry me?"

She'd meant it as a joke, but the energy in the room had changed. Vincent adjusted his position on the chair and looked down at his hands. She hadn't meant to say that. She hadn't meant to imply that there was anything *real* happening here, or that there was any future for them. But the damage had been done. "Look—that was just a joke, Vincent," she said, knowing it sounded lame.

He raised his eyes and gave her a sheepish grin. "At the beginning of next month, I'll probably be at the edge of the earth somewhere, attracting stray bullets. I'm not exactly marriage material, Win."

"Well, I'm not either." Win loaded the dishwasher and went back for Vincent's plate and utensils. She looked down at him. "I'm a little particular about my surroundings. I like things just so. I enjoy being single and having no one to worry about but myself, no one I have to make compromises for. I enjoy hefty doses of retail therapy. I'm not particularly suited for parenthood."

"You've done pretty well with Fifi," he said.

"It's *Lulu,* and I think she's a little less work than a baby."

Vincent nodded but didn't say anything.

"How about you? Had you ever thought of having kids?"

He looked up at her, and his eyes were dark and a little sad. "You know, every once in a while I wonder what I'd be like as a dad, and how I'd take my son here to the cabin, and to baseball games and stuff, like my dad did with me. Then I realize I'm nearly forty and I'm not home enough to even subscribe to the newspaper. I don't have a girlfriend, let alone a wife. So, no. Kids aren't on my radar screen."

Win flipped on the dishwasher, but nothing happened. She put her hands on her hips and shook her head. "What's the deal?" She laughed. "Is there an appliance poltergeist here or something?"

Vincent chuckled and removed the front of the dishwasher, seeing that the touch panel had been disconnected. He plugged it back in. "Artie arranged to have all this stuff not work so that you'd be sure to come get me."

Win laughed. "Boy was I an easy mark."

"I was too."

She smiled up at Vincent. "Remind me to call Artie tomorrow and cancel the car. He promised me he'd bring me home in three days if I didn't like it here."

Vincent reached for her, and Win looked down to see how her small hands were swallowed by his. She thought it was the perfect metaphor for this—Vincent MacBeth was swallowing her. She was being consumed, sucked into a place she'd never gone before.

"So do you like it here, Win?"

"To a surprising degree," she said. "And you?"

"I've never liked it better," he said.

Vincent made a fire. And soon, Win found herself naked again, lolling on the rug on the floor, Vincent's tongue probing and licking between her spread legs as she soared out of her head with the pleasure. She was floating, swimming, drowning, crying out, and then his big body was around her and on her and inside her, and she knew that this kind of sex was very different from the sex they'd had earlier that day. It was sex with connection. It was sex with affection.

This kind of sex felt an awful lot like making love.

Chapter Four

Mac and Win fell into a rhythm that seemed to work for both of them. Most nights he stayed with her, taking his musing responsibilities quite seriously, making her come and shake and sigh and fall asleep in his arms, a big smile plastered across her pretty face. Most mornings, she got up at a preposterously early hour to write before the sun came up. They'd spend the rest of the day in episodic sex that damn near bordered on Zen at times, punctuated by highly productive spurts at the keyboard for Win, who now wore her "lucky jammy pants" all day, every day, and hours of work for Mac at his dad's cabin.

Win often napped in the late afternoon. Mac would return to the house and wake her up by licking the inside of her thighs until she spread for him, eventually welcoming him back into her body.

Mac also talked on the phone with his superiors, who were kind enough to tell him he was headed to the Northwest Frontier Province of Pakistan as soon as he was medically cleared. And every day he took time to visit his dad at the assisted-living place in town. With a combination of speech and handwritten notes, they talked about Realtors and his dad's physical therapy. One day, about two weeks after her arrival, they talked about Win Mackland.

"You like her?!" his dad scrawled the words on a blank page of his spiral notebook. Mac grinned and patted his dad's arm and thought he was looking less tired today. Maybe the fact that Mac had mentioned a woman by name for the first time in thirty years had lightened the old man's heart.

"I do like her, Dad," he said. "She's funny and beautiful and talented. You'd like her too. She writes movies."

His father's words came out garbled but Mac knew what he'd just requested—he'd asked him to bring Win for a visit. It sounded innocent enough, but he wasn't comfortable with the idea. Somehow, bringing her here would be letting her all the way in. Maybe too close. It might give her ideas that there could be something between them once they left the mountain, which wasn't likely.

Yes, she was sexy and great and fun. No, he wasn't relishing the fact that their time was drawing to a close. But in the final analysis, he didn't see how a woman in New York and a man who split his time between the nation's capital and various points in hell could make it work.

"I'll try, Dad," he said.

"Good," his father wrote. *"That's my boy."* Then Old Mac scrawled out on the paper, *"Any movies I've ever seen?"*

Mac sighed, shoved his hands in his jeans pockets, and nodded. He knew his dad was going to love this shit.

"She writes the *Lethal Mercy* movies, Dad. Max Mercy is her creation."

The smile started in his dad's eyes, then spread across his face, culminating in a crooked grin and a robust laugh.

"Thursday after bingo," he wrote in his notebook.

The next afternoon, Mac tackled a job he'd been putting off to the last minute—emptying the old rolltop desk in his father's bedroom. It was crammed full of cancelled checks from as far back as 1970, along with receipts for repairs done at the cabin, deliveries of gravel for the drive, and even a birthday cake ordered from the bakery in town. Based on the 1981 date, Mac figured that particular cake was for his seventeenth birthday, the first without his mother. As he recalled, the cake had been yellow with white frosting, and got thrown in the trash untouched.

Mac stared at the receipt, remembering in vivid detail how he and his dad had come to blows that day. They'd beat on each other standing up inside the cabin, with hits to the face and gut, then tumbled out the front door, down the porch steps, and crashed to the grass, where the pummeling continued. At the time, Mac was still growing into his strength while his dad was still hanging on to his, and it was a fairly even match. It ended when his father sat on his chest and pinned his arms.

Mac gazed out his father's bedroom window now, the view unchanged from his earliest childhood. The funny thing was, he didn't even remember the injustice that had set him off that day. It could have been anything. But he had been pissed as hell—that much he remembered—and certain his dad couldn't possibly understand. Mac sighed, seeing his seventeen-year-old self from his forty-year-old point of view, and knowing he'd been nothing but an angry child that day, raging at a world that allowed his mother to die. Who can a teenage boy blame when disease takes his mother? It was easy to blame his father. So that's what Mac had done—for a lot of years.

Without thinking, Mac folded the bakery receipt and stuck it in his wallet. He continued on with the desk, eventually stumbling on an old black-and-white photo of the cabin, its paper edges yellowed and dog-eared. The two men standing in front of the cabin were his grandfather and his father, who was no more than seventeen himself. Mac let go with a surprised laugh. His grandfather had to be about forty in the picture—Mac's age now. They looked like each other—eerily so. A date carefully written on the back read *August 1946*. His grandfather must have just built the place, home from the war. He'd been a navy man, too.

Mac collapsed into the desk chair and let the photo dangle from his fingers. He had to be insane to sell this place! So what if the proceeds would pay for anything his dad might ever need? Selling a fraction of the property would accomplish the same thing.

Mac stood up and paced, eventually putting the photo in his wallet next to the bakery receipt. No, he probably would never have a son to give this place to, but his dad had given it to him two weeks ago. It was his place now, and his decision to make.

He couldn't wait to tell Win.

Vincent was unusually quiet driving back from the assisted-living place Thursday, and Win occasionally glanced at him behind the wheel of his big black, shiny truck. His shoulder had healed well, and he sat straighter than he had three weeks ago. She studied his strong, dark profile, and smiled to herself. It was astounding that in such a short amount of time she'd become accustomed to this man. She could read him. She knew him.

And it was obvious that bringing her to meet his father had been difficult for him.

"You okay, Vincent?" She reached over and touched his hard right thigh, stroking him through his jeans. "Your dad is sweet. He seems to be doing well."

"Yeah."

"You know, if you're hacked off at me for something, the least you could do is tell me. That way I can be pissed at you too, and we could have our first real fight. It might be a cleansing experience."

He turned her way and gave her a half-smile. "Do we need cleansing?"

"Apparently so."

He put his big rough hand over hers and squeezed. "I'm not angry. What time are you leaving tomorrow?"

Win looked out the window, realizing that he must be feeling the same sense of dread she was. How could these three weeks have gone by so damn fast?

"Artie said he'd send the car after lunch."

"All right."

Vincent raised her hand to his lips and Win blinked away tears, keeping her gaze directed out the window. She didn't want him to see her cry.

"How about we take Fifi for a walk when we get back?"

Win turned to see him grinning at her. She smiled back. "I'm sure the Fif-ster would love that."

She packed a lunch of cheese, crackers and fruit, tucked it into Mac's backpack, and they set off through the woods. It was a warm and bright day, the light subdued by the towering stands of trees, and Win suddenly wondered just how beautiful this place might be in the fall. With a twinge of sadness, she realized she might never have an opportunity to find out.

"I'm not going to sell the cabin, Win."

Vincent had been quiet for several minutes and his words surprised her, both in their content and the fact that he spoke at all.

"What? When did you decide that?"

He shrugged, and Win wondered if the backpack was digging into his shoulder. "Want me to take that for a while?"

He smiled down at her and brushed a hand through her hair, which she imagined was wild and woolly in its freed state. "I can handle it, cutie."

She laughed. "Cutie, huh?" She rubbed into his touch, hating the idea that today was the end of all this. "So what're you going to do with the cabin? Rent it out?"

Mac nodded. "I had this crazy idea I thought I'd run by you." He stopped where he was walking and grabbed both of Win's hands in his. He kissed her on her forehead, and the gentle ownership she felt in his touch shocked her. Win suddenly had the wildest thought. What if he was going to ask her *that?* Could it be? Was he going to get down on one knee right here in the woods and ask her if she would . . .

". . . consider renting it from me?"

Win whirled back from La-La Land. The man was talking real estate while she was thinking real love! She sighed. "What in the world would I want your dad's place for?"

The biggest, most devilish grin spread across Vincent's face. "You could keep an eye on it while I'm away. Maybe you could pop up one weekend a month to write. You know, for inspiration."

Win scrunched her eyes and put her hands on her hips. "Would these monthly visits coincide with your shore leave, by any chance?"

Vincent laughed. "Shore leave? I'm not on ship duty, baby."

"Whatever you call it, then. My point is, will you be here when I am?"

"I can try." Vincent's smile disappeared and he looked down at his boots. "I'll give you all the money you need to keep things repaired, decorate it any way you want. Maybe Barbara Jacobs could help you with that."

Win laughed. "I sure hope you won the Lotto while I wasn't looking."

"Naw. But Dad and I have decided to sell one hundred acres. With the market the way it is right now, that will take care of everything he might need with plenty to spare for knickknacks."

Win frowned at him. "And all this luxury would run me how much a month?"

Vincent shrugged. "How's a dollar sound?"

"Better than Manhattan rentals, that's for sure." Win cocked her head and studied his face, a face she was going to miss like hell. "Once a month at best, eh?"

Vincent's gaze turned serious, and he stroked her cheek. "Sometimes, I don't know when I'll be leaving, when I'll be back, or how long I can stay stateside. There will be times I can't tell you where I'm going. I won't be reachable while I'm away."

She blew out air and looked around at their surroundings, noting Lulu was tugging at the leash. "Sounds like the makings of an ideal relationship."

"That's my reality. That's who I am."

Win swung her gaze back to Vincent's face—her fantasy man made real, and a real man with a life that was anything but fantastic.

Vincent cleared his throat. "I guess I was thinking that if you used the place, we'd be connected. There'd be a reason for us to bump into each other."

Win felt her face heat up and her eyes grow wet. This was not how she pictured their time together ending—in some kind of messy, snotty, emotional meltdown. She couldn't help it though, and she felt her lips tremble.

"Oh, Win. . . ."

Vincent had placed his hands on her shoulders but she smacked them away. *"Bump into each other?"* she shouted. "We spend three weeks getting about as close as two people can get and now you just want to *bump into each other?"*

He laughed. "I love the way your accent shows up when you're upset."

She huffed and took a few steps back from him. "I do not have an accent, and for your information, I am not upset. I am merely mad as a hornet and embarrassed that I just wasted three weeks of my life with some emotionally unavailable GI Joe action figure!"

Vincent didn't move. It looked like every muscle in that formidable body was tensed and ready.

"And I don't reckon *anything* of mine is going to be bumpin' up against *anything* of yours, *anytime* soon!"

Lulu went airborne at the end of the leash when Win spun around—only to find she'd backed herself right up against the creek. She had nowhere to go but the moss-covered rocks, and her mind raced. What did a woman do when faced with the fact that she'd fallen in love with a man whose life didn't mesh with her own? Were sudden moves a good thing or a bad thing? Should she just go back to finding another perfectly serviceable metrosexual boyfriend with a compatible lifestyle?

Or should she forget about men entirely and just get a full-time dog?

Win decided to jump up on a moss-covered rock, noting a moment too late that she'd somehow jerked Lulu around so much that the dog's leash was tangled in her ankles and she was close to toppling over into the creek.

Suddenly she was up off her feet and pressed against Vincent's body. His mouth was hard on hers, kissing and kissing and kissing until she couldn't breathe, didn't want to breathe, and her arms went around his neck and he flipped her so that she was chest-to-chest against him, her feet dangling above the ground. He pulled his mouth away and said, "Stand for a second so I can take off your jeans."

"Whaa—?"

He had her belt undone and her jeans and panties around her feet in seconds flat, then began to undress himself.

"Wrap your legs around me, Win."

She did, because she really wanted to, and realized that in the script, this was the scene where Max had leaped into the air, snatched Eva by the hair to save her from tumbling to her death into a raging canyon river, only to be smacked hard across the face.

Win had no desire to smack Vincent. She just wanted to love him.

"I'm going to miss you, baby." Vincent was somehow holding her up with his good arm while undoing his belt, then shoving down his jeans. He lifted her and speared her with his cock, pushing up with his hips so he could give it to her in one slow, deep, complete thrust.

She cried out in rapture and sought out his mouth.

They kissed, their mouths desperate for each other. They fucked, Vincent taking Win so thoroughly that he had bottomed out in her and was pushing against her cervix. She had the craziest thought, her mind dark and confused and awash with lust and need, but all she could think of was how badly she wanted to feel him come inside her, splash up into her, be a part of her forever.

"Win, sweetheart—" Vincent moved with her, turned, and lowered himself on a big rock. He kept his hands on her hips. "I'm coming in you, Win."

"God, yes!" She grabbed his face and kissed him hard, feeling herself tense and jerk and squeeze him just as he let out a joyful roar and exploded inside her.

It was stupid, stupid, stupid. They hadn't used a condom and she could easily be pregnant. But as Win burrowed her face into the crook of his neck, felt his breath against her cheek, sensed the caress of his hand on her bare back, she didn't give a damn. That's how far gone she was.

How much she loved him.

"Uh, Win?" Vincent tapped her on the upper arm.

"I know. But I don't care."

"Not the condom oversight, though that is something we definitely need to discuss, but I think Fifi's gone AWOL."

After an abrupt untangling of limbs and body parts, they threw on their clothes and began to search for the poodle. Win thought that if anything happened to that sweet little puppy she'd never forgive herself—not to mention that Carly would kill her.

Ten minutes later, Win heard Vincent's voice boom through the forest, announcing he'd found the dog. Win ran back to the path to see him holding a very alive Fifi—no, Lulu—in his arms. After a quick examination of her white fluff, Win found the dog untouched by her brief brush with the wild.

That evening, Win unplugged the laptop and packed her bags while Vincent grilled chicken and vegetables for dinner. They ate on the back deck, sharing the sunset and Artie's last bottle of Krug 1990 Blanc de Blanc. At one point, Win used her bare toes to fondle Vincent between his legs.

"Stop, or you'll regret it," he said ominously.

"I regret nothing," Win replied, looking at him over her wineglass.

Vincent's smile became tender, his eyes held hers and he leaned across the table on folded arms. "You know what, Winifred? I don't think I've ever not regretted something more in my life."

She liked that. "And you know what else, Vincent?" Win got up, walked behind his chair, and put her arms around his neck. She kissed the top of his dark, thick hair and prepared to finish the witty retort just on the tip of her tongue. But Vincent chose that moment to let his head fall back against her breasts. He stroked her fingers, sighed, and closed his eyes in bliss.

Instead, Winifred blurted out, "I love you."

The big black limo pulled up the gravel drive right on time, and Mac couldn't say he was sad about it. Ever since Win dropped the "L-bomb" on him at dinner the night before, things had been strained. He knew she hadn't intended to say it, that it was a slip, but the instant the words hit the air, he'd closed up.

Yes, he spent the night with her. Yes, they'd made love and it was un-fucking-believable, as always. He'd held her in his arms and told her he'd miss her and wanted badly to see her again— and it was all true. But he couldn't tell her he loved her. How could he?

He knew that in hours he'd be standing right where he was, in the driveway, saying good-bye. She'd be on her way to Manhattan in just minutes, and he'd start the long drive to D.C., and within days he'd be on a plane to beautiful downtown Peshawar.

She'd been kind enough not to bust him last night, but Mac figured he'd be damn lucky to ever hear from her again.

Mac's mind zapped back to the present when a tall, cool blonde stepped out of the back of the limo, took one look at him, and screamed.

He watched Win whisper to the woman, release Fifi to her hugs and kisses, and figured it must be Carly. He took a few steps closer to her and held out his hand.

"Hi Carly. I'm—"

Carly's eyes went huge and she burst out laughing. Then she said, "Wow, Win. This is a little spooky."

Win rolled her eyes at Carly in a way that made Mac's insides twist. In just three weeks, he'd gotten used to everything about her. Her facial expressions. The sweet noises she made just before she was about to come. The way she smelled after a shower. How her hair curled into corkscrews on hot afternoons. How sweet her ass looked in her lucky jammy pants.

It suddenly occurred to him that he'd identified and catalogued Win's six different laughs, and each one indicated something different, from arousal to anger. Mac couldn't remember ever knowing this much about one woman. Or ever wanting to.

Oh fuck. This was a damn stupid time to realize he loved her back.

Carly was shaking his hand, and Vincent introduced himself, drowning in his sudden awareness.

He loved her. He loved her. She was getting in the limo with Carly and Fifi.

Win turned to him. There were no tears in her eyes. She smiled, and her bravery and levelheadedness made him love her more.

"Good-bye, Mac."

"Good-bye, Win."

"Thanks for the keys to the cabin. I'll keep an eye on it for you."

She stood on her tiptoes and brought her lips to his. Vincent could tell she intended it to be a quick peck, but he wasn't letting her get away with that. He swept her up in his arms, gripping her around the waist with one hand and cradling her head with the other. He kissed her like he could never get enough of her, like he'd miss her so much he might die, like he loved her.

She pulled away, blinked in astonishment, and made her little squeaking sound. "Oh," she said.

"I have your fax, phone, cell, e-mail. You have mine. I'll talk to you soon."

"All right."

"No muse shopping while I'm gone, Winifred."

She smiled again. "Stay away from bullets, Vincent." Her eyes suddenly softened and her lips trembled, and with a whisper she added the word, *"Please."*

Mac watched the limo turn down the gravel lane. "I love you, Win," he said aloud, hoping none of the squirrels heard him. "And thank you, Artie."

Then the car disappeared in a cloud of dust and shade, taking away the most amazing female he'd ever known.

The November rain sliced through the dark city sky in hard sheets, and the pounding was so loud that Win could barely concentrate. She'd transferred the latest version of the screenplay from her desk top to her battery-operated laptop, just in case the power went out. The storm was that bad.

The dogs were causing a ruckus, and Win spun around in her desk chair to make sure they weren't gnawing at the table leg again. She laughed at the comical sight of Lulu and her own dog rolling on the carpet, the shaggy, eighty-pound Fifi gently cradling his tiny playmate in his oversized front paws. These days, when Carly went out of town for the weekend, Lulu hung with Win and Fifi instead of going to the kennel. Win figured that, with Fifi in her life, what difference would a few additional pounds of dog make?

She returned her attention to her computer screen, grabbing her wayward curls and twisting them into a roll at the back of her head, which she secured with two pencils. She had two days left to finish this last round of revisions on *Have Mercy,* and she had to say she was pleased with the changes the studio had suggested. Nothing too rash, and even some tidbits she wished she'd thought of herself.

Executive producer Marla Chen said she loved how Win had kept Max Mercy's razor-sharp edge while making him sexier, sweeter and more likable than ever. She predicted women were going to cream in their jeans.

Win's gaze wandered out the dark window to the rain-blurred city lights. It was times like this that her mind wandered to Vincent and the effect he had on her own jeans. The effect he still had. It didn't escape her that so much of him had gone into this script that he should be mentioned in the credits. She promised herself she'd look into it.

Win smiled, leaning back in her chair with satisfaction. Since Vincent, there'd been no David Bowies in her life. No magazine editors or artists or graphic designers. The only two men who mattered were Fifi, who'd showered her with gratitude since she'd freed him from death row at the animal shelter, and the memory of Vincent.

And the writing had been going great guns. Not only had she tackled the revisions, but she'd started on a new project. It was a straight love story—pure romantic comedy—and unlike anything she'd ever written. When Artie looked over her first few scenes, he winked and said, "Finest stuff you've ever done, doll."

She was startled from her pleasant daydream by Fifi's wall-shaking bark and Lulu's earsplitting yip. Under the cacophony, she heard the knock on her door.

"Who is it?" she shouted, rustling the dogs into her bedroom and shutting the door. She hoped it was just her neighbor, Mrs. Fortner, because she sure wasn't dressed for visitors. Not that she was expecting any.

She squinted through the peephole but couldn't see a thing. She blinked and looked again, this time seeing a dark brown eyeball staring right back at her.

"Your muse is back, Winifred," he said.

Two weeks had passed since she'd heard that voice—it had been a rotten connection and she hardly heard a damn thing he'd said, but it had been his voice. It had been something. But now he was *here!*

Win's knees shook and her hands fumbled as she unlatched the four locks on her door, trying to steady her breathing, saying to herself over and over, *Have mercy! Have mercy!*—aware that she wasn't looking her best that night.

The door opened and there he was—and he wasn't looking all that hot himself. Vincent was wet as a sewer rat. The left side of his face was bruised. A bandage stretched across his cheek. His upper lip was swollen.

"I do not want to know," Win said, grabbing his arm and hauling him inside, ripping off his coat and kissing him before he could say anything more.

"Watch the lip, baby," he mumbled, crushing her against his chest, lifting her off the floor.

It was insanity. The dogs were barking their heads off in the bedroom. Win was laughing and crying and swooning and she loved this man and he was *here*.

Vincent placed her on her feet, stroked the sides of her face and smiled at her. He let his eyes travel down the front of her red cardigan and her lucky jammy pants, and quirked an eyebrow.

"Rewrite hell?"

She nodded. "Not really hell, though."

"Good. Just left there."

He cocked his head and looked over toward her closed bedroom door, which was being thumped from the inside. "Something you want to tell me?"

Win laughed, her mind clearing a bit, then she smacked him in the chest. "Why didn't you *tell* me you were fixin' to come back to the States? Lord, you burn my ass up!"

A crooked smile spread up the right side of his face. "My plans exactly, my little magnolia. But what's going on in there?"

She walked to the bedroom door, and grabbed the handle. "Prepare yourself," she warned, then pushed.

Vincent was nearly knocked backward by the big sheepdog mixed breed, and had to hold it aside by the collar in order to pet Lulu.

"Hey Fifi." He picked up the poodle and rubbed her little pompadour. "Who's your friend?"

Win walked back to him, relishing this moment. "As you well know, the poodle's name is Lulu." She enjoyed the sparkle in Vincent's eye. "This, however, *is* Fifi."

The big dog was now humping Vincent's right leg, and he laughed. "Fifi's a boy, Win."

"Yep."

"Just wanted to make sure you knew that." He gently shook the dog off his leg, put Lulu on the floor and stared at Win. She looked good enough to eat in those drawstring pants and that little sweater and no bra and bare toes and flushed cheeks. "You know you got pencils stuck in your hair?"

She raised her arms to remove them, which allowed him to watch her breasts shift under the fuzzy knit. He could see her tight little nipples. Win then shook out those gorgeous curls and looked up at him with a seductive smile.

"The cabin is looking good," she said.

"So are you."

"There's furniture in it now."

"Is there a bed?"

"A big one."

"How big's the one in there?" He nodded toward the bedroom door.

"Barely big enough for you, I'm afraid."

Vincent stepped close to her. "Don't be afraid, Win. I'm going to ask you something and I want the truth."

The tone of his voice startled her. She gazed up at him, nodded, and said, "Fine. Ask away."

"Are you pregnant?"

"*What?*"

"I have to know. For two months I've been wondering if I got you pregnant that day by the creek. It has been driving me nuts thinking that I was a world away and you were here, pregnant with my baby."

The pain on his face devastated Win.

"Vincent—"

"I asked you on the phone when we talked, but I don't think you heard me. You said, 'Yes, uh huh,' like I'd asked you about the fucking weather! I've been a crazy man."

"Oh, Mac! I couldn't hear you! I'm sorry!" She frowned at him. "You came all the way to New York to get your answer?"

He ran a hand through his wet hair and shook some of the rain from his fingertips. "I came here to see you and to watch you answer my question."

"Come here, Vincent. Come with me."

She led him by the hand to her bed, got a clean towel from the linen closet and dried his hair. She felt the exhaustion pour off him in waves. There were black circles under his beautiful dark eyes. She fluffed the pillows under his head, straightened his legs, then untied his boots and took off his socks.

She climbed up on top of him, and stretched out along the length of his body. She turned her head to rest her cheek on his chest.

"I'm not pregnant, Mac. If this were a script, I'd be pregnant and you'd be thrilled and you'd tell me you love me and you'd never leave me." She felt a shudder move through his body, and she didn't know if it was relief or disappointment. Maybe he'd never tell her which it had been.

"Is that what you wanted?" he asked.

"I don't know what I want. But it would have been easy to make up my mind if I was pregnant, you know? The decision would have been made for me—I'd be a mother and I'd always have a reason to bump into you."

He laughed, tightening his hold on her. "I love you, Win."

She smiled to herself. She already knew that. Both she and Carly had seen him drop the L-bomb as the limo drove off that day. They'd given each other high fives the whole way back to Manhattan.

"I love you too, Vincent."

"I'm not sure what comes next, though."

Win pushed up on her hands and smiled down at him. Her real-life hero was battered and bruised and needed sleep. He needed her. It was obvious. And she'd never felt more inspired in her life.

"How about we wing it, Mac?" She kissed him on his stubbled chin. "I have a suspicion that whatever we do, it'll be better than anything I could have imagined. And that's saying something."

He chuckled softly. Then Vincent closed his eyes and let the smile on his lips soften as he fell to sleep.

Reno's Chance

Lora Leigh

Prologue

t wasn't a party she wanted to go to, but Raven had promised her best friend Morganna that she would be there. Being there meant she would, of course, run into Reno.

Reno, with the softest gray eyes she had ever seen, the most luscious buff body God had ever given a man. As she left the bathroom, her body washed, scrubbed, lotioned, and perfumed, she assured herself it wasn't for Reno.

But she knew better.

Her body knew better.

She wanted to come up with an excuse to stay home, but she knew she wouldn't. It had been weeks since she had seen him and she missed him.

They were friends, she told herself. She was allowed to miss him. It didn't mean anything. Just because her heart hammered in her chest at the thought of seeing him, her breasts became swollen, her nipples hard and tight, it didn't mean anything except he could turn her on.

That was all it meant.

She threw herself on the bed, turning on her back to stare at the ceiling overhead. It wasn't the ceiling she saw, though. She closed her eyes and it was Reno she saw. His head lowering, his lips so full and sensual, taking hers.

She was shocked at the moan that passed her lips, the heaviness that filled her body, the liquid warmth she could feel between her thighs. His hands were broad, callused. How would they feel moving over her naked body, cupping her breasts as his fingers, then his tongue, rasped over her nipples?

She licked her finger and thumb, moving it to her nipple, mimicking what she thought he would do and had to bite her lip to keep from crying out at the pleasure.

"Yes," she whispered instead. "That's what I want, only better."

And it *would* be better. His fingers would be hotter, rougher, more demanding.

Her legs shifted on the bed as her hand moved down her midriff.

Pathetic, her mind jeered.

She could fantasize, she told herself fiercely. That's all it was, just a fantasy.

She touched the bare flesh between her thighs and a broken sigh fell from her lips.

God, she wanted him.

And she could have him. She knew she could. He had been chasing her for nearly two years now. Every time he came home, he watched her with a promise swirling in the stormy depths of his gaze. And that didn't count the stolen kisses, the knowledge that one day soon, he was going to start chasing her in earnest. She knew it was coming. Knew she could fight him only so long.

If she fought him at all.

He made her hot, wet. Her fingers slid across the dewy flesh, gliding along the silken juices that eased their way until they rasped against her swollen clit.

"Reno," she whispered his name, her breathless voice sounding as hungry as her body felt.

But it was Reno she saw. His touch, his fingers that stroked the sensitive little bud that kept her on the edge of pleasure, her release a strangled breath away as she imagined his lips covering hers, his tongue licking, stroking, probing. She gasped, her fingers moving faster, more firmly against her clit as she felt her release peaking.

"Yes, take me." Her head tossed on the pillow, her fingers pushing her pleasure higher. "Now, Reno. Now."

She imagined him moving over her, his cock, broad and engorged with lust, sliding through the wet folds, pushing forward, stretching her, taking her. . . .

Her hips arched as the explosion tore through her, pleasure singing through her body as she whimpered in need. But it wasn't enough. It was never enough. The release, despite the pleasure, was tinged with a hollow emptiness, a knowledge that nothing could match the real thing. That if Reno were with her, taking her, she wouldn't be whispering—she would be screaming.

Her hand fell back to the bed as she took a deep, weary breath.

He was all she wanted in the world, all she had ever really needed. And he was the one man she could never allow herself to have.

Chapter One

"eed a ride?"

Raven McIntire stiffened in shock at the raspy, dark voice behind her. She turned slowly, her breath halting in her throat at the sight that met her eyes.

Reno Chavez. Six feet three inches of tough, powerful muscle and finely honed strength. Thick, midnight black hair cut close to his head showed off the strong, harsh features of his face. Brooding gray eyes, high cheekbones, lips that drew the eye time and time again. He was a well-built, powerful male animal and he knew it. Even more, Raven knew it, and had been hopelessly drawn to him for years.

How did you fight the man your heart ached for? The one who had been your best friend, your confidant, your protection as a teenager? The first man you ever fantasized about, and the only one that made you hot enough to whisper his name in the dark safety of your bed?

It wasn't easy, but she had been managing it. Well, sort of. He did manage to sneak the odd, knee-weakening-make-her-want-to-beg, kiss whenever he had the chance. She had sworn she wasn't giving him any more chances after the last one. But she was still standing there, staring up at him like a lovesick fool.

He tipped the bottle of beer to his lips and drank, his eyes locked on hers as she stared up at him in fascination. A woman couldn't help but be fascinated by him and she was no exception. The only difference was, she liked to think she was smart enough to stay away from the bad boys and keep on the safe side of the emotional court.

"I called a cab." She lifted the cell phone she held in her hand as she flashed him a bright smile.

Reno had always been a bad boy. A devil-may-care charmer who had stolen her heart when she was no more than a teenager and continued to hold it. Even now, after he entered the one career that made him off-limits to her. She knew the perils of loving a Navy SEAL, and was terrified of the cost of giving into the seductive war he had been waging on her for the past year.

He continued to watch her as her gaze flickered nervously to the street. She was standing on the porch of his sister, Morganna's house, having ditched the party nearly a half-hour before. She wasn't a party girl, no matter how she tried to pretend for her friend's sake at these little get-togethers.

She wore the short, flirty black skirt with its low-rise waist and the matching, snug, sleeveless top with its high-rise hem. Her tanned belly was bare clear below her navel, the little diamond navel ring she wore glittering in the overhead light of the porch. And there was no mistaking the fact that he noticed. His gaze kept drifting down, his eyes heavy-lidded, making her belly tingle in response.

It reminded her too much of the touch of his lips, his hands moving over her back. The last few times he had been home after assignments, he hadn't let a chance to touch her go by. He was trying to seduce her, and Raven knew it. Knew it and had no idea how to combat it.

"Stop looking at me like that, Reno," she ordered him, frowning as his gaze lifted to hers again.

"But I like looking at you, Raven." A grin tilted one corner of his mouth as he stared down at her. "I like looking at you a lot. Did I ever mention how much I miss the days when you flirted and teased, instead of running from me?"

She snorted indelicately. "I bet you do. You have enough women chasing after your tight butt. You don't need me." She glared at him suspiciously. "How much have you had to drink anyway?"

"Not near enough," he sighed as he reach out, pulling at a curl that fell over her shoulder. The action had her heart racing, her womb clenching in hunger. "Do you realize this is my first night home and my bed is occupied? I went to find the earplugs to drown out that crazy music and crash for a few hours. But I think the bed is going to need de-lousing first."

His lips twisted with a grimace, though his gaze was rueful as he stared down at her. And he did look tired, exhausted, in fact. Raven knew he wouldn't be likely to sleep here until tomorrow night, not if his bed was in use.

She crossed her arms under her breasts, knowing that what she was about to do was dumb. Really dumb. But if she had a weak spot, it was Reno. It was a weakness she fought continually, but a woman could only be so strong. And, she didn't have a chance against an exhausted vulnerable Reno.

"Look, if you mean it about the ride, I have an extra room. You can crash there until you're rested enough to de-louse your bed," she offered. Hell, she couldn't see the man suffer. He fought for God and country. It just wasn't right.

He tilted his head slowly, those gorgeous gray eyes of his softening marginally.

And she was softening, as well. All she could remember was the touch of his lips, his hands, the heat of that hard, corded body the last time he had been home. What he made her feel was dangerous, addictive.

"You don't have to do that, Raven. I'll toss Morganna out of her bed."

"Good luck." She snorted at that one. "Last chance, Reno. My cab should be here in the next five minutes, and if you don't have me on the road by then, I'm taking my offer back."

A grin quirked his lips. "You drive a hard bargain, Raven. My bag is still packed," he said lightly. "I'll go grab it and my keys. Stay put."

Evidently, the lure of a quiet bed was too much to resist. She sighed as he turned and reentered the house, his tight buns flexing beneath his jeans as he moved. Damn, that man was packed from head to toe. He was definite male candy and she had a horrible sweet tooth.

She throttled a purely female groan of frustration at the thought. He couldn't have a clue just how hard she had lusted after his male form over the past years, or how hard denying him over the last few months had been. The only thing that had saved her from drowning in her own drool was the fact that she knew he was way more man than she could handle. That had been forcibly brought home to her just after her eighteenth birthday, nearly seven years before, when she surprised him by bursting into his bedroom in her excitement to see him. Reno was six years older than she was, a grown man, sexual and intense, even then.

She shivered at the memory. She had shuddered, eyes wide as she stared at the curvy blonde tied to his bed.

"Perv," she had snapped before turning and literally running.

He had been naked, aroused, hard and thick and long and tight . . . and hard and thick and long . . . She closed her eyes and clenched her teeth as her clit began to throb and her pussy spilled its slick juices along the sensitive folds between her thighs. She wasn't going to think about it, she told herself fiercely. If she did, she would never get any work done tonight.

"Let's go." He stepped outside, his duffel bag slung over his shoulder, the keys to his pickup in his hand.

This was stupid, told herself silently. But she couldn't stop the rush of pleasure as his hand settled in the small of her back and he urged her to the side of the street. Callused and wide, his fingers nearly spanned her lower back, the strength in them sending a thrill shooting through portions of her anatomy that she wished weren't nearly so responsive.

He led her to the wide, double-cab, black pickup she had admired earlier. She should have known it was his, she thought in resignation. It was as strong as he was. A man's vehicle.

Opening the door, he gripped her hips before she could do more than gasp, and lifted her into the seat. Eyes wide, surprise whizzing through her, she stared back at him, aware that her response to the action must be plain on her face. Dammit, she was supposed to be playing it safe.

"Scoot in," he whispered as his hands slid slowly from her bare waist, and he stepped back, his hand going to the door.

Drawing in a deep breath, she swung her legs into the truck, moving in just enough for him to close the door. Her flesh tingled where he touched her, heated and ached for more.

"Dumb, Raven," she whispered to herself as he loped around the truck. "Really dumb."

He opened his door, tossed the duffel bag in the back and stepped easily into the cab. He had no problem navigating the height from the street because his legs were so damned long, she thought irritably.

The truck pulled from the curb as she sat nervously, staring out the window, calling herself every kind of fool she could think of. This was kind of like the lamb inviting the wolf into its pasture, she thought in disgust.

"Thanks for the bed, Raven," he said softly as he turned at the corner, his voice sending shivers down her spine.

That voice should be illegal. Someone should put duct tape over his lips and a sign on his body that declared him dangerous to the female sex, because that's exactly what he was.

"Not a problem." *Liar, liar,* she raged silently. There wasn't a chance in hell she was going to get any work done with him in her house.

She tugged at her skirt as his eyes strayed to the bare flesh of her lower thighs. Dammit, she knew this skirt was a bad idea. It was sexy and fun and showed her body off to its best advantage. And Reno was definitely taking advantage of all the bare skin flashing.

She could feel his gaze flickering over her legs, her profile, and though he kept both hands carefully on the wheel, she could almost feel them coasting over her body instead. Callused and warm, rasping against her flesh as she arched to him.

She clenched her teeth, pushing the vivid fantasy back as she restrained the shiver that would have worked over her body. Flames licked just beneath her skin, sensitizing her flesh, reminding her why she didn't have a love life. Because she knew, clear to her soul, that no other man could make her want him as intensely as Reno could. Without a touch, without a word. Hell, he didn't even have to be in the country.

Pathetic. Stupid. Reno was so far out of her league that they didn't even exist within the same reality. He was a warrior, a fighter; his world consisted of blood and death while hers existed within the security he helped create. And to be honest, he terrified her. The needs and desires she had when she thought of him, the fantasies that taunted her in the deepest part of the night and the sexual hunger she could feel building within her were too intense, too damned strong.

"Here we go." He pulled into the parking lot, swinging the truck into the empty space in front of the town house. "I really appreciate you letting me stay over."

She glanced up at him. Damn, he did look tired. But still sexy as hell. She was such a lost cause where he was concerned.

"Not a problem," she said again as she gripped the door handle and swung the door open. "Come on and get settled in. I have to work some tonight, but I'm pretty quiet on the computer."

She pulled her key from the minuscule purse she carried at her hip. Behind her, she was aware of Reno moving silently. How the hell did he do that? There wasn't even the sound of his shoes on the pavement.

She unlocked the door, flipping on the light to the small living room as she led the way in.

"Come on up. The bed is made and everything, so you can crash whenever you want to."

She moved up the stairs, uncomfortably aware of him following her. She could feel her butt burning. Oh God, was he looking at her butt? Unconsciously she clenched the cheeks of her ass then forced herself to relax. Dumb. Dumb. Dumb. He hadn't even touched her and she was ready to rape him. This was so pathetic.

She opened the door to the spare bedroom, the one directly across from her own, and stood aside as he brushed past her. His arm slid over her breasts as her breath caught in her throat. She barely managed to throttle a hungry moan at the contact.

"Well. Good night." She had to get away from him. She had to close him up, get him out of sight.

He dropped his duffel bag to the floor and turned to face her, a slow, predatory move that reminded her of a wild animal or a hunter on the prowl. Why did she feel like the lamb?

He smiled then. A wry quirk of his lips, really, as the gunmetal color of his eyes gleamed with amusement.

"Good night, Raven," he said, his voice huskier, deeper.

The sound echoed in her pussy, her very wet, very aroused pussy. This was not good. Not good at all. She escaped the room, now heavy with his male presence and the predatory lust she saw reflected in his gaze. Morganna had warned her that Reno wouldn't wait long before pushing for what he wanted. He had made his intentions clear to her, informing her in that brisk, no-nonsense voice of his that he wouldn't let her run from him much longer.

And she had most likely just played into his hand.

Raven gritted her teeth as she paced the living room, pushing her fingers through her hair and again calling herself every type of fool she could think of. She was no match for Reno, and she knew it. How was she supposed to fight him? Hell, he was every woman's fantasy come to life, and he was now flat in the middle of her home, right across the hall from her bedroom, his hard body aroused. Yes, she had seen that bulge pressing against his jeans, the way his eyes darkened as he watched her, the determination in his gaze.

Reno was through playing, and Raven had a very bad feeling she wasn't going to get far resisting him. But what bothered her even more was the fact that she wasn't entirely certain she wanted to resist him. And that scared her more than anything.

It was her own fault, she reminded herself with harsh criticism. The day she had turned nineteen and learned that he wasn't staying home after his tour in the Navy was finished, that he was actually taking the BUDs training to become a SEAL, she had been enraged.

Not Reno. Not the man she had pinned all her dreams on. She couldn't lose him as her mother had lost her father. As she had lost her father.

"Don't go. I'll do anything," she remembered whispering tearfully, staring up at him, her hands on his chest, all her naive beliefs that her love for him would keep him with her, filling her.

He had smiled that crooked little grin she loved so well as he touched her cheek and lowered his head. She knew he had meant the kiss to be light. To be comforting, rather than exploding out of control as it had.

"I'll be back," he had sworn. "I will, Raven. For you."

She had slowly backed away from him, shaking her head, as her lips throbbed from the kiss that had sent a swelling wave of hunger rushing through her.

"If you go. I won't be here." She had choked on her tears, her fears. "I won't be here for you."

"You'll be here," he had whispered then, his voice immeasurably gentle, confident. "Just as I'll be back, Raven. You'll be here. And once I have you, baby, I won't let you go."

She had made certain he never took her. That he gained no more than the stolen kisses he managed to get when he caught her unawares. That he took no more of her heart than he already possessed.

She was going to drive him insane.

"Damn woman," he growled.

She had been running from him for years, and he had been aware of it.

But he had made up his mind on a cold winter's night as he lay alone in his bed, smiling like a fool over a teasing remark she had made one evening. He had made his mind up. Raven was his, and she was going to stay his.

She had been too young then, only seventeen, unaware of how sexual he was, of how dominant he could be. He wanted the woman he saw emerging within her, not the child she still was.

At the time, he was on leave from the navy and knew the course he wanted his life to take. As soon as possible, he was heading for SEALs training and a military career. It would be years before he could have her. Years, he knew, before she would be mature enough to accept loving him, despite the career he had chosen. But when he had told her his plans two years later, her reaction had only reinforced his belief that she needed to mature first.

She was mature now. And stubborn. Stubborn enough that he knew, if he waited any longer, she would slip out of his grasp forever. With each year, she set herself more firmly against him, more determined that he wasn't the man for her, simply because the career he had chosen was the same one that had made her parents so miserable.

He wasn't going to let her run any longer. She was stronger than her mother whether she knew it or not. And he knew damned good and well that she loved him. Otherwise, he would have had a lover to deal with, rather than just her stubbornness. And dealing with her just might end up driving him over the edge of frustration.

His cock was throbbing and that flirty little black skirt she was wearing wasn't helping matters. It barely covered her ass, showing her long, beautiful legs to advantage, at the same time baring her lower stomach like a feast to a starving man.

Long, golden brown hair, thick and filled with riotous curls, fell down her back, while her blue eyes watched him with wary arousal. She tried to hide it, but it was there, just as clear as the press of her tight, hard nipples against the snug, matching top.

The flush of her creamy cheeks, the soft part of her pink lips. She was a temptation he wasn't going to deny himself much longer. He had waited too long as it was. What good did it do a man to fight the endless wars, to survive the wounds and the loss of friends when there was no warmth left in his life? Only fantasies. And it was time to make the fantasies come to life.

His dream of being a SEAL, a warrior, had been fulfilled. It eased that pit of fury he felt each time he heard of the injustices that plagued the world. Now he had his biggest dream to fulfill. That of possessing Raven, heart and soul.

He was in her home. That was the first step. Undermining the enemy's defenses was best done from inside, as SEALs had proved more than once. Slipping under the wire, undetected, silently setting up the explosion to come.

And she *would* explode.

He grinned at the thought. Of making Raven so hot, so wild, she went up in flames in his arms.

Damn, he could feel his balls drawing tight against the base of his shaft, his own release begging for freedom. He had a limited amount of time to make this work. For the time being, he was on leave, but that would end the minute his team was needed. He might have a few weeks, at the most, to work with.

And if he didn't touch Raven soon, feel her lips under his, her body pressed against him, then he was going to be a candidate for the asylum.

He shifted his shoulders in an effort to relieve the tension building there. He was exhausted. He had expected to come home and rest at least one day before putting his plan into motion. Instead, he found his bed occupied, his sister in a frenzy, and the object of his obsession standing before him like the most erotic fantasy he could have imagined. Damn, that skirt.

Reno was an ass man and he knew it, and Raven's ass had tempted him for years. Perfectly rounded, taut and tempting. Her breasts were his second favorite. Full, rounded globes, her nipples pressing hard against the material of her shirt.

Son of a bitch. His cock was so damned hard, he would never manage to sleep tonight. He shook his head at the arousal beating through him and Raven's obvious determination to close him out of sight. He knew his sister's best friend better than she thought. She wasn't working, no matter what she said, so he had no problems whatsoever disturbing her. He was a man on a time limit, and he wasn't given to being wasteful with his time.

Anticipation surged through him as he strode to the bedroom door and opened it quickly. The stairs were just to his side as he turned the corner and started down them. He heard her voice, lowered, a feminine hiss of fury as she talked on the phone.

"Dammit, Morganna, the man is exhausted. He has shadows

under his eyes and his face is almost dead gray. What the hell were you thinking? You knew he was coming home. He told you he was coming home."

Reno stopped halfway down the stairwell, his head tilting as something melted in his heart. He actually felt the muscles of his chest, his heart, expanding then relaxing at the realization that she was ripping his sister's ass over that party.

"I don't care how pissed off you were at Clinton. That's no reason to treat Reno like that. For God's sake, he needed to sleep and you let your friends take his bed. What kind of sister are you? . . . Well you shouldn't have had the party to begin with. Smack Clinton around. Having a party is not going to get his attention, you nitwit."

Actually, it would, but Reno saw no reason to point that out. Her brother Clint would make his move when he was ready and not a minute before. He was just as stubborn as Raven. Maybe more so.

"Get his bed replaced, Morganna. He cannot stay here. . . ."

The hell he couldn't.

"Don't give me excuses. I want zero excuses. I want a phone call in the morning saying his bed is ready for him to occupy. Period. Or I swear to God I'm going to tell Clinton all about your lurid little fantasies that you force me to listen to."

Lurid fantasies? He grimaced. He did not want to know about his baby sister's lurid fantasies. It was time to cut this conversation short.

Sighing silently, he moved down to the next step heavily, allowing her to hear him practically stomp down the stairs. When he rounded the closed-in space to the small living room, she was off the phone and staring at him with wide eyes. It was the cutest sight.

Wariness and hunger reflecting in her deep blue eyes, her breasts moving hard and fast, peaked with hard little nipples as she watched him nervously.

"You're supposed to be sleeping," she snapped, a frown forming between her brows. "I hate to hurt your feelings, Reno, but you look like something the cat dragged in."

A smile tilted his lips. She made him smile, made him want to linger in the warmth she filled him with.

"I feel like something the cat dragged in." He agreed with her there. "Am I disturbing you?"

Her shoulders lifted in a defensive shrug. "Not really." She cleared her throat nervously. "I was just yelling at Morganna. Unfortunately, I think she's too used to it. She wasn't paying much attention."

"That's Morganna for you." He watched as her gaze flickered over him, touching him with curious, hungry eyes before forcing her gaze away, staring at every point in the room, except him.

Damn, he loved how shy she could be. How sweet she was. How prickly she could get. He figured he had loved Raven all her life in one form or another. But what he felt for her now consumed him. The plan he had set in motion tonight was risky, and he admitted it, he was taking a chance, but he was damned tired of waiting for her to realize how much they meant to each other.

She was watching him warily now, biting her lower lip nervously as her gaze flickered over him again.

"You're acting like I'm going to pounce on you, Raven." He moved closer to her. He wanted to touch her so damned bad, it was killing him.

Stopping in front of her, he reached out, one finger twining in a tight curl that fell across her shoulder. Her breath caught, a flush washing over her face.

"Aren't you?" she snapped. Fiery, accusing, Raven was nobody's fool. She might be stubborn, but she was smart as hell. "Every time I turn around, you're trying to grope me."

He spread his hands out innocently. "I'm just standing here talking to you, baby. If I was going to pounce, you'd be flat on your back on that the couch rather than standing there deliberately provoking me. And as I recall that last kiss, you were groping right back."

It had been right after his last assignment. He had returned home a week late to find Raven sleeping on the couch, having evidently waited with Morganna until he arrived.

How was he supposed to resist her? Years of fantasies, of aching hunger, and there she was, a temptation to his body and to his heart, that he couldn't ignore.

She hadn't sniped at him or tried to run from him. Sleepy, seductive, she had lifted to him, her lips opening eagerly for his kiss when he knelt beside the couch. He would have had her in his bed minutes later if Morganna hadn't interrupted them when she did. That kiss, her eagerness for him and the soft breathy sound of her voice as she whispered her pleasure had sealed her fate. She was his woman.

She frowned darkly. He frowned right back at her.

"I am not provoking you," she informed him imperiously. "You're tired and disagreeable. And I really think you should head on to bed and go to sleep."

She wasn't running from him, but he could see the indecision in her eyes, the sweep of arousal and emotions filling her. She wasn't going to back down easy, and she wouldn't give in without a fight.

"I should be," he agreed, his voice rough. "I really should be, but this is a hell of a lot more important right now."

His head dipped down before she could move, if she intended to move. Her eyes widened, her lips parted and he caught the gasp that escaped her throat.

Bombs exploded in his head. Fire rushed along his nervous system until it centered in his aching cock. She was ambrosia. She was the elixir of life.

His arms circled her, tight, as he restrained his need to eat her alive. His lips moved over hers, his tongue spearing deep as a shattered moan escaped her throat and her hands tightened at his waist before moving to his back.

He could taste coffee, mint and woman and the alternating flavors exploded on his senses, going to his head like the strongest narcotic. Reno bent over her, surrounding her; he wanted to draw her into every cell of his body as her lips opened, her tongue met his and his senses flamed. Sweet, velvet heat. The taste of her went to his head, the feel of her causing his erection to pulse and pound with a hunger barely leashed.

"Reno?" Her voice was dazed as his lips slid to her cheek, to her neck.

Her head fell back as his teeth raked her shoulder, her body becoming liquid, pliant. His. He allowed his hands to move, rather than holding her to him, roaming her back instead, pulling at the short length of the skirt until one hand could smooth over her bare buttock. *Bare? Fuck!*

His hand clenched on the curve as she trembled against him, a thin wail of pleasure escaping her throat a second before she jerked out of his arms.

"That was damned unfair." Raven stared back at him, shock and pleasure racing through her system as she fought to make sense of the impulses that still pounded through her body. He made her drunk, made her greedy for more of his kiss, his touch.

Oh God. That kiss. Her hand rose to her lips, her fingers feeling the swollen curves as her shoulder tingled from the rasp of his teeth.

Dammit, she was supposed to be denying him, not falling into his arms like a wimpy sex kitten. But it never failed; he touched her and she melted. She lost her mind, her sanity, her ability to remember the fact that Reno would never let her escape with any part of her heart intact.

He was watching her with blatant hunger. There was no apology, no attempt to hide the lust that burned in his eyes and darkened the features of his face.

"Who said I was going to be fair?" He growled, coming closer, looming over her as she backed into the entertainment center behind her. "Raven, are you wearing panties?"

Heat flooded her face, her body.

"Yes!" she gasped. "I am. Dammit, Reno, you aren't supposed to kiss me like that."

Like he was starving for the taste of her, ready to consume her at a moment's notice. How was a girl supposed to keep her sanity when a man stripped her control with no more than the touch of his lips?

"Why?" His voice was dark, incredibly deep. It vibrated in the pit of her stomach, causing her womb to spasm in need as her pussy creamed heatedly. The panties in question were going to be soaked if this didn't stop.

She breathed in deep, striving for control as he moved closer, pressing her into the shelf of the entertainment center as she felt the length of his erection pressing into her lower belly.

"Do you know how long I've waited for you, Raven? Since you were seventeen, teasing me, tempting me to take what I couldn't have. You're not a kid anymore. You're a woman."

She couldn't handle this. How was she supposed to fight him *and* herself? Especially when she wanted him so desperately?

"Find Gina what's-her-name," she snarled back, remembering the day she had burst into his room to find him naked, preparing to take another woman.

"You were a kid. I was a man, Raven. You are not a child any longer."

She shook her head. This wasn't happening.

He was destroying her defenses. He was going to break her heart.

"You tied her down," Raven gasped. She didn't want to be tied down. She really didn't. No matter how many times she dreamed about him tying her to his bed, torturing her with his touch.

"Mmm," he murmured against her lips, his tongue stroking over them slowly. "Yes, I did. Just like I want to tie you, Raven. Stretched out on my bed, unable to do anything but feel me. Feel me now. I'm dying to touch you."

His hands slid to her buttocks as he lifted her, notching the hard length of his cock against the swollen pad of her pussy as her clit throbbed in pleasure, in need. Her hands gripped his shoulders, her nails biting into the fabric of his shirt as, helplessly, her legs parted, her thighs gripping his outer legs as his hands held her closer, his fingers massaging the flesh of her ass as she shuddered in his arms.

She couldn't get the picture out of her head. Her tied to his bed rather than Gina Delaney. Her legs spread for him, the bare folds of her cunt wet and glistening as he came to her, his cock like a living arrow preparing to impale her.

"Reno. Reno, wait. . . ." His lips were at her collarbone, his tongue stroking the sensitive skin as he thrust slowly against her, stroking her clit into full blazing life.

Every cell in her body was screaming for his touch. Her breasts were swollen, her nipples . . . God, her nipples were on fire.

"Ah, Raven," he whispered, lifting her closer, pressing deeper between her thighs as she shuddered, her thighs clenching, her hips moving against his, rubbing his shaft against her clit as she fought to breathe through the incredible sensations. "Baby, I don't know if I can let you go now."

"We have to wait." She shook her head, struggling against him and herself as she felt the hands at her rear parting her flesh, sending a heated strike of pleasure whipping through the tight, forbidden little entrance there.

"Wait for what?" he growled. "For another excuse to run? You run every time I come home, Raven. How am I supposed to seduce you when I can't even find you? Dammit, the waiting is over."

Chapter Two

Okay, a command, given in such a sexually rough, dominant voice should not have the juices spilling from her pussy like warm honey from a comb. But it did, and they were, even as he picked her up off her feet again and moved quickly to the couch, laying her down as he loomed over her.

His face was savagely cast, his cheekbones high and sharp, his lips full and hungry. She could feel every erogenous zone in her body perking up and taking notice of the commanding male form that had her in his grip.

"Reno, this isn't boot camp," she protested, even as she tried not to moan when he pressed her thighs part, his hands gripping her hips, holding her still as her skirt pooled inches above the decent line.

Could he see the crotch of her panties? Were they as wet as she suspected? She shuddered at the thought of him seeing the proof of her desire.

"Hell no, it's not," he growled. "Damn good thing too, baby. I'd have to punish you for insubordination first thing. I might anyway. . . ." His voice dropped, becoming raspier, sexier. "I could really get into spanking that pretty little ass, Raven."

No. No. No spanking. So why were the cheeks of her ass clenching as though it might be fun?

"Pervert," she gasped instead as his head lowered, his lips pressing over her navel as his tongue curled around the small diamond navel ring and tugged.

Her hips came off the couch, a high, broken cry leaving her lips as her hands gripped his head. To pull him back. Yes. Make him stop. So why the hell was she holding him closer, her fingers clenching in his hair as reality began to recede?

It was so fucking sexy. She had never known anything so erotic as Reno's lips on her stomach, his tongue flicking over the ring as his hands moved to grip her thighs, parting them further, sliding high.

She shuddered in his grip, her knees bending, her skirt rising above the crotch of her panties as his fingers smoothed over the flesh of her inner thighs.

"Perfect," he whispered as his lips began to move higher. "There you go, baby, just lay there and let me make you feel good. Do you know how much I've wanted to just make you feel good? Make you burn for me?"

His tongue swiped over a nipple as he neared her breast. Even through the material of her short tank top, the sensation was incredible. Hot enough to send the blood surging through her body, her nipples hardening further as an unfamiliar burst of heat surged from her nipple to her pussy.

"Feel good?" His voice was a rough growl as she stared up at him.

His hand hooked into the stretchy fabric of her top and began to lift it.

Raven whimpered. She couldn't help it, and the helpless sound of arousal infuriated her. She heard her own hunger, her own weakness in the sound. The complete inability to deny the whiplash of emotions and erotic pleasure that seared her senses. Her hands gripped his wrists, but she couldn't whisper the words she knew it would take to stop him. All she could think about was his tongue licking over her ultrasensitive flesh, sucking her into his mouth, stroking the intensity of pleasure higher.

"There we go, baby," he crooned as she released his wrists, allowing him to pull the material over her head and toss it aside.

God. She was practically naked in front of Reno Chavez. His stormy gaze was eating her up, his hands trailing incredible shards of pleasure over the sides of her breasts as he watched her with a lust-filled expression.

"Reno . . ." She whispered his name, terrified to believe it was actually happening, he was really here, his hands moving quickly over the buttons of his shirt and stripping it from his shoulders.

She reached for him. She couldn't help it. All that tanned, hard muscle with the light arrowing of short, dark hairs was too much to resist. She sat up, barely noticing the surprised pleasure in his expression an instant before her breasts raked over his chest. Her hands gripped his neck and she pulled him down to satisfy the overwhelming need for his kiss.

Within seconds he had her flat on her back again, but she had what she needed. His chest sliding over her nipples, his tongue plunging into her mouth, twining with hers as her hands roved his shoulders, her nails raking, her sensuality taking over as her greatest fantasy began to come true.

It wasn't smart. Holding her heart back from him would be the hardest thing she had ever done in her life. But she needed this. She needed him. Once and for all she needed to exorcise the ghosts of her own fantasies. She had known since she was no more than a teenager that Reno was her greatest weakness. And now she knew he could destroy her.

She moaned in protest as his hands pulled at her arms, bringing them from around his neck as he gripped her wrists in one hand and stretched them over her head, his eyes lifting as he watched her with narrow-eyed hunger.

"Stay." His voice was impossibly dominant as he issued the sensual order. "Keep your arms up, your hands right there. Don't make me tie them, Raven." Then he smiled, a slow, intensely erotic curve of his lips that had her fighting to breathe. "Or is that what you want?"

To be tied up? Hell no! But she couldn't get the thought out of her head. As she clenched her hands, keeping her arms in place, she could almost feel the restraints holding her, sending her imagination flying until she felt him move.

"Oh God. Reno . . ." His fingers released the little purse at her side, then slid the zipper of her skirt down.

"I want you naked, Raven," he told her firmly. "If you intend to say no, baby, you better do it now."

No. No. No. No. Her head was screaming the word, but it wouldn't come to her lips. Instead, she gripped the armrest of the couch, shuddering as he eased the skirt over her thighs, moving away from her to strip the material completely off her body.

"Sweet mercy," he whispered as he stood by the couch, staring down at her.

Raven knew the point of no return had already been reached. There was no turning back now and she knew it. She didn't want to turn back.

She watched, breathing harshly as he toed his sneakers off, and his hands went to the waistband of his jeans. As though in slow motion, she watched, the metal buttons were flicked open, the jeans parting, revealing the dark material of his snug boxer briefs.

Seconds later, hooking his fingers in the waistband of the briefs, he peeled off both jeans and underwear, the thick length of his erection, the purplish head bulging, heavy veins straining against satiny flesh, was free.

"I want to touch you," she whispered, her gaze locked on his cock. "Please, Reno. I need to touch you." Her mouth watered with that need.

"Later, baby," he groaned. "If you touch me now, I'll lose it."

He knelt on the floor then, spreading her legs until one rested on the floor, the other, knee bent, still on the cushions of the couch. Leaning forward, his tongue flicked out to lick over her nipple before drawing it into the incredible heat of his mouth.

"Reno. Oh God. Reno. It's so good. . . ." She writhed beneath him, unable to keep from watching, her eyes locked on his lips as he drew her nipple into his mouth. His tongue rasped it as he sucked it deep, sending sharp fingers of lightning-hot sensation rushing straight to her cunt.

It was incredible. Unlike anything she had known before. Anything she could have imagined.

He growled, the sound vibrating through her, throbbing through her clit and causing her hips to arch with an involuntary violence.

"Easy, baby," he whispered, kissing his way to the other mound, his tongue licking over the tip before he drew it in as well.

"So good," she whimpered. "Reno, I don't know if I can stand it."

She was arching to him, trying to press her flesh deeper into his mouth, willing to beg if that was what it took as she watched him tug at the peak, his cheeks working rhythmically with his tongue to make her crazy.

"You can stand it, baby." His voice was deeper, more sexual as his lips began to drift down her stomach. "I've dreamed of eating you like candy."

He was going to kill her. She was certain of it. She stared at him, dazed, out of her mind with the sensations spearing through her like wicked fingers of fire as his lips trailed to the elastic band of her minuscule thong.

"So pretty," he whispered as his head lifted, his hands moving to her inner thighs, spreading her legs further as his lips smoothed over the crease between her leg and the heated flesh of her cunt. "So sweet and hot."

"Oh sweet God . . . Reno . . ." His lips capped over the hot mound, covered by the silk of her panties as his tongue pressed against the tortured nub of her clit.

She tried to close her legs, to clench against his head, to hold him in place while she rubbed against him and rocketed through space. His brief chuckle was her warning that he wasn't going to allow that. His hands tightened on her legs, holding them in place as his tongue prodded at the tormented, nerve-ridden flesh.

"Reno, really. I swear. I don't think I can take it," she cried out desperately. "I've waited too long. Fuck me now."

He jerked up as he stared back at her, his eyes nearly black as his gaze clashed with hers. The groan that tore from his throat was tormented as his hands ripped the panties from her and he moved quickly over her.

She felt the broad head of his cock part the swollen folds waiting below. She was slick, incredibly wet as he pushed against the hungry opening of her vagina.

"Damn, you're hot," he whispered as he lifted her legs, bringing them to his hips, holding her still as he pressed closer, grimacing as the crest penetrated the snug opening.

"Now, Reno," she begged shamelessly, her nails digging into the couch as she strained closer. "Please. Now."

A throttled groan left his chest as he surged inside her, hard and deep, forcing his way past unused muscles as the fierce, thick length of his cock impaled the tight sheath.

Raven's eyes widened as a shocked cry of pain left her lips. She struggled beneath him, her hips writhing as her hands flew to his chest, pressing against him as she fought to adjust to the fiery, involuntary stretching of her vagina.

"Fuck!" He stared down at her in shock, his hands at her hips, flexing, gripping her tight as his erection throbbed almost violently inside her.

"Reno." She tried to smile as she forced herself to relax. She had read about this. It was supposed to hurt the first time. She knew it would hurt the first time. Everyone said it would. She had to relax.

She felt her pussy ripple around him as she concentrated on the muscles there, forcing herself not to clench tighter around him, but to allow the flesh to accommodate him, to clasp him snugly rather than fighting against the penetration.

"You should have told me." He was panting above her, the struggle for control obvious on his face. "Dammit, Raven, you weren't supposed to be a virgin."

Her eyes narrowed. She could feel the pleasure building now, the tension gathering in her clit, in her womb, the release that had tormented her since his first touch.

"And you're not supposed to be an asshole, but you are," she gasped. "Now finish it, dammit."

She flexed around him, moaning at the incredible sensation, the snug fit, the feel of him inside her, a heavy thick weight pressing against delicate, sensitive nerve endings.

A strangled scream left her throat as he began to move. The short, incredibly firm strokes made her crazy. She couldn't stand it. She strained against him, her hips meeting his as she fought for breath.

He was being careful. Dammit, she didn't need him to be careful. This was her first time, her first real climax, her first everything. She wanted it all.

"Harder," she panted, twisting against him as her fingers gripped his shoulders. "Do it harder."

"I don't want to hurt you, Raven." His voice was more an animal growl than a groan. "Dammit, wait."

"No." Her head thrashed against the cushions. "Harder, Reno. Fuck me. Fuck me like we both need it. Do it now."

As though her words triggered the desired response, he moved over her, bracing one elbow at her head, tucking the other beneath her rear to lift her to him as he nearly pulled free.

The hard stroke of his cock over the tender nerve endings had her arching closer, eager for more, a second before his control disintegrated.

Raven held on to Reno as he began to ride her hard and deep. She was shocked at her own cries, primitive, desperate—but even more shocking was the pleasure ripping through her.

The pressure building in her clit as his pelvis stroked against it was almost painful. His hips lunged against hers, driving his erection to the hilt inside her over and over again as she felt her mind begin to unravel. She couldn't survive it, surely no one could take such pleasure and ever be the same again.

The sensation built in her womb, her clit, the overfilled recess of her pussy as she felt the muscles there tightening, the tension coiling. . . .

"Raven." His head lifted, his gaze spearing hers as her eyes drifted open. She was so close. So close. "Are you protected?"

The words barely registered; the meaning was lost to her.

"What?" she gasped. She needed more. She tightened further as his cock surged inside her with a rhythm that left her fighting just to hold on to her sanity.

"Protected, Raven," he groaned, his hand tightening in her hair as he forced her attention to him. "The pill. Goddamn, anything. Are you protected?"

Protected. The pill. Thank God her doctor had prescribed them to regulate her monthly cycles. "Yes . . . ," she wailed as the pleasure began to clash and careen inside her. "The pill. Yes. Oh God, Reno, harder. Harder . . ."

He gave it to her harder. Bracing his knees on the couch, the hand at her hip clenching with bruising strength, he gave her what she needed.

"Fuck. Come for me, Raven. Come now, baby. . . ."

There was no need for the harsh command. She was holding on the edge, desperate to fly to the center of the shocking heat consuming her. She didn't come. She didn't release. She dissolved. She fragmented. She exploded. She lost herself as the pleasure became a white-hot conflagration that ripped through her soul and sent her flying to space and beyond.

She was only distantly aware of him looming over her, driving harder, deeper, as a new, surging flood of heat inside her sent her higher. All she knew was perfection. Merging. A complete, terrifying release that kept her floating as the pleasure slowly receded, leaving her limp and wasted beneath him. And certain that nothing would or could ever be the same again.

Chapter Three

*I*t was one o'clock in the morning, there wasn't a chance in hell Morganna was conscious enough to even answer the phone, let alone understand Raven's bitching. And the man slowly easing from her body looked like a sated demigod as he sat on the couch at her feet.

Uncomfortably aware of her nudity, Raven hauled the thin blanket from the back of the couch as she sat up herself, pulling it around her almost desperately. She could feel his eyes on her, watching her with that eagle-like glare of his.

"You should have told me." He sighed then, running his hands over his hair as he breathed out roughly. "You weren't supposed to be a virgin, Raven."

She turned and gaped at him in disbelief, nearly speechless at his comment and the irritable tone of his voice.

"Well, excuse me, Mr. Experience," she snapped in reply. "What does my being a virgin have to do with anything anyway? What was I supposed to do, excuse myself and go get fucked by someone else before you had your turn?"

He grimaced before turning his head to look at her. And she really wished he wouldn't look at her that way. All satisfied and sated and considering another round.

"I wouldn't try it now if I were you," he grunted, reaching out to touch her hair as she pulled back from him. "I wouldn't be happy."

"And your happiness matters, of course." She rolled her eyes at that.

She ached in places she had never known existed. A deep, pleasant ache. She wanted to curl up on the couch and sleep for a week, to relish the bone-deep feeling of completion that she couldn't extinguish. Damn him, he should come with a warning sign.

He didn't answer, merely watched her. And that was more nerve-racking than the sound of his voice. He could always do that to her. Look at her as though he saw into her soul, or he was a part of her soul. She shivered at the thought.

"I'm going to bed." She pushed herself to her feet, wondering if she could actually walk now. "God, I must have been insane."

She wavered as she stood, forcing her legs to steady, wishing she could force the ache building in her chest to go away as easily as she made her legs obey her. Holding the blanket to her tightly, she made it the first step.

"I don't think so." He stood up, placing himself in front of her, giving her an up-close view of that gorgeous chest as he did so.

She could feel their combined juices easing from her pussy now, dampening her thighs, reminding her of the pleasure of moments before. That memory sent a shiver racing down her spine and a coil of heat building in the pit of her stomach again.

His hands gripped her upper arms, his fingers caressing her sensitive skin as she lifted her gaze to his.

"Reno." She swallowed tightly. "We need to think about this. I need to think about it."

She couldn't deal with him now, she had to make sense of this, she had to find her bearings. This was Reno, for God's sake. She had known him all her life, lusted after him since she was fifteen and shed tears for him while he was on assignment. This was the only man who could break her heart, who could destroy her soul.

He snorted in reply to her desperate words.

"Yeah, like I'm going to give you a chance to come up with excuses to run from me."

The world spun around her as he lifted her into his arms, turned and headed for the staircase. She clutched his shoulders, fighting to force back the melting sensation in the center of her chest. He was carrying her, with little or no effort. Taking the stairs quickly and moving into her bedroom.

"I'll help you shower."

"I don't need any help showering." The panicked sound of her own voice shocked her.

He moved into the bathroom. "Then I want to sleep with you Raven. Just sleep. I want to hold you close and feel you breathing against me." He sat her on her feet, his hands cupping her face, lifting it until he could stare down at her intently. "I'm not going to let you go tonight."

She shivered. She tried not to, but she couldn't help it. She had known he was bossy, dominant, a man who knew what he wanted and how to get it. She just hadn't expected that phenomenal will of his to turn on her in quite this manner.

"You forget, I've run for a reason." Her hands gripped his wrists as she stared up at him. "We'll break each other's hearts, Reno."

She could see the exhaustion marking his face, clearer now than it had been before. A haunting hunger filled his gaze, and Raven knew in the bottom of her soul that she wasn't going to deny him. For now . . . for this moment . . . he needed her. Surely, for the short amount of time he would be here, she could protect her heart. Couldn't she?

"This is a good idea, Raven." He lowered his head, his lips whispering over hers. The kiss was soothing, calming. Emotion raged just beneath it, subtle, but intense. Emotions she refused to delve into.

"One of these days, your bossiness is going to get you into trouble," she warned him as he pulled back, a small smile playing about his passion-swollen lips as he moved away from her to adjust the water in the shower.

She could do it. She took a deep, fortifying breath. It was too late to turn back now anyway. She could have tonight, enjoy his touch, his laughter, the qualities that made him so very unique to her. And when he left, she could let him go without the tears or the rage or the fear. She was strong enough. She didn't have to love him.

"Come on, baby." He stepped into the shower, his hand catching her wrist as he pulled her in after him.

"Do you ever ask for anything?" she asked as he sheltered her from the spray and began soaping a washrag.

His smile flashed, filled with amusement and warmth.

"When I have to."

Raven frowned at that.

"All of you macho SEAL-types are so damned bossy. Reminds me why I steered clear of them."

Her brother Clint was a SEAL; most of her friends' brothers were in one part of the armed forces or another. They were all bossy, domineering men who forged their own paths, whether in life or in love. They left, and sometimes they never returned.

"You weren't steering clear of me, Raven," he told her then, his hands incredibly gentle as he pressed the washcloth to her chest and began to wash her. "I just let you think you were."

She snorted mockingly. She would argue, but that washcloth felt so good, rasping over her flesh, washing away her thoughts as easily as it did the sweat from her body.

She tilted her head back, allowing him to have his way. She had fantasized about this too much, and unfortunately, he was better than the dreams had ever been.

"You should be falling on your feet," she whispered, the sound of her voice punctuated with a gasp as the cloth moved between her thighs, cleaning her slowly.

"Maybe," he growled, "I should rest."

He knelt in front of her, spreading her legs as he lifted one, propping it on the small shelf at the side as the washrag moved over the bare flesh of her pussy.

"Damn, Raven. Do you know how pretty you are? Silky and soft, and so responsive to my touch." He shifted, allowing the spray to rinse her as he dropped the cloth, using his hands to help dispel the suds there.

Arousal built within her quickly. She knew what he was going to do and she didn't know if she could bear it.

His fingers moved over the narrow slit, parting her swollen flesh as she fought to get her bearings, to breathe. If she could just breathe, she could maintain her control.

"I've dreamed of tasting you . . ."

Oh God.

"Fucking you with my tongue, sucking that pretty little clit into my mouth . . ."

She felt her juices gathering, weeping with sensual abandon from her sensitive cunt as her head rolled against the wall of the shower. The explicit, diabolical words made her weak, made her long for him to do it with every fiber of her being.

Her hands braced against the wall and the shower door. She couldn't touch him. If she touched him, she would beg, plead for him.

"Reno . . ." Her thin wail filled the shower stall as his tongue swiped through the slit, circled her clit, then disappeared.

Her eyes drifted open as she stared down at him, her legs weakening at the erotic sight of him kneeling before her, his tongue moving in again, circling her clit as he stared up at her.

Not fair. Oh God. She couldn't stand it.

Her hands moved involuntarily, her fingers digging into his scalp as she parted her legs further, pressing him closer.

"More . . . ," she panted. "Lick me more."

He hummed in approval, his tongue dancing in the slick cream that began to coat her as her hips tilted further.

"Oh yes," she moaned. "Like that, Reno. Lick me all over."

She was trembling, watching him, feeling his tongue circle her clit, lick along the narrow valley, circling the sensitive opening of her vagina, teasing her with the threat of a sensual thrust into the suddenly hungry depths. His hands were at her buttocks, spreading them open, sending chills racing up her back at the flare of heat that invaded the tiny entrance there. The sensations were building, pulling at her, ripping away the veil of distance she tried to maintain as he teased her with his tongue.

"Reno, do it," she whispered desperately as his fingers slid lower, parting the folds of her pussy as his tongue teased and tempted. "Please. Please do it."

"What, baby?" he whispered wickedly. "Tell me. Whatever you want, I'll give you."

Her eyes fluttered; her knees weakened. His tongue stroked, taunted, yet never gave her what she knew would throw her over the edge. She wanted it inside her. She wanted to feel his tongue shoving hard inside the snug depths of her pussy as she watched him. Watched him eating her like he loved it, lived for it.

"Do it," she cried out fiercely. "Dammit, Reno, stop teasing me. Please."

He flickered over the opening, licking at the juices falling from her as she shuddered at the pleasure. So much pleasure.

"Fuck me with it." She thrust her hips closer, her hands pressing against his head, her gasping moans turning to a shattered scream when he did as she begged. His tongue plunged deep, filling her, pumping inside her as her orgasm took her by surprise, hurtling her into a rapture she could only give herself to.

"Son of a bitch!" He was on his feet, lifting her, bracing her against the wall a second before he wrapped her legs around his hips and plunged deep inside her.

Shocking. Burning. He filled her to overflowing and then made her take more. Delicate tissue parted, clenched, hugging him heatedly as he began to move, sending her flying again, ripping away, layer by layer, the shields around her soul.

"Ah God, Raven baby . . . so tight . . . so hot . . . hold me, baby. Hold me and mean it."

She couldn't do anything less. She held on to him as though her life, her very heart depended on it. And in a way, she knew it did. He was filling her soul, the one thing she had sworn she would never allow to happen, was happening.

Her legs wrapped around his waist, tightening, her arms around his neck locking in place, her lips searching blindly for his as she convulsed again, jerking in his grip, trying to drive him deeper, harder, as the world rocked around her in a release that seemed never ending.

Reno pumped inside her, hard and fast before his groan filled her senses and the heat of his release filled the hungry depths of her pussy. She milked him, moaning in exhaustion as the tremors of release shuddered through her again, leaving her limp, ragged in his hold as his arms tightened around her.

Moments later, she was only distantly aware of him pulling free of her, cleaning her again, then himself, before he shut the water off and dried them with quick, economical movements.

A smile curved her lips though, as he picked her up in his arms and carried her to her bed. Curling against his chest, his hands buried in her hair as his arms surrounded her, sleep overtook her. Warm, sheltered, free of the teasingly erotic dreams that used to haunt her, she slept in her warrior's arms.

Reno stared into the darkness of the bedroom, Raven's warmth tucked close to his heart as he sheltered her against his chest. She slept naturally, easily. Not that he expected the battle to be over by any means.

A sleepy smile quirked his lips. He'd better rest tonight, because he had a feeling that come morning, she would be just as prickly as ever. Not that he intended to let it do her any good. He was a part of her, whether she wanted to admit it or not. Just as she was a part of him.

And being a part of Raven was like being reborn. Never had he known anything as sweet, as hot, as soul-fulfilling as being her lover.

He had warned her, the night Morganna had interrupted them, that her days were numbered. He wasn't waiting any longer to claim what he had known for years was his.

She shifted against his side, a murmur of pleasure leaving her throat as his hands rubbed lightly down her back, and she settled against him once again.

"I love you, Raven." He whispered the words he knew she didn't want to hear. Gave them to her while she slept, knowing that, for now, it was the only way she would accept it.

"Reno . . ." His name as it left her lips filled him with pleasure. Even sleeping, she knew where she belonged.

Chapter Four

She had slept with Reno Chavez.

She hadn't just slept with him, she had been taken by him. Held by him. Fucked senseless, to be honest, she snapped silently.

Raven leaned on the kitchen counter the next morning, her head cradled in her arms as she waited for the coffee to finish, for the rich fragrance teasing her senses to become an elixir that would hopefully clear her head. Bring her sanity back. It would be really nice if it could turn back time.

She moaned pitifully.

She couldn't even claim she'd been drunk; she hadn't so much as touched a beer while at Morganna's. She had been stone-cold sober until Reno kissed her. Until his hands stroked her body, bringing her nerve endings to life and a ravenous hunger clawing at her womb.

She pressed her thighs together at the memory, hating the feel of her loose shorts rasping against her flesh. She wanted Reno's hands. Even the loose shirt was uncomfortable on her sensitive body. She could strip it off. She could undress, go to him. . . . She gritted her teeth in mental refusal.

She was not going to think about it. She was not going to relive each and every slow slide of his cock inside her vagina, stroking the pulsing nerves there, stretching her, filling her, making her burn. . . .

Her fists clenched as she rolled her forehead against her arm.

She couldn't have made a bigger mistake if she had actually put effort into coming up with one. Sleeping with Reno was tantamount to jumping from a plane without a parachute. It wasn't just risky; it was suicide to her emotional well-being.

He had been hard-headed as a boy, bossy as a young man, and now he was so firmly dominant, it was enough to make her teeth clench. What happened to the nice young man who put Band-Aids on her knees and bought her ice pops from the corner store? Why did he have to become the big tough SEAL who insisted on a career that risked his life every time he went to work?

"Dumb. Dumb. Dumb," she muttered as she lifted her head, staring at the slow stream of black liquid that ran into the carafe.

"When are you going to break down and buy a real coffee-maker?"

She stiffened at Reno's amused voice, refusing to turn and face him, to stare at that incredibly sexy body. The same one that had risen over her last night, pushing between her thighs as he filled her with the hard, broad flesh of his cock. She shivered at the memory.

"This one works," she mumbled. And it had been her mother's before she died five years before.

There was no way she was going to consider facing the day without coffee. She needed it. It was essential. Otherwise, she was going to melt into a puddle of aroused goo before she ever managed to push Reno out the door.

He grunted noncommittally behind her.

"We'll get a coffee grinder later and some fresh beans. I'll make you some real coffee."

Turning her head slowly from the shelter of her arms, she stared back at him. Over six feet of lean, smooth, hard muscle. Damn him. He wasn't wearing a shirt. His chest, with its smattering of hair, was displayed in all its dark glory, muscles shifting, tempting, encouraging. . . .

"Don't you have a bed to buy or something?" She straightened quickly, jerked a cup from the hook on the wall and prayed the dark brew would hurry. She had to clear her head, or she was never going to make it through the day.

"Are you trying to run me off, Raven?" She could hear the grin in his voice, see it when she glanced back at him.

"Yes," she snapped desperately. "I am. I can't deal with you this morning. Go torture Morganna."

Like she thought for a minute that he was going to do that. She should have known better, she told herself frantically. He had warned her that last time, when he woke her with a kiss, looming over her like a tide of passion, that her days were numbered. She had tried to convince herself he wasn't serious. She should have known better.

"I don't think so, baby. Do you think I'm going to let you run me off this soon?"

Uh-oh.

She blinked back at him as his expression hardened, his gray eyes turning stormy. She knew that look, and it did not bode well for getting rid of him.

"How soon, then?" She slammed the cup to the counter and jerked the pot from under the small stream inching into it to rapidly fill the cup.

She brought the cup to her lips and sipped too quickly. The hot liquid burned her tongue, but it did nothing to erase the remembered feel of his touch.

"Damn, Clint was right, you're a grouch in the morning," he stated as he moved to the pot himself, causing her to back away quickly. If he touched her, she was a goner.

"I'm always a grouch." She frowned as he poured himself a cup of coffee. "And that's my coffee."

He lifted his brow mockingly. "I know a cure for your grouchiness."

The wicked smile playing about his mouth had her womb convulsing in arousal. Damn him. Damn him. She could feel her body preparing for him, aching for him. Even more frightening was the fact that it felt right. His presence in her kitchen wasn't as upsetting as it should have been. It felt comfortable, impossibly natural. She hated having people around her first thing in the morning, but Reno was different. Which meant he had to go.

"As soon as I finish my coffee, I'm throwing you out." There was just no other answer.

She moved to the table, cradling the cup lovingly as she inhaled the scent. Sanity resided there surely.

"You'll have to grow quite a bit first, darlin'." He wasn't amused; he wasn't smiling. He was staring at her from determined, intense eyes.

"And don't call me darlin'."

He leaned against the counter, his bare ankles crossing as she glanced at his feet. Dammit, even his toes looked sexy.

She sipped the coffee, remaining silent. There had to be a way to get him out of her apartment, short of calling the police. And what was she supposed to tell the police? Excuse me, Officer, but

I let him fuck me last night, so of course he thinks he has rights now.

She rolled her eyes at the thought. Of course he thought he did. She knew Reno. There wasn't a chance in hell he had even considered a one-night stand. He was her brother's best friend. Her best friend's brother. He was playing in earnest.

Panic flared at the thought of that. *Oh hell*. She looked up at him wildly, taking in the small grin quirking his lips and the way he watched her. As if she were his.

"It was just sex."

He laughed. Asshole. He sipped his coffee and grimaced.

"I'm definitely going to have to show you the fine art of preparing coffee," he drawled. "This stuff isn't going to help your attitude at all, Raven."

"My attitude is not the problem. You are," she informed him through gritted teeth.

"I invited you over to sleep. Not come in and take over," she said, feeling desperate as she got up from the table. "You weren't supposed to . . . to—" Her face flamed. "—do what you did."

"What did I do?" His eyes widened, almost innocently. She could see the knowledge glowing there, even as the sweatpants he wore began to tent in the front from his erection.

She swallowed tightly at the sight of it. Her mouth was watering. Oh God, why was her mouth watering? Why were images of going to her knees and pulling the waistband clear of that thick flesh suddenly torturing her? And her mouth was watering. Weak, Raven, she accused herself firmly. You are so weak.

"That," she said, her hand waving toward the erection. "That's what you did last night. You seduced me."

"Seduced you?" He was clearly laughing now as he glanced

down at the tented material. "With my cock? That was seduction? Baby, all I did was kiss you. You kissed back."

"Well that was enough," she sniffed. "Now it's time for you to get dressed and leave."

He set his cup down on the counter, his eyes narrowing, and trepidation skated down her spine. She knew Reno. Knew his looks, his moods, and his stubbornness. She knew when he was about to do something he knew was going to piss her off. And he had that look now.

"Come here." His voice was deep and rich like black velvet.

"What?" she said, staring at him warily.

"I said, come here," he growled. Raven shivered in reaction. Her pussy was gushing at the sound of his voice. She was so easy.

"No." She crossed her arms over her breasts, hoping to hide the telltale rise of her nipples. Damn they ached for his touch, his mouth, his tongue flickering over them.

His brow arched.

"You know," he said conversationally. "I'm dying to watch the bare flesh of that pretty little ass turn red. Get over here, Raven, or I'm going to see just how fast my hand can make it blush."

Reno watched as Raven's eyes flared, the blue darkening, filling with arousal and heat as she stared at him with wild-eyed panic. He wanted to chuckle, but he had a feeling it would push her further into retreat. As though he was going to allow that.

He mentally shook his head, watching her trying to rebuild her defenses to keep him out.

Poor Raven. It didn't matter.

Nothing was going to diminish the heat and the hunger between them.

"You did not just threaten to spank me," she suddenly snapped, blinking in amazement as she watched him.

"Yes, I did," he said refuting her statement blandly. "Now come here." He pointed his finger directly in front of his feet.

Anger sizzled in the air. Pure feminine fury heated the room as her arms dropped slowly to her sides and her cheeks flushed with emotion.

"How dare you order me around!" She was seconds from stamping her foot. Damn, she made him hot when she flamed like that. "This is my house, Reno," she said, pointing at her chest, her own eyes narrowing. "My kitchen, my house, and you're leaving."

Reno studied her before quickly coming to a decision. She was trembling with anger . . . and panic. He didn't want to push so hard and fast that he lost her. So he'd leave, but he wouldn't be gone for long. He'd give her a bit of time to miss him, but he would be back. Besides there wasn't a chance he could stay away long, not after having had her, feeling the heat of her pussy gripping his cock, the sweet tight muscles rippling around him as she came, holding her satisfied body next to his afterward.

He straightened, watching her closely. She stiffened, her foot moving back as though to retreat before she quickly checked the motion.

"Raven, come here," he said more gently.

If possible, her eyes widened even more in panic at his softer tone.

He was very well aware of the risk he was taking. Convincing Raven to open her heart was fraught with danger. Not the physical kind, but the emotional kind. She had seen the result of her mother's life with her Navy SEAL father. The long absences, the fights when he returned home, her mother's inability to accept the danger her father faced and her father's refusal to deal with the situation in any a way except to take more missions, to stay away longer, until finally he hadn't returned. He had been killed while on a mission, leaving her mother to deal with her guilt, and Raven to face the world without a father.

Her lips tightened defiantly before she stalked over to him.

"Now what?" she snarled up at him.

"This."

He lowered his head. He didn't touch her except with his lips. He gripped the counter behind him with both hands, itching to grip her instead. No force, no demand, nothing but the arousal whipping between them, making him crazy, making her hot enough to sear.

Her lips opened on a strangled gasp, her hands reaching for his waist, her fingers curling against his flesh as his tongue surged deep inside. Slanting his head, he pressed closer, groaning when his erection cushioned against her stomach as she rubbed against him, a whimper of lust escaping her throat as he nipped at her lips, stroked them with his tongue, then delved inside for the sweet nectar of her passion.

When she was soft, pliant, molded to his body as her tongue tangled with his, he slowly drew back.

"Reno . . ."

Her soft gasp of protest had him gritting his teeth as he fought every instinct inside him screaming to take her to the floor, to convince her, to force her to admit what she was so obviously denying.

Instead, he drew in a hard breath and stepped away from the temptation of her sweet body. God, she had no idea how hard it was to step away from her, to leave her as aching as he ached for her. But he couldn't, wouldn't risk losing her. If he carried through now, took her to her bed as he wanted to so desperately, then it would weaken not just his resolve, but the inroads he had made into making her realize what they could be to each other.

"Now I'll go." He turned and walked out of the kitchen. "I'll see you in the morning, Raven. I'll bring the coffee."

Chapter Five

Raven stomped around the house for hours, cleaning what didn't need cleaning, cursing men, their arrogance and their damned alpha, dominant, gung-ho, hero complexes. She had cursed both Reno and her brother Clint for years for the very things that made them so special. They were warriors, determined to protect, to make a difference. And they did make a difference. But he was still being arrogant. Relationships weren't war zones.

"There is no relationship, dammit," she muttered furiously, stepping out of the shower and drying off quickly before fluffing her hair.

She was not going to sit around tonight and wait for him. She had waited for him too many nights, pacing the floor with Morganna, chewing her fingernails if they knew he was on a mission, shedding tears when he was later returning home than he had told his sister he would be. She and Morganna both waited for that black government car that would bring the horrifying news of a death.

Now, she was supposed to sit around the damned house and torture herself over feelings and emotions she knew she was never going to be rid of.

She loved him.

Dammit, she did love him but that didn't mean she had to like it.

She jerked the red silk and lace thong panties and bra from her drawer and pulled them on, knowing they looked good on her. Sexy and hot. They made her feel wicked and wild. Almost as wicked and wild as Reno made her feel.

Biting her lip, her hands moved slowly, cupping her swollen breasts as her thumbs rasped over her distended nipples. She closed her eyes, and could almost feel him touching her, making the heated burn ignite fiercely in the depths of her womb.

He wasn't supposed to do this to her. Make her miss him so desperately, make her wish she could accept as easily as he did. But he wasn't the one who would be left to pace the floors, to fill with anger. And that was the part that terrified her. She didn't want to be like her mother, always angry or depressed, terrified when she heard the sound of a vehicle coming up the drive.

Reno and Morganna's parents had died six years before in a car accident. Together. There had been no government condolences, no questions were ever answered regarding how they died. Where they died. The questions Raven's mother had asked every day until her death.

She plucked the sexy little black dress she loved so much out of her closet as the past ate at her soul with a hollow ache. It fell halfway down her thighs, the thin straps barely covering the bra straps as the bodice draped over her breasts. The shimmery black silk felt good on her, looked good on her.

She paired it with the high-heeled, black strappy sandals and drew in a deep breath before shoving keys, cash and ID into a minuscule purse and headed downstairs.

She wasn't married. She didn't have to sit at home and pace the floors and she damned sure didn't have to worry about Reno Chavez or his perceptions and arrogance. Let him sit and brood if he wanted to. She was going to play.

She was bored out of her ever-loving mind, but she wasn't going to admit it to Morganna, who had joined her on her little evening adventure.

"Reno's going to be pissed," was Morganna's only objection to the night's activities as they walked into the small club, the pulse of the music surrounding them, the smoky atmosphere dim and not nearly as appealing as Raven tried to pretend it was.

"He'll live," she snapped. "Your brother is entirely too dominant, Morganna. And I'm still pissed at you for letting your friends use his bed."

"Of course he's dominant," Morganna laughed as they made their way through the crowd to the back of the club and a lone empty table. "He wouldn't do what he does if he wasn't. Admit it, Raven, it's one of the things you love about him."

It was one of the things that terrified her about him.

"No, that's what you love about Clint." She took her chair and looked around impatiently for the waitress. "I like my men a little safer. You know, Morg, the 'stay at home and hearth' type of guy?"

She waved the waitress over, impatient to get on with forgetting about Reno and his arrogant my-way-or-no-way attitude.

"You like fooling yourself is what you like," Morganna laughed after they gave the waitress their drink orders. "But you go right ahead. I like watching Reno in action. He's smooth. Clint should take lessons."

Raven directed a dark look at her friend.

"Drop the subject. I'm here to have a good time, not to talk about Reno."

She danced with the first man who asked, not the up close, slow and sway, but a fast hard beat that filled her veins and allowed her to ignore the memories threatening to overwhelm her senses.

She sat out the slower dances, a rare occurrence for her, which only made her angrier. But she couldn't stand the thought of another man holding her, not yet. God, how pathetic was that, she wondered as she moved to the hard beat echoing though the club.

She swayed in time to songs, her hair flowing down her back, caressing her upper shoulders, reminding her of Reno's touch. She closed her eyes and saw his face, only to snap them open and glare at her present partner.

She glanced across the room and her heart shuddered in her chest as she swore she caught a glimpse of him moving through the crowd. No one could move like Reno, with a male predatory grace that drew the eye and had women panting to rub against him like cats.

Shaking her head, she pushed the suspicion away.

She didn't know why she was letting this affect her so drastically. The physical attraction had bloomed between them for years now. She had known that she would eventually end up beneath Reno in bed; she just hadn't expected the raw power of it.

She moved back as the rawboned, broad young man she was dancing with reached out to clasp her hip, flashing him an irritated frown when he pouted back at her. She wasn't in the mood to be groped. She wanted to dance, expend the energy pulsing in her body and forget about the one man she knew would be cemented in her brain forever now.

As the band paused, preparing to strike up another number, a hard hand suddenly gripped her wrist, pulling her around as she gasped in surprise.

Oh hell. Reno was pissed.

She stared up at him, aware of the immediate hardening of her nipples and their ultrasensitivity against the lace of her bra. Between her thighs, her clit began to throb with the same furious, hard beat of her heart.

"Well, fancy seeing you here," she yelled out above the music as he began to drag her across the dance floor. "Let me guess, Morganna called you."

"Morganna shows good sense at the oddest moments." His head turned, eyes narrowed on her as he began to pull her out of the crowd. He stalked across the room, heading for the shadowed corner of her table. Rather than being pushed into one of the chairs there, she found herself flattened against the wall as his head lowered, his lips at her ear.

"What are you doing here?" She stared up at him defiantly. "I don't remember inviting you."

"No, you were too damned busy running away from me," he snapped.

She should have told him then and there she didn't want him, didn't need him, but the words wouldn't come out of her mouth.

"Jealous, Reno?" She was breathing harder, her nipples pebbled and pressed tight against her dress.

"Not jealous at all," he assured her tightly. "You wouldn't let another man touch you, would you, Raven? You know who that sweet little body belongs to, don't you?"

"Yeah." She smiled slowly, aware of the drowsy passion that reflected in her expression. "Me."

He nipped her ear firmly, sending shudders racing through her. "I'm going to paddle your ass for that one."

"Oh, spank me." She gave a mock shiver, her voice sarcastic despite the tremors of trepidation skittering up her spine.

She gave a startled jerk as he imprisoned both wrists in one hand, holding them above her head as the other moved to the back of her thigh, running up the skirt of the dress to cup one rounded cheek of her ass firmly.

The feel of his hand, callused and warm, had her breath catching in her throat. The implied threat in the action should have pissed her off, at the very least should have made her more nervous than aroused.

"Oh baby, I *will* spank you." To prove his point, his hand moved back before delivering a light, warming tap to her flesh. "You have no idea how well I'm going to spank that pretty little ass. If you wanted to play the vixen, sweetheart, then you knew where I was. You could have come to me."

Her head fell back against the wall as his fingers slid beneath the edge of her panties and trailed down the narrow crevice separating her buttocks.

"I wanted to forget about you, not run to you," she snapped breathlessly, fighting herself and the weakness that struck her knees as his fingers probed ever closer to the slick curves of her cunt.

She could feel her flesh heating further, the thick juices coating her pussy, preparing her for him as her mind filled with the erotic images of the night before. Reno coming over her, parting her thighs as he slid between them.

Her breath hitched in her throat as her vagina spasmed in greedy hunger.

"We're going to discuss that one as well, darlin'," he growled at her ear, pressing his hips against her lower stomach, letting her feel the thick erection behind the fly of his jeans. "We're going to discuss all your little bad habits, in depth." Two fingers plunged inside the weeping entrance of her cleft, stretching her sensitive flesh as he pushed her to the edge of climax.

The music surrounded them, the awareness that anyone could be watching. Not that they would see much the way Reno had positioned her.

"Reno . . ." Her gasping wail was low, a throttled cry of need as his lips slid to her throat, his teeth raking as he took gentle nips, then soothed the little fire with the warmth of his lips and tongue.

"Damn you, Raven." His voice was rough, the edge of control apparent in the husky baritone. "You're pushing me too far, baby. Only you would refuse to settle back and see where the hell this could go. Why do you want to push me?"

He thrust his fingers in her weeping pussy, holding her on the edge of sanity as she fought to keep from screaming out her demand that he take her. There and then.

"I'm not pushing you," she gasped. "You keep pushing. . . . Ah God, Reno." She had to bite her lip to keep from begging as he slid his fingers from her, panting as his lips continued to caress her neck, his breathing heavy and labored.

She stared up at him as he pulled back from her, lowering her arms, but still holding her wrists prisoner with his powerful hand.

"Show-off," she accused darkly as her gaze flickered to her bound wrists. "Why didn't you just bring the handcuffs?"

"Don't tempt me." His smile was all teeth. Predatory, intent. "Now come along like a good little girl, Raven."

She frowned at the heavy mockery in his voice. He might be a bit more than pissed, she thought, which only caused her own temper to rise. He had no right to be angry with her; it was her choice how she spent her time, not his. And she would be damned if she would put up with this attitude because she decided to spend time dancing rather than waiting around on him.

"Hey, dude, you got no right to be hauling her out of here." The big boy from the previous dance stood in their way, bringing Reno to a slow stop.

Raven glanced over his shoulder, wide-eyed. The younger man wasn't as tall as Reno, but he was thick and heavy, built like a damned linebacker and staring at Reno like a bull on a rampage.

"Sorry, dude, but the lady belongs to me." A normal rational man might have paid attention to the warning in Reno's voice, not to mention the savage look on his face.

"I didn't see no brand, asshole," the younger man swayed drunkenly in front of him, causing Raven to stifle a groan of mortification.

Reno would never let her live this one down, and neither would Clint, once he got wind of it. Dammit, why did these things have to happen to her?

"You just didn't look in the right place," Reno informed him, his voice deep, deadly. "Count yourself lucky. If you had, I'd have to rip your throat out."

Raven's eyes widened. This Reno was scary. He looked ready to fight, to defend, to claim.

"Uhh, Reno, let's just go." She pushed at his arm, aware of the grip he still retained on her wrists.

"Tough little man, aren't you?" the boy laughed, and Raven

groaned miserably. The other man had to be drunker than she thought, to even consider insulting Reno so rudely. Besides, Reno was at least six inches taller than the other man. Sometimes wider did not mean better.

Before she could do more than gasp in surprise, she was free, and Reno had the boy by the throat. Slowly, he took the younger man to the floor as beefy hands wrapped around his wrists and brown eyes began to bulge at the lack of oxygen.

"Don't mess with me, boy," Reno growled mercilessly. "Or my woman. Period."

When he released the younger man, Raven glared at him.

"You're insane," she said, slapping at his arm with enough force to sting her hand as he stared back at her in surprise. "Your woman, my ass! You are a bully, Reno. A macho, self-serving, arrogant SEAL bully and I'll be damned if I'm going anywhere with you."

She turned and swept through the crowd, her face flaming in embarrassment and fury, even though her body was still heated, throbbing.

My woman.

Something inside her had melted when he rasped the words, his tone thick with possessiveness and male fury, while another part screeched in horror. He had claimed her. It wasn't just sex to him, he was serious about this, and that point had just been driven forcibly home. Not that she hadn't been aware of it already. But now, she knew it down to her soul. All her dreams, hopes and fears were tied up with one man. With Reno.

She was screwed.

Chapter Six

Reno stayed carefully behind Raven's car as he followed her home, his hands gripping the steering wheel.

She was right. He had been pissed, jealous and riding the fine edge of his control; otherwise, he would have handled the younger man with a bit more discretion. Truth was, he wanted to kill that kid for daring to try to come between him and Raven.

He wiped his hand across his face as he fought his raging emotions. Never had he had felt the adrenaline pumping through his system as it was now. His cock was harder than it had been at any time in his life and the urge to fuck Raven until she was too exhausted to fight back was nearly overwhelming.

She was driving him insane, not that he had expected anything less from her. He had known that stealing her heart wouldn't be easy, and binding her to him even harder. She looked at him and saw her parents. The father who left to fight, the mother who screamed and raged and drank too much while he was gone until the day he returned in a casket.

It was the danger of the job that some women couldn't handle. And he would have worried that Raven couldn't handle it, if he didn't know for a fact that each mission Morganna knew he was on, she and Raven waited out together. Laughing, joking, calling him names and insulting him to hell and back, as reported by his sister. But she handled it. Just as Morganna helped Raven handle Clint's absences. They had a support system they had relied on most of their lives.

She was stronger than she thought was, Reno reflected, as he pulled into the driveway behind her car. He watched, eyes narrowed as she flounced out of the car, that little black dress flirting with her upper thighs as it whipped around her in a cloud of silk.

More slowly, Reno got out of the truck. Slow and careful, he cautioned himself. He had lost it at the club. Hell, he had nearly fucked her in that dark corner for everyone to see.

"Go away, Reno," she snarled as she unlocked the front door. "I don't want to see or talk to you.

At least she didn't try to slam the door in his face. She pushed into the house, leaving it wide open for him. Reno controlled the smile that wanted to touch his lips. She could yell until hell froze over, but he knew her. Inside out and upside down, he knew her, loved her, and he would be damned if he was going to let her find excuses to throw him out of her life.

"Aren't you tired of being such a coward, Raven?" he said as he followed her inside, closing and locking the door behind him.

She whirled around, the long, sleek golden brown curls that made his hands itch fanning around her slender body.

"Me? A coward?" An imperious thumb pointed into her chest. "I'm a realist, Reno. Unlike you, I prefer to see the truth rather than the pretty lies you want to feed me."

He crossed his arms over his chest, slowly. "When, Raven, did I ever lie to you?"

"Every time you touched me," she yelled back at him, thinking of the past two years, the teasing kisses and flirtatious touching. "Pretending it was something light, something friendly. You want it all, don't you, Reno?"

"Hell yes!" He snapped, facing her across the room, knowing if he got too close, there was no way he could keep from touching her. "I never pretended any different, Raven. You were the one who kept running, who kept refusing to face facts. You're the liar, Raven, not me."

"I never lied to you." Her hands swiped through her hair, frustration and pain evident on her face. "I told you I couldn't handle you. I couldn't handle the kind of relationship you want from me."

"Fuck that," he growled. "I don't want just a damned relationship with you, Raven. I want forever. And you knew it all along."

Raven stared at him wide-eyed.

"No . . ."

"Yes, by God, you did," he bit out. "You'd flit around, teasing and flirting, a little kiss here and there, a pet and a pat and you thought that would be enough to hold me off. Now you're finding out otherwise and it scares the hell out of you."

Determination straightened her shoulders and glittered in her eyes. "I want you to leave." Her voice was rough, ragged with emotion. "Leave and don't come back, Reno."

A mocking smile twisted his lips. "Yeah, I guess you do." He crossed his arms over his chest again, restraining the need to hold her, to promise that everything would be okay. "If I leave," he continued, "you'll keep hiding your head in the sand, pretending that somehow, someway, if I'm killed in action, then it won't hurt. You'll survive it without a bottle in your hand and your heart will remain intact."

He watched her pale, the color leaching from her face as she stared back at him in shock.

"Do you really think you can do it, Raven?" he asked softly. "Do you think it won't hurt? Do you think you have your heart packed away nice and tight where nothing or no one can break it?"

"Stop." Her voice shook, breaking his heart. But her rejection hurt worse. It seared his soul.

He moved toward her then, gripping her shoulders before she could evade him, staring down at her as he fought his own raging emotions.

"Will it work?" He wanted to make her see the truth. "Look at me, Raven. If I die tomorrow, will it hurt any less than it would if we had a year or twenty together? Will you lay me in the ground any easier?"

"Oh God!" She shuddered, her eyes filling with tears as she stared up at him in misery. "I couldn't stand it. Don't you see, Reno? I couldn't stand it if something happened to you."

Those tears. He couldn't handle her tears. God, don't let her cry— it made him want to kill someone. And since he was the one causing the tears, that didn't leave many options.

"You don't understand," she said, dashing away her tears. "What if I'm like my mother? I don't have the courage to face that."

"The hell you don't," he said, and swooped down, taking her lips, forcing her head back against the wall as he took the kiss, as he needed to take her heart. Fully. Completely. And her response was everything he knew it could be, everything he knew she kept hidden inside her soul.

Her lips opened, her tongue reaching out for his, suckling him inside the warmth of her mouth as she lifted to him, pressing the hard tips of her nipples into his chest as her arms wrapped tight around his neck, her hands gripping his head.

With a ragged growl, he pulled her closer, lifting her into his arms and turning for the staircase. If this was all he would have, then he would take it. But by God, he would show her. If it was the last thing he managed, he would show her exactly what she was throwing away.

Chapter Seven

The expression on his face was like none she had seen before. Powerful, dominant, the hard planes and angles tightened into sharp relief as he moved.

"Reno." The protest was halted by the simple means of his lips covering hers again as his hands gripped the rounded curves of her buttocks, pulling her up and flush against the thick cock ridged behind the fly of his jeans.

Heat flared instantly, spreading from her pussy through the rest of her body as her hands gripped his shoulders and she arched closer. She couldn't imagine never knowing this again, never being held by him, loved by him.

Twisting in his grip, she fought him for the kiss, as desperately hungry for him as he seemed to be for her. His hands clenched the flesh of her rear, pulling at the curves until an erotic, sharp little tingle pierced the small entrance of her anus at the separation of the flesh.

"Feel it, Raven. Feel how sweet and hot it is. That doesn't just go away, baby; it haunts and eats at the soul and makes you so fucking hungry for it, you think you'll go crazy without it. That's how I've been. That's what tears at me every minute we're apart. Needing this. Your taste, your touch."

She stared up at him, knowing she couldn't refute his words. The memory of those brief, heated kisses in the past, his arms surrounding her, had tormented her. She needed him, needed him until it terrified her, but it made her aware of the weakness of her heart and the battle she was losing to hold it aloof.

Then the world spun around her as he lifted her in his arms, ignoring her instinctive protest as he strode across the room and quickly upstairs.

"Reno . . . you're taking over again," she gasped as he stepped into her bedroom, lowering her feet to the floor before pulling her back against him once again.

"I'm not taking *you* fast enough." He growled, bending his head as he tilted hers back, catching her lips in a kiss that stole her objections, just as it stole her breath.

He chuckled, the sound rough and strained as she worked her hands between them, moving for the buttons that held his cock prisoner. She wasn't going to stand there, allowing him to control her, to dominate her so easily. She couldn't deny the pleasure, but she could make him just as crazy as he was making her.

"No, no. Bad girl." His hands caught hers as he turned her around quickly, pulling her back against his chest as one hard arm locked around her waist. "Look in the mirror. Look how pretty you are, Raven."

She blinked at the image in the large mirror that sat atop the chest. Reno's hand moved along her shoulder, lowering the strap of her dress down her arm until the draped bodice fell away from the swollen curve of her breast.

The red lace of her bra showed up clearly against her pale skin, the picture reflected back at her was one of a forbidden taste of sensual excitement. He stood head and shoulders above her, staring down at her as he stripped the dress from her upper body, his lips moving over her neck and shoulder as the material dropped to the floor.

Raven stared into the mirror, seeing him as he surrounded her, a broad, powerful male animal intent on possession. His gaze met hers in the mirror, his gray eyes nearly black, his expression tight, the skin stretched tight across his high cheekbones, the fight for control blatantly evident.

She felt the breath lock in her chest at the image he presented. Boldly, unapologetically male. Possessive. Dominant. He held her and meant it.

"Such a pretty little bad girl," he whispered then. "Do you know what happens to bad girls, Raven? Bad little girls who refuse to admit what they see staring them in the face?"

She almost came from the sound of his voice alone. She felt her womb convulse, stealing her breath and her senses as his hands smoothed up her waist and cupped her engorged breasts in a firm, heated grip. Devilish thumbs rasped over the peaks, sending flares of brilliant heat washing through her.

The sight of those broad, darkly tanned hands cupping the swollen mounds of her breasts was highly erotic. He was so strong, yet his grip was firm, gentle. There was no pain, no sense of force, just pleasure and hunger and need that spread from those hands to her body and left her trembling in arousal.

"You really are a pervert." Unfortunately, it was turning her on more than it should.

"Oh baby, you have no idea," he whispered, his eyes, so filled with emotion and lust, meeting hers in the mirror as he loosened the catch of her bra. "But I intend to show you. I'm about to let you get very well acquainted with every perverted fantasy I've ever had about you."

The bra dropped to the floor.

Raven gasped at the sight of the bare skin as his fingers, the backs of his fingers only, traced the curve of her breasts, rasped over the hard points of her nipples. Electric pleasure sizzled though her nerve endings, sending pulses of sensation whipping over flesh. She could feel her juices easing past her vagina, dampening the bare folds of her pussy as she pressed closer, rubbing her buttocks against his erection.

He wasn't the only one who could tease. She might not have his experience, but her arousal made up for it. She needed him, needed his touch, his kiss, the flames of pleasure that surrounded her and struck into the core of her being as he held her.

"Vixen," he growled roughly, pressing his cock tighter against her rear. "You keep teasing me with that little ass and you'll get more than you bargained for."

Her eyes widened as she blinked at his image in the mirror. He looked serious.

"You wouldn't." She arched against him as one hand slid down her stomach, his palm cupping the heated contours of her pussy through the lace and silk of the thong that seemed more a tease than any actually covering.

She stared at the image they made—sexual, hungry. His hand cupped her possessively, his fingers curving between her thighs, rasping against the material of the panties over her swollen flesh.

"Don't bet on it," he growled at her ear. "But first, I have to show you how I punish bad little girls."

She had only a second to gasp in shock as he lifted her from her feet, backed to the bed and sat down heavily before pressing her over his legs.

"You wouldn't! Dammit, Reno!"

His hand landed on the upraised flesh of her butt, sending sensation shooting to her clit. She jerked, shocked, amazed. She had known, that first time he spanked her so long ago, that a little pain could be an incredible turn-on. But this was different. His bare hand applied to her naked ass sent her flesh blooming with heat, and her pussy spasming in pleasure.

"Beautiful," his fingers trailed over the rounded flesh before his hand lifted, falling again on the opposite cheek with the same devastating effect.

"Reno, this isn't a good idea." Her pussy was creaming furiously as she shuddered in his grip.

He slid his fingers slid under the silken strap of material that ran between the cheeks of her rear. "Are you sure, Raven? I think it's a very good idea."

Raven groaned as she felt the silk of the thong rasping over her cunt, caressing the swollen nub of her clit as she writhed on his lap. Just when she thought he must have surely forgotten his previous intentions, his hand rose and landed on her bare butt again, causing her womb to convulse as she felt her juices flowing from her pussy.

She was quivering, shuddering with a fiery pleasure as he spanked her with an erotic precision that had her screaming out with each strike against her flesh. The pleasure whipping through her body seared her from the inside out and left her gasping, nearly screaming in arousal.

"Reno, this isn't fair." She moaned, jerking against him as one blow nearly threw her into orgasm, the pleasure-pain was so intense.

"No, Raven, what isn't fair is your denial." His hand landed again, making her burn as she screamed out beneath the fiery lash. "What isn't fair is aching for you, loving you and having to fight you every damned step of the way—" Smack! "—when we both—" Smack! "Know—" Smack! "Exactly how you feel. . . ."

She was arching back to his hand and begging for more, so close to climax, she could feel it shuddering through her, clenching in her womb as he suddenly lifted her, tossing her to the bed as he rose to his feet.

Rolling to her back Raven came to her knees aggressively, baring her teeth in an arousal so deep, so hot, she knew it was burning her out of control. Before he could loosen the first metal button of his jeans, her fingers were there, pushing his out of the way, loosening his jeans until the rigid length of his cock jutted through the open fabric.

Thick and heavily veined, the flared head broad and ruddy, it was a treat Raven couldn't refuse any longer. Her eyes lifted, meeting Reno's stormy gaze as her head lowered, her tongue swiping over the small pearl of liquid that collected on the tip. His fingers threaded through her hair as her lips parted, covering the hot flesh with greedy hunger.

Her lips and mouth moved on him as her fingers enclosed the silken length. He was like iron encased in silk, hot and heavy, an erotic weapon of such sensual destruction that she was left helpless in the face of their combined needs.

Her mouth enclosed him, tightened as her tongue flickered over the sensitive head and she began a smooth, firm, sucking action that had a harsh groan ripping from his throat as his fingers tightened further in her hair.

A sense of power filled her, a heady feminine thrill that she held such a sensual, sexual force in the very palm of her hand. It was exhilarating, shattering, more arousing than anything she could have imagined.

Her mouth moved on him in ever increasing demand, feeling the hard throb of blood just under the flesh, feeling the thick erection pulse and throb as he groaned her name in a thick, guttural tone.

One hand moved to the heavy sac just below the straining shaft, her fingers cupping the taut flesh as her other hand stroked the length that her mouth couldn't consume. She moaned around the fullness that thrust demandingly between her lips, hungry for the heat and taste of him.

"Enough," he suddenly growled, his hands tightening in her hair as he pulled back.

But not before he spilled a few precious drops of semen on her tongue. Hot, salty, male, the taste sent her senses spiraling as she fought his hold, eager for more.

"That's not fair," she gasped as he held her out of reach, his hands catching her wrists to keep her from tempting him further.

"Of course it is." He turned her quickly, pushing her upper body to the bed as he raised her hips, coming to his knees behind her. "Especially when I intend to do this."

In one smooth, fierce stroke he filled her. Raven arched, a strangled scream escaping her lips as she felt his cock fill her to overflowing, powering into her with a force and pleasure that left her helpless.

He filled his hands with the smooth flesh of her rear, separating it as he began to move, creating a brilliant shaft of electric sensation as he parted the entrance to her anus. His thumbs smoothed down the crease until he reached the point where he filled her. There, his fingers slid in the slick cream that flowed easily from her body. He smoothed it back, dampening the little hole over and over again as she bucked beneath him, the pleasure so intense, she wondered if she could survive it.

One hand held her buttocks spread as the other began to spread more of her juices back along the crevice. Below, his cock thrust slow and deep inside the sensitive, hot depths of her pussy. He was making her crazy, moving so slowly, teasing her with alternate deep, fast strokes, then slow easy ones. All the while his fingers played at the tiny entrance above, relaxing her, easing her.

"Do you want to throw this away, Raven?" The question was delivered in a hard possessive voice. "This as well as everything else we've ever shared?"

"No!" She couldn't stop the protest, the need that filled her. Not just sexual, not just the hunger for the biting pleasure of having his cock fill her. But something more, something that went deeper, that grew more intense each time he touched her. It wasn't just sex, no matter how desperately she wished it were.

"Good girl," he whispered, thrusting harder inside her, thrusting against delicate tissue and nerves as she cried out at the pleasure.

She was gasping, crying, begging for more when she felt his hand tighten on her hip. The thumb massaging her anus paused for just a second before it began to push inside with slow devastation.

Raven's back arched, a strangled scream escaping her throat as the piercing pleasure-pain shot up her back before arrowing back down to strike the core of her womb as he began to fuck her in hard, deep thrusts. He stretched her, filled her, thrusting inside her in counterpoint to his thumb as it raided the tender entrance of her ass.

The dual penetration broke the last threads of her control, both physical and emotional. A shattered wail escaped her throat as she clamped down on him, exploding with a force that drew every muscle taut as it shuddered through her body in hard, heavy pulses of release.

Behind her, she heard him groan, felt him swell inside her, then felt his explosion, the hot splash of his semen filling her, branding her. She collapsed beneath him, groaning heavily as his thumb slid from the tight grip of her anus. Seconds later, she heard him breathe in heavily as his cock slid free of her wet vagina and he collapsed on the bed beside her.

"Hell, we're going to kill each other at this rate," he panted as he pulled her into his arms, one hand smoothing back the perspiration-damp hair that fell over her brow.

Raven opened her eyes, dazed, relaxed, knowing she was losing the emotional battle she was fighting, and fighting to make sense of it. He wasn't giving her a chance to think, to consider, to come to terms with the emotions tearing through her heart.

"It hasn't changed anything," she whispered then, watching his eyes darken with emotion. "How am I supposed to deal with this, Reno, when you keep clouding my mind with sex?"

"I'm not clouding your mind, baby." He then pulled her closer in his arms as he sighed deeply against her hair. "You're clouding it yourself. Either you want there to be an 'us,' or you don't. Think very hard before you make that decision, Raven. Fear can be dealt with, but you have to face it before you can defeat it."

She frowned.

"I love you, Raven." He tilted her head back, staring down at her, his eyes dark, filled with emotion, with a savage intensity that clenched her chest and brought tears to her eyes. "That won't change in a day, a week, or a century. But I won't destroy myself chasing after you. You have to decide what you want, and once you do, you have to stick to it. Either way it goes, there's no going back."

Chapter Eight

"We really should get out of bed," Raven muttered drowsily the next morning as Reno smoothed his hand over the rounded curves of her rear and watched her quietly.

She lay on her stomach, her head turned away from him, the long tangled locks of her dark hair flowing around her. Reno trailed his hand from the rounded flesh of her buttocks to her back, his fingers tangling in the rich mass of curls. She looked so delicate, small and tempting as she lay beside him, exhausted from their lovemaking.

This was the picture he would keep in his mind of her. Her beside him, tired and replete, her hair fanning over her back as he touched her, stroked her.

He kissed the curve of her shoulder, allowing himself to breathe in deep, to fill his senses with the scent of her.

"Did you hear me?" she mumbled as she lifted her shoulder against his lips.

Reno smiled at the irate drowsiness. He could hear the threat of laughter in her voice, despite her tone. She liked to play at being tough, unemotional, but he could hear the threads of feelings that she tried to hide.

"I hear you, grouch." He raked his teeth over the flesh he was caressing, smiling at the faint shiver that gripped her body. "You're just a coffee hussy. You think you're going to convince me to fix you some."

Soft laughter greeted the accusation.

"Guilty." She rolled to her side, dragging the sheet around her as she glanced up at him.

Something in his chest expanded, threatening to steal his breath as he stared down at her. Her angel's face staring up at him, those dark, sleepy eyes staring at him from the flushed expanse of her face. She had the power to steal his breath, and often did.

He held her close, his arms tightening around her as she cuddled against him hesitantly. He could feel her breasts pressing against his chest through the sheet she had pulled around her like a shield. But at least she wasn't running.

"I really need that coffee, Reno." Her voice was languid, as lazy as the hand that played almost unconsciously through the mat of hair on his chest.

"You gotta pay for it first." He grinned as she sighed with exasperation.

"You should be tired," she grumped. "*I'm* tired. You didn't even let me sleep last night."

"Of course I did." He smiled against the top of her head as he pushed the sheet away impatiently. "You slept between two and seven while I made some calls and reenergized with a snack."

"You eat too much." Her casual tone was spoiled by the tensing of her body when he mentioned the phone calls.

He wasn't going to let her ignore who and what he was. That

wasn't going to help when the next assignment came up. That, un-fortunately, he knew would be sooner than he had expected.

"I have to keep up my energy," he whispered as he pressed her to her back, pulling the sheet away from her as she watched him, her eyes darkening with arousal.

"How pretty," he sighed as his hand smoothed down her stom-ach, feeling the muscles ripple beneath his fingers as he moved un-erringly to the heat between her thighs.

Her breath caught, her eyes widened as he cupped the damp, bare flesh there. He loved that look, surprise and arousal, a hint of confusion, as though she hadn't yet figured out why the pleasure was so intense.

His head lowered to capture the sweetest lips he had ever kissed as his fingers played erotically in the hottest, silkiest folds of flesh God had ever made. Raven just felt different from any other woman. She tasted different; she smelled different. Everything about her was so unique, so soft and sweet and spicy that it sent his senses spinning. She was addictive. She made his head spin, made his heart pound out of control and his hands ache to hold her forever.

For now, his fingers parted the swollen folds between her thighs, caressing her gently as she gasped beneath his kiss. Her hands clenched his shoulders, dragging a groan from his chest as pleasure whipped through him. He tightened against the surge of lust that nearly overwhelmed his senses.

She arched beneath his hands, her hips pressing closer, the swollen bud of her clitoris rubbing into his palm as she tensed be-neath him. Reno raised his head, staring down at her intently, see-ing the wash of heated hunger suffusing her face as she stared back at him in bemusement.

He slid a finger slowly past the tender opening of her vagina, watching her mouth open as a cry escaped them. God she made him crazy.

His cock twitched in anticipation as he thrust his finger inside the heated depths of her cleft, massaging and caressing the silken tissue that rippled beneath his touch. Her breathing was harsh now, thready little moans escaping her throat as her head tilted back, her eyes closing while her hands moved down his chest, her nails raking over his flesh.

"What are you doing to me?" she moaned, writhing beneath him as he slid another finger inside her, working her muscles slowly, easily, feeling the slick cream of her arousal coating his fingers as she clenched around them.

"Loving you," he whispered as he read the dazed pleasure consuming her expression. "Do you feel me loving you, Raven?"

He thrust in harder, deeper, finding the ultrasensitive mass of nerves, so that when his fingers pressed into it, rotating subtly, she cried out with sensual abandon, arching closer, her hips pumping against his hand as the muscles of her cunt convulsed around his fingers.

"There you go, baby," he whispered, forcing back his own driving hunger to watch hers. "Let me love you, Raven."

He twisted his fingers inside her, sliding nearly free before driving deep again. He watched her face, relished the ecstasy that consumed her even as his own hunger bit deep into his loins. He was dying for her. He would die for her.

Filtering the overpowering lust was the incredible love he had always felt for this woman. She was so much a part of him that he could never imagine life without her now. Couldn't risk that she would turn away when the job became a reality rather than a distant thought.

Gritting his teeth, he quickened his fingers inside her, pushing her over the edge, watching her dissolve as he pulled free and slid quickly between her thighs. She was still convulsing, the muscles rippling and clenching as he positioned the straining length of his cock and pushed inside her.

"Oh God, Reno," she cried out beneath him, her legs raising to circle his hips, her arms wrapping around his neck as her eyes opened, the deep blue burning with emotion and pleasure as she stared up at him. "Don't let me go. Please don't let me go."

"Never, baby. I'll never let you go," he swore deeply as he lowered himself, bracing his weight on his elbows as his hands clasped her head, staring down at her as he began to move inside her with quick, long strokes that sent frissons of sensation shooting up his spine.

She was so tight, so hot. Clenching around his flesh with rhythmic strokes that had him groaning roughly as his hands clenched in her hair.

"Reno . . ." Her nails bit into his shoulders as she stared up at him, her expressive face filled with confusion, with love, with such arousal, it had his scrotum drawing up tight as warning tingles of release began to sizzle at the base of his spine.

"Yeah, baby?" He was fighting for control. Just a few more seconds, he thought desperately. He could feel her tensing further beneath him, her own explosion nearing. "Tell me what you need, Raven," he said, panting. "Anything you want, baby, it's yours. Anything you want."

He watched her eyes turn liquid, tears filling them, but never spilling over as the emotion in her gaze intensified.

"I need you." Her legs tightened around him as the words whispered from her lips, hesitant, filled with longing. "I need you, Reno."

He lowered his head again, his lips whispering over hers as he felt her rising, felt the impending explosion moving through her.

"You have me, Raven," he whispered against his lips. "Forever, baby, you have me."

He pushed inside her harder then, deeper, his strokes increasing until he was jackhammering inside her, exploding with her, his soul dissolving and merging with hers until he had no idea where Raven ended and he began, all he knew was that he would never, could never, let her go.

Raven walked into the bedroom that afternoon, coming to a slow, careful stop as she caught sight of Reno packing the duffel bag that had lain nearly empty since the first night he had spent with her.

He was dressed in the camouflage fatigues, black boots and dull green shirt that were trademarks of his job. As she watched, he lifted his holster and the deadly weapon it contained and packed it carefully.

He was leaving. No warning, no time for her to prepare for it. She stared at him, fighting the building dread that rose within her.

He flashed her a strained smile. "I should be back in about a week. Command called about an hour ago. There should be a car to pick me up soon. I'll be at the base tonight, before we head out first thing in the morning. I left you a present in the kitchen."

She swallowed tightly, shoving her hands into her jeans pockets as she pushed back the emotions roiling inside her. Fear, pain, desperation. They hadn't had enough time together, less than a week, not even long enough to build up the memories to hold her through the long, empty nights.

"Sure." She smiled back, certain she came off as perfectly relaxed as if he had told her he was heading to the corner store. She would not be like her mother. She would not send him away, worried, stressed, uncertain about her state of mind. "Be careful."

She leaned against the wall memorizing his face. The curve of his lips, his dark stormy gray eyes, the strong arch of his brows.

He watched her carefully, his expression concerned. Tense.

He shrugged his shoulders as though shifting some invisible weight.

"I'll be back," he said again.

She smiled back at him. "Of course you will."

He seemed to relax then, at least marginally, the smile on his face curving more naturally. This was who he was. He was a warrior. You can't tame the wind, and you can't housebreak a warrior. She had to accept that.

"I love you, Raven," he said then.

I love you, Raven. I love you, Raven.

The words rebounded through her soul.

She drew in a hard, deep breath. "Did you get everything packed?"

She moved quickly to the dresser, opening and checking drawers. "Clint is always leaving his stuff strung around the place when he visits. I swear, he's a slob. I pick up after him for a week after he leaves."

Nerves were jumping beneath her skin as she fought to hold on to her composure. She wasn't going to cry, she wasn't angry, but she was suddenly realizing how much more she stood to lose than she ever had.

"Raven." His hands landed on her shoulders, holding her. "I love you."

She stilled, then turned to him, staring up at him desperately as he watched her. Something inside her was splintering, fragmenting. What was it? She wasn't angry as her mother had been when her father went on assignment. Raven had been through this too many times with both Reno and Clint. Admittedly, she didn't have as much to lose then as she did now, but this part she knew how to handle. Didn't she?

"Don't you go and get yourself hurt, Reno," she fairly snarled up at him. "I won't be happy."

His off-center smile had her heart clenching with love.

"I'll make sure of that," he whispered, his voice quiet, almost saddened as he watched her.

His head swooped down then, his lips catching hers as her breath caught in her throat. Her throat tightened and something in her chest exploded as his kiss consumed her. Her arms went around his neck as she lifted to him, helpless, aching, as his arms jerked her closer, his hands nearly bruising as they roved over her back and shoulders, imprinting his touch into her soul forever.

A horn blew outside. Once, twice.

He pulled away from her, turned, grabbed his duffel bag and stalked from the room. Seconds later, the front door slammed and he was gone. Raven stared at the window across the room, the shards of sunlight cut across the bed, small motes of dust dancing in the air.

The silence was oppressive, heavy.

She forcibly held back her tears, the pain. She could survive this. She wasn't angry, but God she missed him already.

As she stared at that bright swath of sunlight, a memory broke free, surging past her defenses. She had been young, so young. Barely ten as she lay on her bed that weekend, listening to her parents scream at each other. Her father had to leave again, another mission, another fight. Her mother was crying, begging him not to go. His voice had echoed with his frustration, his own anger. He had to leave. It was his job. No, her mother had screamed, it was his mistress, and she wouldn't share him. He might as well not even come back.

He hadn't come back. A black car and two military counselors had arrived instead. Her father had died in an unknown country, and he was never returning. He wouldn't come home. She wouldn't hear her parents arguing ever again, or sit on her father's lap while he read her stories. He would never tickle her again or call her his dark angel. He was gone forever.

Which was worse? The worry or the loss? She had always wondered that. Especially with Reno. If she let herself love him, which would be worse? Never having him or knowing there would never be another chance?

She moved from the bedroom, down the stairs and to the kitchen. The soft noises coming from the other room warned her of what to expect, but nothing could contain the rush of emotion when she stepped into the room.

The box sat by the door, barely large enough to contain the ball of fluff attempting to break free. Attached to the side was a note, written in Reno's distinctive scrawl.

To keep your feet warm until I return. Love, Reno.

"Until you return," she whispered, staring at the golden retriever pup as it began to howl pitifully for release.

"Well, little guy," she whispered, kneeling beside the box as she touched a soft silky ear hesitantly. "At least we'll have each other."

She drew him from the box and stepped outside, feeling the late summer heat on her face, the breeze whispering over her damp cheeks. But they weren't. She'd promised herself she wouldn't cry.

But the tears fell as she cuddled the pup, staring into the brilliance of the late summer sky.

"I didn't tell him I love him," she finally admitted, the pain exploding in her chest as she realized Reno was right. There was no hiding from it. No hiding from him. She loved him, and she hadn't even told him.

"It's an easy in and out." Reno faced his men in the small conference room, standing in front of the large monitor that displayed the target they were being sent in to hit. "We have two hostages to rescue and a laptop used by the cell commander. Laptop is priority. We'll go in quiet, set the explosives, grab the laptop and the hostages and run. Pickup will be waiting on us here." He pressed the button that switched the picture to an area nearly ten miles from target. "Two Black Hawks will be waiting to fly us out to a waiting ship."

He lifted the stack of files on the desk beside him.

"Read this carefully. We have intel reports on entrances, exits, weak spots and so forth. We'll meet with the assist team when we reach the ship and finalize plans there."

"The cell commander is wanted for war crimes, Major," Ace spoke up, his deep voice echoing in the small room. "Are we just after the laptop or his head as well?"

"The assist team will be in charge of that," Reno informed him. "We'll be going after the hostages. But you don't take chances. The opportunity is there to take that laptop, you get it. We stick with our target op and adjust as we have to."

"And pop the bastard if we get him in our sights," Joker, the explosives expert of the team spoke up. He wasn't joking. This particular terrorist commander was brutal, without mercy. He wouldn't be shown any.

As Reno opened his mouth to dismiss the men, a sharp knock had his head lifting as the door opened.

"Major Chavez, we have a situation that demands your presence," an MP snickered from the doorway. "General says now."

Frowning, Reno nodded to Ace as he handed the files to him to distribute to the other three men and made his way to the door.

"Situation?" he asked warily.

"Situation, sir, of a very delicate sort." The MP nodded, amusement dancing in his eyes. "This way, sir."

As they neared the general's office, a frown worked between Reno's brows at the sound of an irate female voice.

"General, I don't care how busy he is. You were my father's best friend and I'm not above pulling strings. If I don't see him before he leaves in the morning, I promise you, I'll be making a visit to your wife, your daughter and your son. They like me." The voice was husky, and filled with feminine fury.

He heard the general's voice, low, soothing.

"I'm not in the army, general," she said. "I don't need rules quoted to me. I need strings pulled. I want to see him. Now."

A grin tugged at his mouth as the MP chuckled.

"She's been ripping on the general for an hour," he whispered as they neared the door. "Want to bet he chews on you next?"

Reno grimaced but something in his heart was loosening. He wouldn't bet against the MP, but he would bet it just might be worth it.

He knocked on the door lightly.

"Enter." The general's voice was frustrated and clipped.

Reno stepped in, saluting smartly, then turned to stare at Raven. She was cuddling the puppy he'd bought her like a baby. Her face was wet with tears, her deep, deep blue eyes filled with misery.

"Raven?" He stepped toward her, pulling her and the puppy into his arms as he stared back at the general. "What's happened?"

"Major, I'll leave you to talk to Miss McIntyre." The general sounded stern, but Reno caught the soft look he cast at Raven. "We'll talk later."

"Yes, sir." Reno nodded as the general left the room and he turned his attention to the pup wiggling between them.

"Raven? Baby? The puppy is going to be smashed," he whispered as he gripped her arms, pushing her back enough to release the wiggling little mass. "What's wrong? Is Clint okay?"

The tears rolled silently down her cheeks. There were no sobs, just a hitch in her breath as she stared up at him.

"I forgot," she hiccupped then. "You left, and I forgot to tell you. . . ."

She shuddered as her voice broke.

Reno moved to the couch, pulling her to his lap as she cuddled against his chest.

"I love you," she cried desperately. "God help me, Reno. I don't want to lose you. I can't lose you. I can stand anything but you leaving, maybe being . . . hurt . . . ," her breath caught, "and not knowing I love you."

Reno closed his eyes, his arms tightening around her, his heart exploding with joy. She knew she loved him. That was all that mattered.

"It's okay, baby," he groaned, kissing her forehead gently as her head tilted back, the wealth of long silken curls flowing over his arm. Her hand lifted to his face, her lips trembling as he wiped the tears from one silken cheek.

"You knew all along, didn't you?" she whispered then. "That I loved you."

"All along," he agreed with a smile.

His lips lowered to hers, moving over the soft curves, nibbling at the damp softness as the feel and smell of her sent his senses rioting.

"Hell, if I fucked you in the general's office, he would court-martial me for sure," he sighed, smiling down at the seductive softness in her expression.

"Yeah. He probably would." Her smile trembled, but it was still there.

"Wait for me, Raven," he growled, his voice husky, deep, knowing every day away from her would be hell. "I'll be home. Wait for me."

"Always, Reno." She kissed him. Her head raised, her lips moving against his with incredible passion and loving heat. "Always."

Chapter Nine

"You are in so much trouble."

Reno tossed his duffel bag to the corner of the bedroom as he stalked inside the room, his brows lowered into a dark frown as Raven reclined back on the bed, her knee bent, her naked breasts thrusting forward in invitation as his hot gaze raked over them.

Damn he looked good. The camouflage pants made his legs look sexy as hell, planted apart as they were, the bulge between his thighs filling out the front of the material.

"Oh really, Reno, it wasn't so bad." She rolled her eyes at his miffed state. "It was just a little present."

She restrained her smile as he dug his hand into his pocket, no small feat with that erection tightening the material. Her mouth watered at the sight of it. He had been gone for nearly two weeks this time. Too long as far as she was concerned, and she was wet and hungry for him. The adult toys he had been so kind as to teach her to use the last time he was home did little to bank the fire that thinking of him caused.

She blinked as the small velvet box landed on the bed beside her. She almost had to bite her lips to keep back her smile.

"Is this a proposal?" She arched a brow as she glanced back up at him.

Oh yum. He was undressing. There went the shirt, revealing the golden expanse of his chest, muscles rippling beneath the sun-darkened flesh.

"I'm going to spank your ass," he grunted as he bent to unlace his boots. "Do you want to know where I was when that box dropped out of my duffel bag, Raven? I was in the middle of communal quarters, sweetheart, with three different teams. Can you imagine the fun those men had at my expense?"

She lifted the box, opening it, and grinned at the sight of the wedding set she had found in his dresser drawer just before he was due to leave. The short letter she had wrapped around it was missing.

Who's hiding now? she had written.

He had been so very careful of their relationship over the last three months, never pressing her for anything, but she had seen how he had steadily cemented his presence into her life.

His clothes now shared space with hers. His guitar was residing under her bed, and his prized trophies from high school and college had made their way to her small shelf downstairs. He even had his own computer desk for the laptop he often worked on. This was his home. He hadn't asked to inhabit it, he had just moved in, just as he had taken her heart, a little bit at a time. But he never mentioned taking it further, never pushed her, though she could tell he wanted to.

She looked up as his pants cleared his hips and his erection sprang free. Thick, the broad head flushed to a near purple hue, it looked intimidating, ready to conquer. She was more than ready to be conquered.

"Turn over," he growled.

He had that intimidating, dominating look on his face now. The one that made her cream furiously and made her blood pressure shoot through the roof. She loved it when he looked like that, and she loved what resulted.

"Do I look crazy to you?" She flipped the box closed as she watched him mockingly. "Why buy the cow, Reno, if you're getting the milk free? I think perhaps you should sleep in the spare bedroom tonight. Better yet, Morganna's not having any parties this weekend. Maybe she can spare a bed."

She moved to get off the bed, knowing the game and loving it. She saw that twinkle in his eye. The happiness that tugged at his fiercely controlled lips and the lust that flushed the hard cheekbones of his face.

Her feet barely touched the floor when she felt his arm hook around her waist, dragging her back to the bed as he flipped her onto her stomach in one smooth, economical move.

She screeched in mock protest, struggling against him as she felt his muscular legs bracket her, holding her to the mattress.

A second later, his callused palm landed on her rear with stinging force. Heat whipped through her buttocks, sizzled along her nerve endings, then down to her clit with vicious force.

"Reno, that's cruel and unusual treatment." She bucked against his hold. "There's laws against this."

He smacked the other cheek, causing her to wiggle fiercely as her vagina began to ripple in desperate need. Damn him, he knew what this did to her.

"Your proposal sucked, Raven," he drawled lazily as another blow landed, making her moan at the border between pleasure and pain.

"It beat yours," she cried out, pressing back, feeling the tip of his erection as it slid against the crease of her damp thighs.

He was hard and hot, and her body was starving for him. She pressed back again, moaning heavily as two more strikes landed on her upraised ass, making her clench at the fire blooming there.

"I was wooing you," he half snarled.

He was always like this after a mission, more dominant, so eager for her that he took her breath away.

"You call that wooing?" She was panting now. His hips shifted, pressing his cock against her eager entrance as she fought for that first hard thrust. "I could die an old maid waiting on you." The next smack landed with burning force on her ass as she felt her womb contract almost violently.

A second later, her back arched as a hoarse scream tore from her throat. The full, heavy length of his cock surged inside the slick, tight confines of her vagina triggering an explosive climax that left her shaking in reaction, shudders of pleasure vibrating through her entire body.

"Oh, you're not done yet, baby." He slid free of her, flipped her to her back and lifted her legs as his head lowered.

His tongue attacked the sensitive folds with ravenous greed, licking around her straining clit as his murmurs of approval hummed against her flesh. Deep, penetrating thrusts of his tongue had her lifting her hips in supplication moments later, only to have him retreat to torture the burning nub above once again.

He was voracious. A sensual, sexual demon intent on draining her of every last vestige of resistance against him. Not that the resistance was anything more than feigned. She loved this side of him, provoked it often and gloried in his possession of her.

She could feel her heart hammering against her chest as her hands lifted from the bed, her fingers moving for the aching tips of her breasts, knowing he was watching. It inflamed her all the more to know that she could push him over the edge, that she could make him as crazy with need as he made her.

He was her lover, her heart and her soul.

She pinched at her nipple as she heard him groan roughly, tugging at the tender points as her eyes opened, her gaze meeting his as his tongue circled her straining clit. He would make her come again, make her scream for him. He always did.

She could feel perspiration gathering on her body as the heat inside her began to build. Her muscles tensed, her breathing became broken whimpers of agonizing need until his mouth covered the erect little clit, his tongue flickering as he sucked it firmly.

She screamed for him as she exploded. Rocketing into the stars with a force that left her dizzy as she felt him thrust inside her, hard and deep, penetrating her to the very core before his hips began to move with furious thrusts.

It didn't take him long. The need was too great; the absence had been too long. He pushed her into a final, exhausted orgasm before giving in to his own, groaning harshly as he buried inside her, his cock jerking in reflex as he spilled his semen in the gripping depths of her pussy.

Seconds later he collapsed beside her with an exhausted sigh, pulling her to his chest as they both fought to bring their breathing under control.

"I need coffee," she muttered sleepily, burrowing close, her hand going to the scar on the right side of his chest.

The bullet he had taken there could have taken his life if it had been a few more inches toward the center. It had been a close call. A terrifying one, but she had survived it without recriminations. When he came home, she had babied him and loved him, and treasured every day she had with him after that. She vowed she would never waste their lives as her mother had hers.

"Coffee hussy," he chuckled into her hair. "What do you do when I'm gone?"

She breathed out pitifully. "I suffer, Reno. It's a tragic, horrible sight to witness. Poor Morganna even feels sorry for me."

She shivered as his hands caressed her back, one running low to her hips before smoothing over her buttocks.

"You're marrying me." His voice suddenly hardened. "Notice, I'm not asking. I'm telling you."

"I already proposed, big shot. You dropped the ball. Remember?"

He grunted at that. "Minx. The men are still laughing over that note you left. Don't you know I'm fearless? I never hide."

"Coward." She yawned, unconcerned, nipping his chest as her lips closed. "Do you know how mad I got when I found that box? It's a good thing you were getting ready to leave that day or I might have had to hurt you."

He gripped a handful of hair, tugging her head back as she stared up at him, her legs smoothing across his as she felt his erection growing, pressing against her lower stomach.

"I love you, Raven," he whispered then, his voice no longer filled with amusement, his gaze velvet soft as he watched her. "Forever."

"You took a hell of a chance, Reno," she whispered. "I didn't know myself how much I loved you. What if I hadn't realized?"

A smile curved his lips. "I would have fucked you into submission."

She rolled her eyes, one hand pressing against his shoulder as though to push him away.

"Get serious."

"Withheld the coffee?" he suggested darkly.

She stared up at him in some concern then. "You wouldn't do that."

"Oh yes I would have," he growled. "But more importantly, I wouldn't have given you a moment's peace. You're mine, baby, and I don't let go of what's mine."

He kissed her then, a kiss filled with promise, heat and magic as her heart dissolved within her chest and flowed into his. It wouldn't do him any good to let her go, she thought, because she had no intention of releasing him.

"I love you, Reno," she whispered against his lips again. "Forever."